The Perfect Game

TERRENCE O. MOORE

ISBN:1461099285
ISBN-13:9781461099284

IN LOVING MEMORY

Neva Elizabeth Moore
Cari Linnea Moore

CONTENTS

ACKNOWLEDGMENTS

I should like to thank my friends Bryant Ambelang and Lance Brownlee for reading the manuscript and Miss Chelsea Samelson for her cover design and sound advice. I am grateful to my father for his faith over the years, his colorful perspective on life, and his teaching me the game of baseball. Above all, I thank my wife for her editing, her encouragement, her insights, and her love.

Better than any other sport activity, baseball expresses the heart and character of the nation. To those who play it, watch it and take satisfaction from it, baseball truly mirrors an American way of life.

It is engaging both as a game to watch and a contest in which to participate. In the latter, it embodies the disciplines of teamwork, it challenges players towards perfection of physical skills and brings into play the exciting contest of tactics and strategy.
—Little League Baseball, *Official Regulations and Playing Rules*, 1983

I TRUST IN GOD
I LOVE MY COUNTRY
AND WILL RESPECT ITS LAWS
I WILL PLAY FAIR
AND STRIVE TO WIN
BUT WIN OR LOSE
I WILL ALWAYS
DO MY BEST
—Little League Pledge

Those who say that we're in a time when there are no heroes, they just don't know where to look.
—Ronald Reagan, First Inaugural

Be ye therefore perfect, even as your Father, who is in heaven is perfect.
—Matthew 5:48

Chapter 1: The Sermon

Trammel tried to keep his mind from wandering that Sunday morning, on the first weekend of summer break, as Pastor McGuffey delivered his sermon on the Good Samaritan. Normally the boy paid close attention to the preacher's words and lessons. He had read or heard most all of the parables from the Gospel and liked the way Pastor McGuffey applied them to real life. Even today Trammel thought he knew what the preacher was talking about. Parts of the sermon commanded his willing ear.

"The insincere question of the lawyer, like so many of *our* excuses, keeps him from doing God's work," observed the thoughtful pastor. "'Who is my neighbor?' leads to an endless cycle of protesting: 'Well, he is my neighbor, but he doesn't need my help,' or 'Why should I help this particular neighbor rather than this other one?' or 'I'm just as bad off as any of these people.' But when we listen closely to Christ's answer we see that the real way of following the commandment 'Love thy neighbor as thyself' is not to beg the question by asking who my neighbor is but to bring the commandment back home to myself by simply asking, *'Am I being a neighbor?'* Am I following the example of the Good Samaritan, or am I instead looking for any old excuse *not* to help my fellow man: because I am too busy, or I didn't see him, or I didn't happen to run across anyone lying on the side of the road today, or yesterday, or ever?"

And yet this particular Sunday did not favor the boy's normally fixed attention. This particular Sunday was the day of Opening Ceremonies at the local Little League. The boy would be pitching in the much touted and anticipated Opening Day Game for the senior league that previewed and served as a surrogate for all the boys' efforts that year. Opening Day did not mark the first game of the season—the regular season games had been going on for the last two weeks, and practices had begun more than a month ago— but rather brought all the players and their families together on the first day of summer break. The day was meant to celebrate the great American pastime and the competitive spirit of emerging manhood, to allow kids to eat hot dogs and old men to tell and retell tales of their own victories and defeats.

The game was supposed to have been played yesterday. Opening Day had always been on a Saturday. And Little League games were never scheduled for a Sunday. Only yesterday it had rained. A mighty Texas thunderstorm had rolled into the area early that morning, and the downpour had continued throughout the day. Fortunately, the league had shown enough foresight to put the tarps down. Given that the directors of the league were not the strict Sabbatarians their fathers had been, that most fathers could never make it to an Opening Day on a Monday afternoon, and that a week from now would be far too late and wreak havoc on the league's master schedule, the Opening Ceremonies, with a dispensation from the state headquarters in Waco, were postponed only for a day.

Trammel's father was not in church with the family that Sunday. He and some other fathers, including the coach of Trammel's team, worked steadily all morning to prep the field for the big game, and at that moment Trammel's father was raking out the mound. He was, if anything, more on edge than his son. The two had had nothing to do the previous day but sit around the house wondering when the rain would stop. For his part, Trammel watched a Western marathon on one of the cable channels. It was a good thing he had seen most of the movies already since his father's various instructions, between the several calls that went back and forth among the coach, Trammel's dad, and several of the other fathers, made it hard to concentrate.

"Ya know, Tram," the father would say, pacing back and forth between the kitchen and the family room while throwing a baseball into his own well-worn glove, "I thank y'oughta start out wi' the fastball, 'en gib 'em a knuckle on 'a nex' pitch." As if to punctuate the importance of his statement, the father would spit a stream of tobacco juice into his aluminum Dr. Pepper can, the top having been cut off with a can opener for that purpose, which he left precariously on the edge of the kitchen table. "'At'll shake 'em up an' make 'em look perty silly. 'En finish 'em off wi' the fas'ball agin. 'Course you'll have ta mix it up so 'ey don't solve ya."

Another moment would pass. "'Course 'at's only wi' the real sticks. Once ya get ta the bottom a' the order, ya can't th'ow nut'n' but heat."

"Yes, sir. I got it, Dad," the boy would intone mechanically.

For a few minutes the father would look out the window, only to see the ceaseless rain. After a couple of throws into his own glove, he would offer the young pitcher his further reflections. "Ya know, Tram, Toby's a perty good stick. But if ya dust eem back a little on 'at first pitch, 'e won't wonta mix it up with ya no more. You'll pick eem apart on 'at outside corner. 'E'll go out lookin', I tell ya."

"Yes, sir. I got it, Dad."

It was not that the boy was not interested in his father's sage advice. He simply knew it by heart. His father had been teaching him in this way for years. And for all the talk of baseball being a "thinking man's game," Trammel found football to be the more difficult science. He had discovered that, aside from the vagaries of human error and chance, baseball consists in a few basic principles to be followed with prudence. When Trammel was pitching, the game was more psychology than anything else. He knew the opposing players, and even those he did not know he could read like a book. Thus he controlled the events by figuring out which of his two or three best pitches each batter dreaded and were least able to hit and consequently throwing those pitches in the right order—and without mercy: with all the "killer instinct," to use his father's phrase, that a thirteen-year-old boy could muster.

Trammel's decided abilities as a pitcher owed partly to his own physical strength and coordination, far superior to that of other boys his age; partly to untold hours of throwing a baseball; partly to the oft-reiterated instructions of his father, who had himself played college ball; and partly to his own innate intelligence, a keen capacity to read his fellow players few Little Leaguers possessed. That rare combination of advantages made him one of the best young ballplayers in North Texas, which meant one of the best young ballplayers anywhere. As young as he was, only a junior player in the thirteen- and fourteen-year-old division, Trammel was beginning to "jell" as an athlete, especially as a pitcher. When he had first started pitching, the whole enterprise seemed to be a puzzle consisting of ball, plate, and catcher's mitt. The batter existed as a happenstance, either to hit or not to hit whatever Trammel was throwing. Getting the ball across the plate was challenge enough. Over the last couple of years, Trammel gained a great deal of control over his pitches and likewise came to understand that the disposition of the batter should govern his choices on the mound. It was then that his father, also his coach, instituted the regime of called pitches so familiar to Major League baseball fans, and Trammel occasionally felt the confidence to shake those calls off whenever he possessed the better strategy.

In church that day, Trammel's thoughts did not settle on any subject in particular. Rather, a general sense of impending action made it impossible for him to concentrate on anything for more than a few minutes, though normally he would think a topic through to its logical conclusion. Game days were always this way for him. Nothing mattered on game days except for The Game, so everything else—schoolwork, chores, conversations with family and friends—were all put on hold. The boy did not dread The Game, but it did cause him a marked degree of unrest. Trammel simply wanted The Game to start so he could do what he had to do, bask for a moment in the glory of winning when it was all over, and then go back to his normal routine of practicing for perfection.

As he lost focus on what the preacher was saying, Trammel felt his mother, sitting on the other side of his sister, looking up from her shorthand and casting a sidelong glance at him. The boy instantly fixed his eyes on Pastor McGuffey. The pastor was like family; at least Trammel had known him that long. The native Texan and graduate of Princeton—both the university and the seminary—had married Trammel's parents, a year after his being called to this church, and had baptized both Trammel and his little sister. Pastor McGuffey had been to their home several times for dinner, always staying to talk with the parents "about church stuff" after the children went to bed. He took a keen interest in the boy's achievements in sports and in school. Most of what Trammel knew about faith had come from the pastor or the boy's mother.

"I must confess, and as most of you already know, I was not the saint of my family. That role was assumed by my sister early on. And were it not for the goodness of her heart, I would have thought she was trying deliberately to *show me up*. She worked in soup kitchens and went to homes for the elderly; she organized canned food drives at her school and Goodwill pickups around the neighborhood. She was always helping and always being a neighbor. I knew I could never be like her. When I was in high school I preferred to hang out with my friends, just goofing around, or to spend time on my real passion, which was chess."

Trammel recalled that Pastor McGuffey was an accomplished chess player and had from time to time offered to teach him to play. From what he had heard about the game he thought he might like it, but he had not as yet found the time or shown the inclination.

"But when I was in college," the pastor continued, "and began thinking about going into the ministry I figured it was time I gained some hands-on experience at being a neighbor. So I started visiting the terminal ward at a local hospital. As it turned out, the first patient I met, a fourteen-year-old boy with a malignant tumor, had taught himself to play chess. He sat there with the chessboard in front of him, no one else around him taking the time or knowing how to play. So I played chess with him—during his time in the hospital—every day for the last couple of weeks of his life. He enjoyed it very much, and right up to the day of his death he was interested in learning new moves. His mother was able to see him happy and could even get some rest whenever she knew I was in the room. We never talked about his sickness or his approaching death; we did not talk about Christ or the life to come. I was no preacher then. In fact, we hardly talked at all. But even to this day I have the satisfaction of knowing that that poor boy, who still had so much *life* in him, did not die without a neighbor, that he did not die without a friend."

The pastor had a way of always making the Bible seem relevant, and to this end he told stories from his own life or from the actions of people he had met, from current events or the lives of heroes, and very often from passages of literature members of the congregation ought to have read. In at least one family these lessons did not fall on stony ground. Mrs. Jones—Trammel's mother—took verbatim notes of every sermon, would often type out a transcript later, and frequently used parts of those sermons to teach or to admonish gently her two children.

As it was not a communion Sunday, after the Lord's Prayer the congregation rose to sing the final hymn. The long summer made havoc of church attendance, even among the choir, so no choir sat that day, and Mrs. Jones could be with her family in the pews. That fact did not prevent her rich soprano from filling the sanctuary as others mumbled "How Great Thou Art." Whenever his mother did sit with them in church, Trammel was always initially shocked and somewhat disconcerted by how loudly she sang, a feat vocal teachers would have referred to as "projection," until he recalled what a beautiful voice she had. In fact, Mrs. Jones had majored in music at TCU. She had chosen the college owing to the reputation of its music program, to her winning a prestigious scholarship, and, having grown up in a nearby town that had since become a suburb in the Dallas-Fort Worth metroplex, to her not wanting to be too far from home. A business minor, she had thought of starting her own music company of some sort. At least that was her plan until she fell in love with and married the campus baseball star: a business major, who, while starting out as a loan officer at a local bank as his young wife finished college, got drafted into the Army. During her husband's tour of duty the young woman had a son. That son, now taller than she was, took immense pride in his mother's musical talents, her stunning beauty, and her incomparable gift for bringing light and joy into the world. The boy had grown up listening to her singing and playing the piano. Unless she was working extra hard for a solo in church or for a local function, these performances took place mostly at night, after the children had gone to bed, since that was the only time of day the mother had wholly to herself. Trammel found peace in the music, a peace he welcomed since he could easily get worked up about things he was wrestling with in school or in sports.

As soon as the music stopped and the pastor had given the blessing and charge to the congregation, Trammel quickly put his own and his sister's hymnals away and reminded his mother that they would have to "get a move on" so he could change at home and get to the field on time. Mrs. Jones smiled and thanked him ironically for the reminder, an echo of her husband's several reminders that morning. True enough, after church she did have a tendency to socialize. The family might have to linger there half an hour as she caught up on how people were doing, made plans for the coming week, and told Pastor McGuffey how much she liked his sermon. Trammel would usually go through two or three donuts and a few cups of orange juice in the fellowship hall while his sister flitted about from friend to friend. By the time the mother had finished, it was not rare for Mr. Jones to be already in the car, listening to the pre-game show of the Rangers or the Cowboys, depending on the season.

The plan worked well. Trammel, who possessed a naturally austere countenance and was remarkably aloof for a teenager, could cut through crowds discreetly without anyone wishing to approach him, and the mother on this occasion consented to tagging along behind him. Just as they were reaching the back doors one acquaintance did, however, momentarily break the rhythm. Mr. Harper was a stout, jolly man. The same age as Mr. Jones, though he looked easily a decade older, Mr. Harper had three daughters, all pretty good softball players. He had always taken a keen interest in Trammel's sporting career and had watched the boy play on several occasions. He was thinking about going to the game today, that is, if he could persuade his wife and daughters that the picnic at the lake they had urged on him could wait until the following weekend.

"Hey, Big Tram, I saw in 'a paper 'is mornin' 'at y'all 're gonna give it a shot 'is afternoon. Ya ready fer the big game?" Mr. Harper asked with a smile and a slap on the boy's right shoulder.

"Yes, sir," answered the boy resolutely, looking out through the glass doors onto the softball field behind the church. "I'm plenty ready."

Chapter 2: Opening Day

By the time Trammel's mother got him (and his sister) to the Little League ballpark, about a third of the players on the various teams had arrived. Trammel's father had been checking his watch for the last fifteen to twenty minutes. When he saw the car pull into the parking lot, just off the fenced outfield of the senior league field, he strode out from the gathering of men near the concession stand, glove and ball tucked under one arm and a bottle of Gatorade under the other. From about thirty feet away he tossed the ball to Trammel, who just had time to get his glove on as he was returning a rolled-up bag of sunflower seeds to his back pocket.

"How ya feelin', boy?"

"I'm a'right."

"Not tired?"

"No, sir, I'm fine," replied the boy, spitting the wet shells of the seeds into the air.

"Been drinkin' water?"

"Yes, sir. I jus' had some comin' over."

"Here ya go," said the father, handing off the Gatorade. "Keep 'is on ya durin' 'is dog 'n' pony show 'fore the game an' take a swig ever now an' 'en. It's gonna be a hot one t'day, and I don't wont ya burnin' up, eb'm if ya have ta keep usin' it," the father said, gesturing towards the Port-o-Lets. "We can't have ya dehydratin' out 'ere."

The father had studied his son's constitution as thoroughly as he had his own and knew that however tough he was compared to other boys his age, the fair-haired, fair-skinned boy was no match for the Texas summer sun. If he did not keep pounding water throughout the day, he would gradually lapse into fatigue and end up with a debilitating headache. Mr. Jones laughed in disbelief whenever he remembered that in his own day coaches had not allowed players to drink water during practices, in football or baseball, thinking it was somehow bad for them. So the boys had to sneak sips of water from nasal spray bottles they hid about their persons. In defiance of those old prejudices, Mr. Jones had become something of a hydration fanatic. He always made sure the team had a big cooler of ice water and usually stopped off at the local 7-Eleven before the game to buy the ice himself.

"Let's th'ow a few." This invitation was code for the extensive warm-up routine—including stretches—the father had developed from his own playing days, augmented with things he had learned from a biography of Nolan Ryan. The purpose of the exercise was to get the boy's arm ready for the present game and to save it over decades of use.

As the father and son headed up the hill to the fields of the younger leagues that would not be used today, the mother made her way from the car, carrying a rather cumbersome and unstylish bag designed for mothers of babies and toddlers and thus replete with extra pockets for diapers and infant paraphernalia. In the bag could be found anything her son, one of the other boys, or most anyone in the stands might need that hot afternoon: a can of Off!, sunscreen, several bags of sunflower seeds, aspirin and Tylenol, energy bars, Band-Aids of all sizes, Ace bandages, Neosporin, an empty ice bag, bottles of both rubbing alcohol and hydrogen peroxide, a few packs of chewing gum, a spare pair of sunglasses in case she misplaced her first pair, a pack of Wet Ones, some barrettes and bands for her daughter's hair, as well as some disposable diapers for mothers who might run out in an emergency. Mrs. Jones, you see, was the Team Mom, and as such she had the de facto responsibility of carrying "the Bag." As long as she had the Bag, no office, no succor, would go unattended.

Mrs. Jones entered the back of the concession stand and greeted the other mothers who had already arrived and were beginning to prepare hot dogs and hamburgers and to set out the thirty different boxes of candy and bubble gum that would be sold throughout the game. Although she was not on duty today since her son was playing, she wore the red and white striped shirt with the blue collar that was the uniform of the Women's Auxiliary, the group of mothers who ran the concession stand whose proceeds paid the umpires' wages and for most of the grounds keeping. All these mothers were in uniform today since they would be recognized as a part of the Opening Ceremonies.

At noon the president of the league took his station at the table set up just in front of home plate on the "Big Field" on which Trammel would be playing today. After testing the P.A. system, he commenced the ceremonies.

"A'right now, welcome e'erbody." The high-pitched sound coming from the mike's feedback caused the crowd to grab their ears.

"A'right, now let's try 'at agin. Better?"

The crowd shouted their approval.

"As y'all pro'lly know, I'm Ronny Dodson, the head a' the league here. So I'd like ta jus' kick thangs off by sayin', Welcome ta Dogwood Little League Baseball." Pockets of clapping and a few women's cheers were heard above the general hubbub.

"A'right 'en, let's git 'ese boys ta where they b'long—out on 'a field." Mr. Dodson then began calling out the teams one by one, starting with the tee-ballers and making his way up to the senior league, made up of thirteen- and fourteen-year-olds.

"H & H Contractors, coached by Joe Johnson."

"Barnett & Sons Exterminators, coached by Hank Griffin."

"First Bank a' Texas, coached by Tommy Price."

As each team was called, fifteen boys wearing freshly bleached baseball pants and colored, synthetic, and somewhat scratchy shirts bearing numbers and the names of the team sponsors would trot out onto the field, led by their coach, in most instances a father of one of the boys on the team. Each of these volunteer coaches had himself been an athlete in his day, though with rare exception was now substantially beyond his high-school playing weight. The coaches donned polyester coaching shorts and specially made tee shirts approximating team colors rather than the uniforms the boys wore, these uniforms having to be, for a reason no one knew, passed on to other players from season to season. Every one of the older boys but one had his stirrups, those sock coverings that baseball players wear, pulled up high so as to reveal only two strips of color on either side of the calf. That one exception was

Trammel, who barely pulled up his stirrups, preferring to be counter-cultural, especially when he could be old-fashioned at the same time. Even his father, who was himself old-fashioned and counter-cultural, tried to draw the line at his son's desire to wear black shoes, though the father had worn the standard black in his day. The attempt wholly unavailing, Trammel was the only boy on the field who could have stepped straight out of the fifties. As the first few teams made their way out onto the field, the fans and families clapped dutifully. By and by, interest waned as mothers had to attend to their children's lunches and fathers grew impatient. Genuine interest in the older players renewed the applause, and Trammel's team, Big Luke's Sporting Goods, took the field to cheers of "Go, Big Luke!" and "You get 'em, Tram!"

When he was a younger player, Trammel always found himself crowded into the middle of the field amidst hundreds of other boys. Today, however, his team formed a queue down the right-field line, and he positioned himself in the extreme corner of the field, just a couple of feet off the fence. From this vantage he surveyed the entire scene, somewhat philosophically. The tee-ballers, five- and six-year-olds, seemed tiny to the adolescent boy who had shot up again this past spring and now stood, at five feet ten, two inches taller than his mother and only four inches off his father's height. Among these younger players the gulf in abilities between the natural athletes and the much weaker players—"glove-chewers," his father called them, owing to their habit of gnawing on the leather strips protruding from the fingers of a baseball glove—was far wider than among the boys in Trammel's league. Five or six years of long practices—of playing catch with different players in warm-up, of coaches hitting fly balls and grounders, of having to stand in the box to face a variety of young pitchers, some of them completely wild and unpredictable—normally gave even the "mullets," another of his father's appellations, the capacity to make some close stab at the game.

After all the teams were in place and the gathering had sung the National Anthem, Mr. Dodson turned the crowd's attention to the scheduled introductions and speeches.

"A'right, welcome folks, ta the thirty-sixth season a' Little League Baseball here in Dogwood, Texas," he proclaimed amid substantial cheers.

"I'm Ronny Dodson, the president a' the league here 'is year [mild clapping]. Y'all 'at know me know I ain't one fer makin' speeches, so I'll just say 'at I'm glad ta be out here on such a won'erful Sundee . . . after a pretty crummy Sa'urdee [laughter], t'offici'ly kick off 'is season of all 'ese fine boys playin' 'a great game a' baseball [a few whoops]. Now, a' course, I gotta make some innerductions first. An' 'fore I innerduce anybody else, I gotta brang out 'ese fine ladies 'at make mos' all 'is possible. An' 'at's 'a ladies—I guess I oughta say the young ladies [mild laughter]—a' the Women's Augziwree. C'mone out here, ladies, don't be shy!"

The Women's Auxiliary, in their red and white striped shirts with the blue collars, walked out onto the field amid warm applause and a few whistles from their husbands, waved, got confused for a moment on whether they were supposed to stay out on the field, and then made their way again off the field amid more applause and their own laughter. The president of the league added, "Now 'ese ladies make a lotta hot dogs back'ere in 'at hot kitchen an' sell a lotta candy ta keep 'is league goin'. An' we thank 'em fer all 'at."

"Now 'ere's one other fella I gotta innerduce 'fore I git ta the real speechmaker, an' 'at's 'a young fella 'at sol' 'a mos' candy 'is year, 'cause candy sales is 'a other thang 'at keeps 'is league goin'. An' 'at young fella's gonna git a brand-spankin' new bicycle fer all 'is hard work. Uh, what kind did ya call it?" The great gathering of boys shouted out the answer.

"A *mon goose*? Like the critter?" the president asked in disbelief. "Well, I guess I ain't up on my bicycles. What ever happened ta Schwinn?" he asked as an aside, to nods of agreement among the parents.

"Anyway, we're gonna give 'is champion candy salesman 'is here bicycle fer all 'is hard work. An' 'at winner 'is year is . . ." The president of the league patted himself down in order to find where he had written the name of the champion candy salesman, since it did not appear on the only paper before him—the list of all the teams in the league—until he felt the index card in his breast pocket listing the other matters he would have to address as a part of the day's ceremonies.

"Yeah, here we go. An' 'a winner is, Tommy Foster. Where's Tommy? C'mone up here, Tommy, fer a little reco'nition. Let's give Tommy a big round a' 'plause fer all 'is hard work. Mayor, c'mone out here an' shake 'is boy's hand."

As little Tommy bounded towards home plate in order to claim his new bike and get his picture taken for the local newspaper, Trammel took a big gulp of Gatorade and threw another handful of sunflower seeds into his mouth. The annual candy drive was the bane of his existence for the first few weeks of every season. Every day he would come home from school to be greeted by the unopened boxes sitting on his floor, taunting him to venture out into the neighborhood and plead for people's patronage, his mother asking him occasionally, "Tra-am, have you tried to sell any candy yet?" Once the last week of the drive came around and the coach had made the obligatory call to "wrap up" the candy sales, Trammel would sit down on his floor and open up one of the boxes, only to read with disdain the canned sales pitch written on a small slip of paper conveniently placed on top of the candy in every box:

> " Good morning (or afternoon). My
> name is _____, and I am playing
> baseball this summer in the _____
> Little League. We are selling this
> delicious bar of candy, with nuts or
> without, in order to raise money for our
> league . . ."

Trammel never made it past this point without wadding up the slip, throwing it onto the floor, and protesting, "How stupid!" Uninspired, he would take his annual walk around the block to see if anyone really wanted to buy any candy.

Trammel always thought hard about what time of day would find the least number of folks at home. He ruled out the weekends and dinnertime. The longer he waited after school, the more kids were likely to have made it home, so he often tried to make a pass not too long after three. Sometimes mothers had errands after picking up their children from school. He hated more than anything having the door opened by a kid he knew and having to tell the kid to get his mom, so usually he just avoided those houses altogether. Being rejected was surely bad, but making a sale was actually worse. The lady of the house never had any money on hand. Women might have pockets in their pants, but they never put anything in them, least of all money. So they would say politely, "Could you wait just a minute?" and then be gone for what seemed like hours, going through their purses, yelling to their children to see if *they* had any money, pouring out the contents of piggy banks. Rarely would Trammel get back a simple, single dollar bill. The lady would either need change—"I don't suppose you have any ones, do you?"—or bring back an handful of quarters, dimes, and nickels—"Sorry"—or write a check, a *check*! for two candy bars—"Now who do I make this out to?"

The worst episode had occurred the previous year. Trammel had the bright idea of going out at about 9:30 on the morning of a teacher in-service day when there was no school. He figured all the fathers would be at work and the mothers might have taken their kids to the park or to breakfast or something. Unfortunately, he stumbled into a girls' slumber party at the home of one of his classmates who had just moved into the neighborhood, a girl who opened the door in her pajamas. Then pandemonium broke out.

"Oh, my gosh! Tra-am!"

"Hidee. Yeah, well, uh, I'm jus' here sellin' 'is candy fer my baseball league. I can see you're perty busy, so I'll jus' come back."

"Oh, my gosh, no! Of course, we'll buy some candy. All my friends are over. They slept over last night. Oh, my gosh, hold on!"

From behind the half-closed door, Trammel could hear the girls carrying on.

"You won't b'lieve it! It's Tra-am!"

"Tra-am?!"

"Trammel D. Jones! He's here sellin' candy fer his baseball team or somethin'!"

"Oh, my gosh! WhattuI look like?"

For twenty minutes the girls fixed their hair and changed into more appropriate attire, one of them being sent every now and then to assure the boy standing outside on a day that was only getting hotter that they would be with him in a moment. Finally, they all arrived as a giggling group of smartly dressed girls, wearing far more makeup than was necessary, who collectively paid him with a check for eight dollars, written by the unseen mother of the first girl. Trammel thought he was in the clear then and handed over eight bars of candy, only to be told that each girl wanted him to sign her own personal bar.

"You mean like a autograph?"

"Yeah, like a autograph," giggled one of the girls, handing him a pen.

"Whatcha gonna do with it?" Clearly the girls had not thought that far into the future, but the terms of their contract were non-negotiable. Trammel signed the candy bars as he mentally checked this house off the list—*forever*.

On the last day of the candy sales Trammel would bring his three "starter" boxes to practice, two of them unopened, and hand them into the Team Mom, i.e. his mother. If anyone asked him how much candy he had sold, he would just respond enigmatically, "'Ey wudn't really buyin' 'is year," as though explaining an unsuccessful fishing trip. Salesmanship—he hated it.

In addition to thinking the mass candy drive was stupid in the first place, Trammel considered the celebrity—and prize—offered up to the champion candy salesman a complete farce. The winner was always some kid who was one of the worst players on his team. And yet he would get his picture in the paper, shake hands with the mayor, and get a brand new bike! For what? For having his father and all his relatives take box after box of candy to their offices and push it on their co-workers. Little Tommy Foster had not sold one-tenth of the candy out of all the boxes he had racked up. Couldn't anybody figure that out?

After the obligatory photo op featuring the mayor shaking Tommy's hand and smiling broadly, the boy returned to his team while Mayor Hardly started on his "brief remarks." Trammel took little interest in what the mayor had to say, particularly since his address was the very same as the one he gave last year. It began with his own reminiscences of childhood—"I remember when I was in your cleats, playing on this same Little League field, too many years ago to count." For fifteen or twenty minutes he treated the crowd to disconnected anecdotes, excerpts from his stump speech, laudations on the "great people of Dogwood," and appeals to the boys to keep doing what they were doing. At last came the peroration: "And then some day maybe one of you will become mayor of Dogwood." Trammel had had more than a little coaching in his contempt for this bombast. His father had grown up with the mayor of Dogwood and had nothing charitable to say about his performance on that same Little League field.

"'E 'as a mullet."

"The mayor?"

"A pure-D mullet, none worse. 'At kid cou'dn't th'ow, cou'dn't catch, cou'dn't hit. 'E 'as plum scared a' the ball, always dodgin' outta the box, hopin' ta get a walk jus' ta get on base ever now an' 'en. 'E spent perty much all 'is time in 'a dugout— workin' on 'is future longwinded speeches as mayor a' Dogwood, I 'magine."

After a discharge of tobacco, his father continued, "In football it 'as even worse. 'E never played no pick-up games with us 'roun' 'a neighborhood. 'E did play one year a' Pee Wee. I 'member 'e 'as always wearin' 'a whitest uniform in practice: white pants, white tee shirt, white socks, like 'ey' all jus' been bleached. 'Is helmet didn't eb'm have a scratch on it 'cause 'e never hit nobody. His momma must 'a' dressed eem herself 'fore ever practice. We called eem Mr. Clean. Anyway, one day i'd been rainin' all day, an' 'ere 'as puddles all over the place. Coach didn't ever know what ta do with eem, but ever now an' 'en 'e'd put eem in as a runnin' back since 'e 'as at least good at runnin' away from 'er'body, 'specially when Coach wanted ta practice some D. So I tol' a couple a' my buddies, ol' Charles Ray bein' one ob'm, 'Whene'r 'e comes runnin' 'roun' your end, hol' eem up o'er by one a' them puddles, an' I'll come crashin' in an' give Mr. Clean a bath like 'e ain't never had b'fore.' So 'ey did jus' like I said, an' I hit 'at boy hard, real hard, an' slid eem th'ough the water an' mud an' grass an' all like 'e ain't never been in. I tell ya, 'at kid got up an' 'as so bent outta shape over 'is stuff bein' dirty 'at 'e cou'dn't hardly keep eemself from cryin'. 'At 'as perty much 'a end of 'is football career. When 'e got up in high school I reckon 'e figur'd 'e 'as better at keepin' uniforms clean 'n playin' in 'em, so 'e became 'a *team manager*," the father pronounced with clear disdain in his voice.

"Wha' does 'at mean?"

"Basically, the great future mayor a' Dogwood carried my jock strap."

"Honey, please!" interjected the mother, who had been listening to this tale from the sidelines.

"Well, babe, the boy deserves ta hear the honest-ta-God truth once in a while, not like 'a papers tell it." The mother could not dispute the truth of the account, only wince at its colorful delivery.

As for his son being mayor of Dogwood, such was not the honor Mr. Jones hoped for: "'A'd be a disgrace."

As important as was the mayor's address to Opening Ceremonies, he was not batting cleanup. That important office belonged to Miss Dogwood, or Miss Teen Dogwood, to be exact. Every year the reigning Miss Dogwood had the distinct honor of throwing the first pitch to the opening game's home-team catcher. Of all the excruciating acts to the drama of Opening Ceremonies, Trammel had always considered this one the stupidest. What did a girl have to do with a baseball game, especially a girl who could hardly throw a baseball? As Miss Dogwood strolled out onto the field, however, the young man began to undergo a change of heart. This year's beauty queen was Sharla Lewis, his friend Todd's older sister, who had known Trammel since they were in the same elementary school together: she in the fifth grade, he in the first. A little later she had been his baby sitter for a time, and he used to flirt shamelessly with her before he grew self-conscious around girls. Today, the seventeen-year-old Miss Dogwood did not wear a sequined dress; that would have been overkill and unbearable on such a hot day. But she did don both tiara and sash, emblems of her royalty, over a snug powder blue cotton tee shirt bearing the words "Dogwood Little League," made specially for the occasion, and khaki shorts that lived up to their name, though they were not nearly as immodest and had an effect a good deal more pleasing than that offered by some of the not-so-trim mothers sitting in the bleachers who wore shorts no less revealing. Trammel had to admit to himself that Todd's sister was uncommonly beautiful. He was even more impressed that she borrowed a glove from one of the younger players and threw a decent pitch, with a short wind-up, from the top of the mound, albeit with a feminine flair befitting a beauty queen. In fact, the naturally athletic Sharla, sister to three brothers, had played softball up through middle school, until her dance and music lessons, insisted on by her mother, managed to crowd out the rest of her schedule.

Charlie Thompson, Big Luke's catcher, turned around to offer Trammel a mild taunt, "I 'ope you can git it across 'a plate 'at good t'day, Tram."

Logan Dwyer, the team jokester, added, "I'd rather watch *her* pitch 'n you any day, Tram." The object of these witticisms was not unequal to the challenge.

"Yeah, you might actually git a hit off *her*." Trammel spit a few more shells. "But 'at'd be all you'd git."

As the cheering died down for Miss Dogwood's first pitch, all but the two teams playing in the opening game dissipated from the field. Those teams got down to business in starting to warm up. A few older boys came out to rake and re-chalk the infield and the batter's boxes. Miss Dogwood was detained for some time at the pitcher's mound by a young reporter named Skip from the *Dogwood Daily Sentinel*. Once she had answered enough of the reporter's repetitive questions—questions revealing mainly that Skip had just gotten out of journalism school, had just gotten this assignment, knew nothing about Dogwood or Little League or baseball, knew no shorthand and therefore had to guess at what his source had just said because he could not write it down fast enough, and was still quite nervous around beautiful girls—the beauty queen sauntered directly towards Trammel, who was working on his knuckle ball with Charlie. As he tried not to notice her approach the young man wondered what the platinum blonde, whose hair was even blonder than his, could possibly want with him.

His question was soon answered when Sharla cozied up to him, put a hand on his shoulder and spoke softly into his ear, "You take it to 'em t'day now, Tra-am," the belle incited, elongating the vowel in his name, as did all true Texan girls. "I'm countin' on ya. I'll be watchin' every pitch." This command she followed up with a wink, as yet bestowed upon no one else during her reign, a wink even her boyfriend had never seen. Trammel turned beet red, and the other boys' eyes fixed on him for a few moments in astonishment. Miss Dogwood then glided to the other side of the field and extended her hand to the other team's pitcher—in order to keep up appearances of being no partisan queen.

Chapter 3: "Play Ball!" and A Legend

Both teams having warmed up, Tanner Dodge took the field as home team while Big Luke's players filed into the first-base dugout. The lead-off batter for Big Luke, a short, fast fourteen-year-old named Russ Howell, put on his batting glove and began swinging a couple of bats together en route to the on-deck circle. Trammel did not take a seat on the bench but rather leaned against the chain link and looked out at the opposing players. He was batting cleanup and, besides, was not one to sit down until he knew the game was heading in the direction he wanted. As the opposing pitcher took a few warm-up throws, Russ swung his way to the plate. The home plate umpire surveyed the field and then turned around to give a thumbs up to the announcer's box atop the concession stand directly behind home plate. Over the P. A., an unfamiliar voice pronounced intimately familiar words: "Okay, boys, let's plaaaay sooooommme baaaaaaaseball!"

A murmur of discontent broke out in bleacher and dugout alike. "'E can't say that," objected one of the Big Luke players. "'At ain't his sayin'!"

"Who is 'at guy?" queried another.

Coach Steere, arms folded, leaning against the pole connecting the outfield fence to the dugout, for once took part in the players' dugout chatter. "Some kid in high school 'ey hired. Wonts ta be a profess'nal 'nouncer er sump'm."

The widespread disapproval of the voice coming over the Dogwood Little League public address system was perhaps inevitable. For two decades the only voice fans had heard calling games on the Big Field was that of Mr. Jackson, who had never missed a game as far as anyone could remember. Mr. Jackson had passed away this past fall, and hundreds of boys, including Trammel, and nearly all of the coaches going decades back, had attended the funeral. Mr. Jackson had, in fact, been one of the five founders of the league, Trammel's grandfather having been another one. The two men were somehow linked in Trammel's mind, not only because they were both older, knew each other well, and had lived in the town for a long time, but also because they were the only men he had ever known to be given the highest praise he could think of, that of being called "a legend."

The legend of Mr. Jackson began when he was hardly more than a boy. He had grown up on a farm just North of Dogwood, the youngest of four sons, in the early decades of the century. When it became clear that Americans would see combat in the Great War, the war now known as World War I, he doctored his birth certificate, stole away from home, and enlisted in the Marine Corps. He did see action and was decorated for his bravery at Belleau Wood. Returning home, he worked on the farm for a year but then decided to go to college in order to return to the service as an officer. While in college he played baseball and was even scouted by some professional teams, but he finished in two and a half years and took his commission. Dogwood saw little of him during the years between the wars, except that he used all of his leave every year to return to the family farm and help out during harvest time. On one of those leaves he saw that the daughter of the owner of the feed and seed store, then keeping the books for her father's growing business, had graduated high school and grown uncommonly pretty. The next year, at the same time, the young officer married her. By the second of the two great wars, Jackson had risen to the rank of major and would go on to become a full-bird colonel. He led a battalion in the landings of Guadalcanal and Okinawa, suffering a flesh wound himself in the second of the two engagements. He never talked about his actions or what he saw in those battles and only referred to the war itself in the most general of terms.

On retiring from the service, Mr. Jackson returned with his wife to their hometown, two of their children having already gone off to college, with the third finishing up high school. The locals wanted the war veteran—who insisted on being called Mr. Jackson rather than colonel—to capitalize on his hero status and run for office.

He just replied politely and gratefully that he "had more important things to do than mess around with politics." Other than taking over the family farm, his older brothers having opted for careers taking them into Dallas, his first project was starting the Little League, along with four other men, all veterans. Actually, it was at first called the Dogwood Boys' Baseball League, since Little League was just then starting to spread out of Pennsylvania. Once Little League became a national enterprise, the Dogwood league joined the more famous organization. Buying the land with their own money, the men, along with their sons and some other boys, cleared and leveled what had been pasture, built the backstops and the concession stand, and lay the rock for the parking lot.

Mr. Jackson embarked on other ventures as well. He donated not just money but a substantial collection of books to the town library, particularly in history and adventure literature for boys. Over the years he was more on top of acquisitions in those areas than even the paid librarians, and not a good biography of an American hero or volume of tall tales was published that he failed to donate with his special inscription: "Read this book, young man, and dream big dreams. Mr. Jackson." Not to be outdone, his wife donated the complete works of L. M. Montgomery with her own message: "Read this, young lady, and learn the joys of family and true friendship. Mrs. Jackson."

An even more conspicuous act of philanthropy, with an occasional profit made, was Mr. Jackson's buying and refurbishing in the mid-sixties the old "picture shows." The two one-screen movie theaters that faced each other on Main Street had been the busiest places in town on the weekends when Trammel's father was growing up. One of them, The Select, showed films that adults would be interested in. The other, The Texan, played only one kind of movies: Westerns. These movies were never classic Westerns such as *High Noon* or *The Man Who Shot Liberty Valance*. Those films would run at The Select. Rather The Texan only showed shoot-'em-ups. And no one older than thirteen or fourteen ever stepped foot into the actual auditorium of The Texan. That was not only because the features were lowbrow, but also because of the unrefined habits of those who watched those movies. The young boys, not wishing to miss a single shoot-out, did not go to the restroom whenever nature called, but instead they would run down to the front of the stage and relieve themselves on the spot. The place smelled accordingly. Thus, parents wanting to see a movie on their own, more often the case in those days, simply dropped off their children at The Texan and themselves saw the picture at The Select. It was a perfect arrangement.

In the early sixties attendance dropped off substantially at The Texan until it went out of business. The Select fared a little better. Mr. Jackson bought The Texan for a song and, based on its renewed business and the owners of The Select wanting to retire, took over that cinema as well. With the former theatre, after a much needed renovation and full-scale fumigation, Mr. Jackson simply revamped and improved the original principle. He showed movies that would appeal to children and early adolescents, but he alternated Westerns, adventures such as *Tarzan*, classic cartoons, and true classics like *The Wizard of Oz* in an effort to appeal to different audiences. He distributed to the local schools at the end of each year coupons for dollar movies and fifty-cent popcorn, thereby filling the theatre from noon 'til night for the first month of summer and doing respectable business in July and August. The Select continued to show mainline movies on weekends, a few weeks behind their opening, but also featured classics in the earlier part of the week when the older folks went out. This strategy proved to be a winning one—in terms of business and as a matter of inviting people to spend their time watching good things—until a year or two before Mr. Jackson died. That was right when cable television came to town.

Though Mr. Jackson spent considerable time and not a little money on such projects, his greatest love had been boys' baseball. He had regretted not being able, because of the war, to spend much time with his own sons as they got better at the game. He made up for it by coaching for a decade and a half. He racked up so many championships—due to his superior insights into the game and an unerring eye for young talent—that he decided at last to give the new breed of coaches the chance at a title. Nor did the daily demands of working with one team for victory allow him to enjoy watching the game as a whole and all the boys in Dogwood who wanted to play baseball. So his "retirement," as he called it, from working with one team led to his serving as the all-knowing, all-seeing, somewhat understated, but always fair and accurate official scorekeeper and announcer for the eighty some odd games played on the Big Field every year for twenty straight years. The league recognized the beloved Mr. Jackson with a ceremony at the field following his funeral. A large wooden cutout of a baseball was attached to the side of the announcer's box, noting his title as co-founder and the years he had coached and called games, all beneath the words: "Mr. Jackson, The Voice of Dogwood Baseball." His wife of nearly sixty years teared up at the ceremony and, smiling, pronounced the tribute the best memorial anyone could have ever given him.

Trammel had known Mr. Jackson pretty well since announcing on the Big Field did not prevent him from watching a few games in the younger leagues. He also served as announcer for the all-star games of all the leagues. Trammel was the son of one of Mr. Jackson's favorite players. The kindly old man was in fact extremely gracious with his praise of the local legend's own son, whom he pronounced, "of all 'a boys I've seen on 'ese fields, the *gamest* ballplayer. An' you gotta remember, I watched your daddy play."

Until today the announcer's box had been empty. No current parent could make the time commitment, and there was no natural successor to Mr. Jackson. As school came to an end, this high-school student, résumé in hand, did apply for the job and in an interview with the league board proved that he had all the technical skill needed to call a baseball game. The jarring effect of an unknown voice, particularly one copping the familiar and heart-warming words that had started every game for twenty straight years, could have been meliorated by an apologetic self-introduction on the part of the new announcer, a confession that he could never do half the job that Mr. Jackson had done but nonetheless hoped to keep the tradition of calling Dogwood Little League games going. But no one offered any such advice to the novice, and the new announcer, having never played Little League himself, instead having viewed the game only as a spectator and as a budding sportscaster, held no such reverence in his heart for the true voice of Dogwood baseball.

Amid the indignant protests in the Big Luke dugout, the team jokester, Logan Dwyer, failed to show proper reverence himself in an attempt at raising a laugh. "Yeah, I'd ruther 'ave ol' man

Jackson up 'ere fallin' asleep 'n 'is new kid any day." The crack led to only a couple of chuckles and a terse rebuke from Trammel. Without turning his head, he spit a few shells through the fence and laid down the law.

"Anybody makes fun a' Mr. Jackson," he announced in his longest drawl, "'as gotta deal with me."

Dwyer, jokester though he was, knew he had crossed the line. "Sorry, Tram," the wit offered in a subdued tone. "Didn't mean it like 'at."

No one wished to tangle with Trammel since he was undisputedly—and the opposing players knew this—the toughest boy in all four of the Dogwood middle schools. Indeed, not too many lower classmen in the high school would have been willing to "mess with" him. Like most boys in Dogwood, he had gotten into his share of scrapes in elementary school. He had won all of them but two, and those two had been with much older boys who were bullying younger ones. Even those two altercations, more draws than defeats, served their purpose of showing that Trammel would never give in without a fight, and the bully would not go home without at least a taste of his own medicine. These fights followed a time-tested protocol. Whenever school was in session, boys would have some disagreement on the playground, normally over whether one player broke the rules in one game or another. The two toughest boys would square off, goaded on by their respective supporters. After the exchange of fierce glares, the decisive words would be uttered: "We'll settle 'is off school grounds." Over the course of the day most of the boys of the school—never the teachers—would receive the latest intelligence: "Tram an' Billy's gonna fight t'day after school. Over in 'a park 'cross from Bobby Miller's place." Depending on the justice of the cause, the equality of the match, the animosity of the two boys, or the extent to which they were really friends, much diplomacy could take place. The combatants did not negotiate personally and directly but rather through their trusted seconds. These affairs had to be handled with some delicacy since neither boy wanted to appear the coward or to show signs of weakness. In cases where one boy had gotten in way over his head, it was the privilege of the stronger to show magnanimity and call off the fight, although waiting to see whether the weaker boy would show up was perfectly acceptable.

Many of these disagreements did reach the fighting stage, especially if Trammel was one of the parties. He figured that if any boy squared off with him, especially since he himself did not go around looking for fights, that boy knew what he was getting into. Nor did he participate in any of the strange stalling techniques and refinements of honor immediately preceding the outbreak of actual hostilities: no last minute negotiations, no walking around the field or neighborhood to find the ideal spot of ground for a fight, no prolonged waiting to see who would take the first punch. Only in one of his earlier bouts did he find himself for a short while staring at his opponent, each forswearing the first punch. After a moment's reflection he reasoned that this piece of chivalric pedantry was preposterous: they had already decided to fight, everyone there was waiting to see a fight, so *someone* would have to take the first punch. Why shouldn't he be the one to take it? He did preface his offensive, though, with the warning, "I'm 'bout ta pop ya in 'a mouth, sa git ready." After that, he figured everybody knew the rule: *Trammel takes the first punch.*

As important as these boyhood skirmishes were for the fostering of male honor, they were not that "big of a deal." They lasted typically only through a flurry of punches; the punches did not hurt much; and each boy could go home satisfied at having conducted himself honorably and bravely in a fair fight. As the boys got older, things started to change, and as a result the number of fights decreased substantially. For one thing, the punches started hurting, really hurting, and leaving distinct marks. The fights, though not for great causes, were not over trivial, momentary disputes either, but rather were more likely the settling of some permanent ill will. Foul language often attended them, and teenage boys were more prone to take cheap shots. The passions of adolescents—real fear and real hatred—were more developed than those of younger boys. As a result, fewer fights broke out in middle school, though those few were nastier; and Trammel need not fight at all since his reputation for being able to deliver a sound beating was beyond dispute. An incident this past fall, however, had made him a legend not only in his own middle school but among boys throughout the town.

It all started when Trammel's younger sister, Christie, came home from school crying. She had walked from the elementary school over to the middle school in order to spend the afternoon with an older girl well-known to the family and in Trammel's class. As she was waiting for the friend, a boy came up to her and another girl and began saying filthy things to them. The boy was Greg Peel, an eighth-grader notorious for picking on girls, sometimes by pushing them, occasionally by smacking them on the bottom, but more often by introducing them to dirty words and making obscene gestures at them during lunch and after school. If he saw a lone girl in the hall while on a restroom break, he would just blurt out something foul, and the girl would run away crying. Several upset mothers had called the school to report Peel's lewd behavior, but little was ever done. Trammel knew nothing of these events since the middle school was big, he did not talk much to the girls, and he spent no time in the company of Peel, whom he despised.

That day, however, Trammel's younger sister got a real taste of what it is like to be a girl in a public middle school, and the whole affair was brought home to the Joneses and to Trammel. Once the father got home early, his wife having called him at work, he and the mother had a private talk with their daughter in her room. Trammel knew something was amiss when he got home from football practice that afternoon since his father's car was never in the garage at that time. He could tell they were all upstairs in Christie's room as he could overhear his sister burst out into tears periodically, though his parents' voices were muffled by the closed door. After a quarter of an hour, he heard his parents speaking in low voices in the hall. He could make out none of their conversation, except once when his father's voice escalated in saying, "'At won't do *nut'n*'!" Another hushed exchange took place. Then Trammel's mother went back into his sister's room while his father came downstairs and appeared at the entryway of the kitchen where the boy was eating tostada chips and picante sauce.

"Son, cou'd we see ya upstairs a minute?" the father summoned with rage in his eyes, though speaking softly.

Trammel instantly jumped up, almost choking on a chip while trying to say "Yes, sir." He quickly reflected on what he could have done to upset the family, particularly given that he had only seen his sister that morning.

"Have a seat, son."

The boy sat down on one of the smallish wooden chairs that made up his sister's tea table set, after moving one of her big stuffed animals that had occupied it. His mother had clearly been crying and now looked at her son with peculiar intensity, as though with a strange, sorrowful hope. The father put his hand on his daughter's hair, the girl still sobbing quietly and looking down at the floor with her arms crossed.

"Tell eem whatcha tol' us, Chris. It's a'right. 'E's your brother an' wonts ta take care a' ya."

Trammel's sister looked up, and with tears streaming down her face appeared quite unlike her normally cheerful, happy-go-lucky self. "When I was waitin' fer Julie outside your school today, this boy come up ta us, me and Kelly—ya know the girl with the red hair and freckles—and he started sayin' stuff, ya know, bad words that I've never heard before. And he was sayin' stuff ta Kelly, too, but mostly he was starin' at me the whole time. Kelly said it was this kid named Peel, and later Julie told me he does this stuff ta girls all the time. A lotta times he even touches 'em."

The rage in his father's eyes ignited in Trammel's as the boy thought for a moment.

"Can ya tell me what words?"

The father handed his son a slip of paper on which a distraught eleven-year-old girl had forced herself to spell out the language of sexual vulgarity. Trammel got the picture. His nostrils flared. He looked up at his father, who asked of him one simple question.

"Ya know what ta do, boy?"

"Yes, sir. I know what ta do."

At that moment he shot out of the room headed for the garage and his bicycle.

"Tram!" his father called after him.

"Sir?"

"E's at home now an' won't come out if ya go after eem. A punk like 'at won't ever come out fer a fair fight. You'll 'ave ta git eem tomorra. An' one more thang: 'e'll be runnin'. 'At you 'n count on."

Before first period the next morning, Trammel grabbed Peel by the neck and slammed him into some lockers. Though just as tall as Trammel and considerably huskier, Peel did not consider himself any match for the athletic, sinewy boy who was now calling him out with a quiet rage. The protective brother ordered the creep to apologize to any girl he had ever touched or made an offensive remark to by the end of the day. Peel would still have to answer for what he had said to Trammel's sister, but the "beatin' might not be as bad" if he "did a lotta 'pologizin' all day long."

"Yeah, Tram, no pro'lem," the vulgarian agreed.

The plan, more gracious than his father would have allowed, at first backfired, but in the end it showed Peel's true character. Peel went up to every girl he had offended, and some he had not, and started with the words "I am sorry for sayin,'" only to go on by listing every foul word or act he could think of. By third period a dozen girls had been thus violated and, now that they knew they had a protector, had told Trammel everything, relating offenses going back over a year. Trammel thought about going after Peel in the halls but knew the fight would be broken up too soon for him to make his point. Instead, he began to shadow his nemesis and told the girls to keep far away from him for now.

Trammel had gym last period. He asked the coach whether he could stay out to run a few laps before football practice rather than head back in and wait for the bell. The coach was pretty laissez-faire when it came to what the school's athletes did in gym class since they were always working on their game in one way or another; and though Trammel did not yet play for the school, the coaches had been scouting him for years. The coach did not give the request a second thought. When the doors to the back of the gym closed, the class having been quickly corralled back inside by two of Trammel's closest friends, the avenger took off in the direction of Peel's house, only two blocks from the school. For his part, Peel did not waste a second. As soon as the bell rang, he darted out of the room, leaving his books behind, and scampered through the halls before anyone else had gotten out of class. When he reached the front doors he bolted for home. Fifty yards from his house, still running, he began to laugh a dastardly laugh, confident that he had outfoxed the fox, unworried about what the morrow would bring. He did not even see the flash that leapt from behind a car parked on the street, four houses from Peel's own. The fleeing culprit was lifted off his feet with a shoulder to the rib cage that landed him on his back with Trammel on top of him. The blow and the landing knocked all the wind out of Peel, and, thus paralyzed, he had no ability to use his limbs in self-defense.

Without hesitation, Trammel went to work on the malefactor who had trespassed on his sister's innocence. In previous conflicts Trammel had always played the gentleman boxer. In this fight he wanted nothing other than a bloody vengeance. He used his left hand to put a vice grip on his adversary's neck and jaw and took clean, untrammeled shots with his right all about the face. As Peel regained the use of his arms he tried desperately but unsuccessfully to cover his face and to squirm out of Trammel's grasp. Trammel at last allowed the semiconscious punching bag to regain his feet and thereby was able to administer half a dozen hard blows to the stomach. Finished with that angle, Trammel hurled the beaten foe back onto the ground, a coughing, whimpering, bloody mess of a punk, who for once fully felt the much talked-about "consequences" of his actions. Still not fully satisfied, Trammel gave two swift kicks to the hip that would make it hard to get up and, as a final sentence, spit straight into the foul mouth's face.

"Nobody double-crosses me. An' nobody talks 'at way ta my sister. Nobody!"

When Trammel's father arrived home that evening, he asked for a progress report. He got little more from his son than a cryptic "I took care of it, Dad." A fuller answer came when the phone rang, and before he could get the receiver to his ear, Mr. Jones heard an enraged Mr. Peel cursing at the top of his lungs. Trammel's father took the phone out into the garage and held it at a distance until the ranting stopped. The heavy door to the garage was not enough to keep Trammel and his sister from hearing the measured but forceful response of their father.

"Listen ta me, shit-bag. I been doin' a little homework a' my own t'day, an' *you* damn well know your son's been messin' with girls fer a long time. If *you* 'as half a father an' half a man, *you*'d 'a' whooped his ass a long time ago so my son wouldn't 'a' had ta. Next thang *you* gotta know is all 'is big talk is fine comin' over the phone, but if you show your damn face 'round here, you'll be wakin' up tomorra in 'a hospital. I don't know 'xactly what happened t'day, but I know my son's gotta a damn sight more mercy in eem 'n I do, an' I'm already 'bout sick a' *you* an' 'at punk kid a' yours. An' as fer all 'is talk 'bout 'a law, *you* go right ahead an' report my son ta the cops. An' when 'ey start askin' questions 'bout why 'is all come about, you'll be explainin' to 'em why 'at fine son a' yours 'as been shakin' 'is winkie ta twelve-year-old girls all over town. We'll see which charge sticks: a good ol' fashioned ass-whoopin' er indecent exposure. So I've heard 'bout enough from *you*, tough guy, an' since I've spoke my piece, I reckon I'll go have dinner with my family." Clunk.

The last charge was an unsubstantiated rumor that Trammel's father had come upon in the course of his own investigation that day into the record of one Greg Peel. No doubt, Peel had made obscene gestures to girls on numerous occasions; this accusation, whether true or not, was assuredly the best way to keep the police out of a private feud. Mr. Jones re-entered the house with a proud twinkle in his eye. He called his two children over to him, then acting as though they had not been eavesdropping; the mother was still at choir practice, though due home at any moment. With an arm around his daughter and a firm grasp of his son's shoulder, he said, as cryptically as his son had, "Well, boy, I reckon ya did take care of it." That weekend father and son went to their favorite sporting goods store in Dallas to get Trammel a shotgun he had been looking at for some time.

The Peel saga did not quite end there. The next day at school everyone wanted to know what had happened. Trammel was not one to give a blow-by-blow account of his victories, especially not a fight of this magnitude. His terse response did, however, add yet another of his colorful expressions to the school's vocabulary.

"Yeah, I *peeled* eem perty good. I don't reckon 'e'll talk dirty ta no girls no more."

For at least a year after this event, whenever one boy threatened another with physical violence, chances were the verb *to peel* would make an appearance. When Peel did not show up to school the next day, or the next, the boys could not help but wondering how disfigured and bruised his face must have been. Rumors circulated over the number of stitches, whether he had one black eye or two, whether a tooth had been knocked out. That Friday evening and the next morning swarms of boys on bicycles rode by

Peel's house in an attempt to see the extent of the damage for themselves. The first forays tried sympathy and coaxing.

"Mrs. Peel, we wonted ta check on Greg ta see if 'e's a'right."

"Mrs. Peel, Greg ain't been at school fer a couple a' days, an' we wonted ta tell eem 'bout some homework an' stuff 'e's been missin'."

When the boys were refused even a cameo appearance, they tried traditional methods. Circling in the street in front of the house on their bicycles, they yelled out taunts:

"C'mone, Peel, we know Trammel got 'a worst of it. 'E damn near broke 'is hand on your face."

"'Ey, Peel, my li'l sister's out here. Ya wonta come talk dirty to her?"

By Saturday night the house was dark. The boys figured that the Peels had skipped town for a few days. Greg Peel never again walked the halls of Dogwood West Middle School. He transferred the next week to Dogwood South, though he still did not attend classes there for another week. Even so, the boys at Dogwood South reported that Peel still bore the marks of a brutal beating.

As Trammel surveyed the opposing team that Opening Day, "drawing a bead," as his father put it, on each one of the players who would stand before him at the plate, he noted that Greg Peel was in left field.

Chapter 4: "Rattle 'Em"

As he watched Andy Daniels (once again swinging for the fences) whiff away at his third strike, Trammel, viewing the scene from the on-deck circle, knew this would be "a ball game." Trammel's coach uncrossed his arms, put his hands to his hips, and leaned forward in the posture he always assumed when he needed to remind a player of a lesson that had been taught a hundred times before.

"Daniels!   What're ya *thankin'*, son?" the coach bellowed before the hapless player had made it even half-way back to the dugout, both hearing the new voice of Dogwood incant the ignominious phrase "three up, three down" over the loudspeaker. "How many times I gotta tell ya? What we need is *base hits*, not 'is Babe Ruth stuff! When ya make it ta the big leagues, I'll letcha know."

"Sorry, Coach," replied a hung-dog boy as he slunk back into the dugout and retrieved his glove. But there was no stopping "Andy Dan," as his teammates called him, this first time out. Both sets of grandparents were in the stands, and the prospect of a home run his first trip to the plate on Opening Day, whatever the odds against it, was just too tempting for his burgeoning sense of glory.

The first two Big Luke players up to bat had fared no better. Russ Howell grounded out to second, and Jeff Banks popped up to short.   Tanner Dodge boasted probably the best infield in the league, all fourteen-year-olds who had played, whether as back-ups or as starters, on the first-place team last year. They worked together as a team should.

Whether the Tanner Dodge bats were as active as their gloves Trammel would soon find out. Approaching the mound, he leaned over to pick up the ball that had just been tossed to the ground by the other pitcher. Trammel flicked it to Charlie Thompson, with a shake of the head. The catcher turned sheepishly to the umpire.

"'Scuse me, sir, I mean ump. Cou'd we git a differ'nt ball?"

"What's wrong with 'at'n?"

"Ain't nut'n' wrong with 'a ball, 'xactly. It's jus' 'at Tram, 'e's perty superstitious an' don't like playin' with no ball 'at's got such a bad stank on it, ya know, from what jus' happened."

The umpire was not unused to adolescent and, more often, baseball superstition and thus obliged Big Luke with another ball taken from the inside of his chest protector. Trammel, defying league custom, took only three warm-up pitches—all fastballs— the three pitches signaling to the other team the number he would need to dispense with each one of their batters. On meeting Charlie's glove, each pitch sent out a loud crack whose significance was not lost on the opposing team. As the infield finished up tossing the ball around and a batter made his way to the plate, Trammel waited atop the mound, glaring in the general direction of the opposing team. The effect was unsettling.

The first batter up was Stevie Johnson, who was, like Big Luke's Russ Howell, a short, fast kid. He wore two batting gloves and two wristbands, kept his cleated shoes ever so white, and chewed bubble gum, blowing big bubbles throughout the game, even between pitches while at bat. As such, he was what Trammel's father called a "hot dog," that is, one who is more involved in the histrionics and accoutrement of baseball than the game really warrants. Trammel hated hot dogs. He would have liked nothing more than to knock the gum out of Stevie's mouth, and would have if he could have figured out a way of doing so without putting one of the fastest kids in the league on base. Stevie took his time making his way to the plate: what with practice swings, adjusting the fit of each one of his batting gloves, knocking the dirt off the bottoms of his cleats (though apparently just taken from the box), pulling up the sleeves of his undershirt so as not to restrict his movement, and a couple of more practice swings just for good measure, all the while blowing green bubbles half the size of his head. Of course, he also had to glance back at his dugout to make sure he understood his instructions. Trammel glowered at the boy without moving a muscle, save for the fingering of different pitches, though his mind had been made up on what to throw for days.

Contemptuous of this affected imitation of the pros, Trammel commenced his wind-up the instant the boy stepped foot in the batter's box, barely giving his own catcher and the umpire a chance to get into their respective crouches. Even before Trammel had released the fastest fastball he had yet thrown that season, Stevie slipped his right hand up the bat handle as he brought his left down around his waist. Rather than swinging his right side around so as to face the pitcher in the way young players usually do, the boy put his right foot back and crouched into a runner's stance not far off from what the pros would have done. From the four corners of the infield, synchronized with the bellow of Trammel's coach, the cry went out.

"Buuunt!"

On cue, the whole team swung into motion. Charlie, Trammel's catcher, sprung up from sitting on the backs of his ankles to a wider stance that would enable him to launch in any direction if the batter made the mistake of popping up. Billy at first and Jeff at third raced down the base lines, hoping to field the ball in time to throw the runner out. Muñoz, at second, rushed over to cover first, while Todd in right ran in to back up at first. In such a scramble it was not uncommon for the fielder to over throw first or the covering second baseman to miss the ball entirely in his mad dash. Though the other fielders had a head start on him and had been instructed on what parts to execute, Trammel moved no less decisively than they. Seeing the attempt at a bunt, he altered his rhythm in no way, but used his momentum to fly off the mound. Knowing before anyone that the pitch was headed for the outside corner of the plate, he guessed correctly that the bunt would come down the first-base line. Reaching the ball, a slow dribbler perfectly placed for a base hit, Trammel grabbed it with his bare right hand and hurled it, side-armed and without looking, six inches to the inside of the bag and waist high. Billy, the first baseman who had been in his own hot pursuit, dove out of the way of the oncoming ball. In flight, the ball passed the runner and landed safely into Muñoz's glove just a split second before he put a toe into first and crossed the swift runner's path.

"You're ouuuuut!" growled the base umpire as the fans on the Big Luke side, already on their feet, shouted in relief.

"Did y'all see that? Did y'all see that?" asked the rookie announcer rhetorically. "Now, that's the way a team ought to cover a bunt." Had these same words been uttered by Mr. Jackson, they would have been taken as an oracle. But the crack in the young man's voice suggested he had rarely seen a bunt being covered at all, much less like that.

"Now 'at's what I mean by playin' team ball!" yelled out Coach Steere. "Way ta git in p'sition." Such words coming from a coach who was four-fifths vigilance and a mere one-fifth praise signaled that he was proud of his team, though there was no time to dwell on that pride now. "Tram, ya know 'ey're tryin' ta shake ya up out 'ere. Don't let 'em git in your head, now. 'Ey tried it once. 'Ey'll pro'lly try it agin."

And similarly, Trammel's father, sent out his own warning: "Way ta go, Big Tram! You watch fer 'at bunt agin now, boy." Mr. Jones was in his usual post, to the right of the bleachers and leaning into the fence, his forearms just above his head.

"You think they'll try to do that again, dear?" Trammel's mother asked, mystified.

Without turning around, after spitting a stream of tobacco juice through the fence, the tall, muscular man shared his insights into the game with his wife, sitting in the stands six feet behind him.

"'Ey'd be stupid not to. It almost worked 'at time. B'sides, Coach Roberts over 'ere's no dummy. 'E's smart enough ta know 'e can't beat Tram's arm, so 'e'll pro'lly try ta rattle eem a little here at first; git some ducks on 'a pond, ya see."

"You don't think it'll work, do you?"

"I'd be surprised if it did," the father answered, spitting another stream without taking his eyes off his son. "Our boy don't rattle."

In fact, the boys of Tanner Dodge had been working on their bunts all week long, each one laying down two or three in every practice and then, rather than taking the field after completing their turn at hitting, going live on the bases. Tanner's coach perhaps did lack confidence in his boys' hitting against the young fastballer, but he knew they were savvy base runners. He was counting on getting a few on base whereby they might steal their way to home or at the very least cause Trammel, in pitching from the stretch, to slow his fastball or lose his deadly accuracy. The whole was aimed at Trammel's inexperience in playing the game with "loose" bases; that is, runners who could steal at will rather than wait for the pitch to cross the plate as in the junior leagues. It was a good theory but one that had yet to be tested. In Trammel's first two outings on the mound that season only three hitters had gotten on base—two in the first game, one in the second. Since none of them had been particularly fast or daring, and as their coaches did not wish to risk losing a sure runner, they had stuck to the bag. What Coach Roberts did not know was that Trammel and his father had been practicing throwing out base runners since the end of football season. Christie having proven far too slow and too unwilling to dive back into first when the time came, Trammel, at his father's suggestion, invited over friends on the weekend to act as base runners. As these lessons became more and more advanced, a full complement of fielders was needed. While the teams had not yet been picked (though Trammel had already been unofficially "drafted" by Coach Steere to play for Big Luke), and since no official member of the league was present, these sessions turned into a good four or five months' worth of weekend practices before the league allowed the season's real activity to start.

Trammel, hearkening to the counsel of his coach and his father, began sizing up the next batter, another one of Tanner's short, speedy fourteen-year olds. He ruled out the fastball since the advantage of that pitch was lost in the player already having his bat in place. He considered a curve but thought that the hitter would still have time to chase the pitch after it broke. He thought the best option would have been a sinker, if he could time it just right. But Trammel did not yet have a good sinker and would never try one in a game without it being honed to perfection. He was relieved to hear Coach Steere call for the knuckleball, using a code word so mixed in with all his incessant instructions and urgings that only an NSA analyst from M.I.T. with a top-secret computer program could have broken it, and even then not that early in the season. If Charlie, who knew it was coming, had enough trouble catching Trammel's full-blown "Roger the Dodger" knuckle, as he styled it, then the hapless batter would have far less of a chance of getting a good piece of the ball and less still of putting it into play where he wanted it to go.

If baseball is ever a comedy, it is most assuredly so when there is a knuckleballer on the mound. The fluttery pitch makes fools out of hitters and catchers alike. To add a hitter trying to bunt into the mix is to move from the comedic to the absurd. Expecting a fastball, the Tanner player had his bat around all right, too early in fact. The slower pitch, the slowest and most erratic Trammel could deliver, made the wait on the wanton ball excruciating, at least for the hitter who was trying desperately to draw a bead on it. Luck was not with him. The ball took a dive right as it crossed the plate, just as a sinker would have, and the hitter dropped his bat downward just in time to chink it. The ball bounced off home plate and dribbled a couple of feet forward. Hesitating a split second to see what had become of his nervous effort, the hitter sped forth more with a sense of duty than of hope in the outcome. Charlie sprung over the plate on the runner's heels, snatched up the ball that had already died in the grass and had to wait a moment until Muñoz again had first covered. Then Charlie, who had been at nearly every one of Trammel's winter practices, threw out the Tanner runner with seconds to spare.

The young announcer almost said, "Was that a bunt or a hiccup?" thought better of it, and gave the more sedate report that Tanner Dodge had tried to bunt again and again been thrown out at first.

Two at-bats, two pitches into the game, the theory had been tested and found wanting. Big Luke's infield was clockwork against the bunt. And Trammel had a pitch that would bedevil all their attempts at this seemingly sure way of getting on base. Furthermore, if his knuckle was really working today, there was little the opposing batters could do but swing and pray. As the third hitter approached the plate, he turned around suddenly, no doubt on a verbal cue from his coach. He looked intently towards the dugout and was greeted with a barrage of gesticulations and slogans, the vast majority signaling nothing but used to disguise the one message the coach meant to convey. The hitter nodded and took his place in the batter's box. It was Glynn Stockton, Tanner's shortstop and one of the best players in the league. Glynn was the one player on the team who, as Trammel's father had reminded him more than once, would be able to hit Trammel's fastball with more than luck on his side. The two had not played against each other for a year because of their age difference, but two years ago their many encounters, as pitcher and hitter, had been essentially a draw. Off the field Glynn was a pretty cocky kid, a little less so around Trammel, but during a game he was all business.

Coach Steere called for the knuckle again. Had it been Charlie's signal, Trammel would have brushed it off, but he dared not question his coach's wisdom or authority. He threw a similar pitch as the last one, though even a little lower so that Glynn could not get under it enough to send a line drive into the outfield, or worse, send it out of the park. To no one's surprise, Glynn squared his body all the way around for a bunt as the Big Luke infield dashed into position, but the hitter pulled his bat back just before the ball crossed the plate. Though low, the ump liked the pitch enough to sing out, "'At's ooone!'"

Both Coach Steere and Trammel, to say nothing of Mr. Jones, sensed something was wrong. Glynn's motions had been a little too deliberate, and he could have handled the knuckle much better than the previous hitter. The Big Luke coach let out a high-pitched whistle, a general signal that meant, "Do the opposite of what I am about to tell you." He called out to his team, "Okay, Big Luke, look alive out 'ere an' watch 'at bunt agin! Ya know what's comin'!'"

"A'right, Tram," the coach continued, "'e didn't like 'at last pitch. I wonder if 'e's gonna be so picky on 'a nex' one." Along with this reflection, he adjusted his hat in such a way that called on his pitcher to throw a curve, not a pitch he called for very often, but just the pitch Trammel had been considering. As Trammel began his wind-up, Glynn squared around for a bunt, far in advance of when he should have. The first and third basemen held their places. By the time Trammel released his pitch, the feint was over and Glynn was back in his regular stance, ready to unload on a soft knuckleball. He realized in a split second, though, that Trammel had put much more speed on the ball than had been hoped. Unfazed, the hitter swung with conviction at what looked like a fastball coming in waist-high and straight down the middle. The ball broke just as he was in full swing and, rather than hitting it with the meat of the bat, he was just able to reach it with the end. Even so, it was enough of a swing to send the ball off like a shot about a yard off the first-base line. But there it met the glove of Billy Swanson, the tallest kid on the Big Luke team and by far the best basketball player, who leapt into the air just in time to rob Tanner Dodge of what would certainly have been a double, maybe even a triple and a threat to home if the right-fielder had bobbled the ball or missed his throw.

"Saved by the bell, or rather the Bill," the clever announcer crooned, "on a great grab out of the Big Luke first baseman, Billy Swanson."

"Can't somebody shut 'at guy up?" Trammel complained as he headed for the dugout, as disgusted by the novel commentary as by the Tanner Dodge dodges and shenanigans, knowing well that the inning could have come out much, much differently. Had just one pitch, one grab, one player been even a fraction off, there was no telling what could have happened. No doubt there was a good measure of luck in there somewhere as well.

Before Trammel could get in the dugout, Coach Steere, his arms folded and resting on his considerable girth, took the boy aside, motioning for him to stand a little ways down the infield fence—away from the hearing of the other players.

"Ya know 'ey're jus' tryin' ta git in your head, Tram, tryin' ta rattle ya."

"Yeah, well, I'm fixin' ta rattle '*em* sump'm awful."

"'Course ya are. But I ain't worried 'boutchur hittin'. You'll git up 'ere an' give us a good base hit in a sec'. I'm talkin' 'boutchur pitchin'. If ya keep your cool out 'ere on 'at mound, 'ere ain't no way 'ey're gonna be able ta keep 'is up. An' 'en, after 'ese stunts ain't worked, 'ey got nut'n' ta fall back on — *nut'n'*. 'Ere's pro'lly only one er two kids over 'ere 'at can hit 'at fas'ball. An' we can figur' out other ways ta take care a' them. So you jus' stick ta your game. It's *your* game, not 'eirs. Got it?"

"Yes, sir. I got it, Coach," replied the young athlete, anxious to get his bat and give the Tanner team a taste of their own medicine.

As Trammel had been heading back to the dugout, Mr. Jones had instinctively started in that direction, too, thought better of it, and sat down next to his wife on the edge of the bleachers, a seat that hardly got warm during the game. Having been his son's coach every year from tee-ball until just this season—and his personal trainer since the boy was just over a year old and showed a natural talent for picking up a ball (the first word other than "Ma-ma" that the boy said) and hurling it across the room—the father did not easily fit into the role of mere fan or spectator. Yet his sizable promotion of a couple of years ago, which had required much more and less predictable travel, had gotten in the way of his handling a whole team. So he had to cede his game time command over his son to other men. Yet he was glad that Trammel had ended up on Mr. Steere's ball club. He had known Steere since their own playing days when they had been rivals. Now that Mr. Jackson had passed on, Coach Steere was the only man in the league who knew the game as well as Trammel's father.

Trammel took only a couple of practice swings in the on-deck circle as the opposing pitcher finished his warm-ups. Before walking slowly and resolutely towards the plate, he glanced over at his father, who had given up sitting in the bleachers and was now in his customary position again, leaning into the infield fence just off the dugout.

"Jus' a smooth, eb'm stroke, now, Tram. You watch 'at ball all 'a way in. 'Is is jus' battin' practice."

Trammel nodded slightly and confided in his father that look of assurance sons give.

Stepping up to the plate, Trammel sized up the situation. The players were all on edge since it was the beginning of an inning and Trammel was a "real stick." He thought he might shake things up a little more. Just before Trent, the opposing pitcher, released a decent fastball, Trammel gave an eye for an eye. Using his left leg as his fulcrum, he slid his right foot back directly behind him and leaned towards the plate, spreading his hands apart, so there could be no question what he might do. The call for a bunt went out, and the players across the field shot into their places. Trammel, having lowered it, pulled the bat back just in time to keep from committing himself to a "swing," and the pitch barely missed the outside corner. Backing out of the box, Trammel looked behind him to the Tanner dugout to sense Coach Roberts's reaction. It was obvious that the hitter was not taking instructions from his coach but rather acting on his own. Thus his intent was by no means clear. Was Trammel intending to show the Tanner team how really to get on base with a bunt and steal at will? He was certainly fast enough. Or was he going to rearrange the field and put the team off balance so that he could pick them apart? He was capable of either.

The next pitch revealed what Trammel had already decided long before the game had begun. Notwithstanding the feinted bunt, Trammel had no one's number more than Greg Peel's, who was not a particularly good ball player to begin with. The pitch came in as another fastball, this one grazing the inside corner, which Trammel sent screaming out past Peel against the left-field fence. By the time the centerfielder (having to make up for Peel's dilatoriness) got to the ball, Trammel was rounding first and seeing whether he could stretch it to third. He took second with ease amid calls of "The play's at third! The play's at third!" and came to a crouching halt ten feet past the base to watch what would become of the throw. The center fielder, a lanky boy named Tommy who had a great arm, sailed the ball into third on one hop, so Trammel sidestepped back to second, kicking up dust, his eyes daring the third basemen to throw the ball his way. This tense moment was clearly not the last encounter these two ballplayers would have this inning.

"Trammel Jones with a stand-up double, and we finally have a duck on the pond in this ball game," came the narration from atop the concession stand.

"'At's Trammel *D*. Jones," the boy muttered aloud. "*D* as in Dick."

The second baseman, still covering the bag, could not help but laughing. "Y'all don't like 'is new guy neither?"

"Ta tell 'a truth, I can't stand his sorry ass," Trammel affirmed.

"Yeah, I know whatcha mean. . . . Say, Tram," second continued, "'at 'as a perty good hit, but I can't have ya stealin' no bases out here. 'At's all 'ere is to it."

"Man can't steal what's already his," was the reply.

"Is 'at right?"

"Yeah, I reckon 'at's right, 'nless y'all can prove otherwise."

This exchange between the two boys, friendly yet not without taunt, concerned the very issue on everyone's mind. Trammel would assuredly make an attempt on third. It was in his nature to do so. He would rather take third on his own than have to wait on the chance of one of his teammates advancing him. He would need someone else's help to make it home, but third he regarded as well within his grasp.

As though reading the boy's mind, or not being able to keep Trammel from his honor, Coach Steere called for Muñoz, now at the plate, to take the pitch. The coach gave the signal twice because the scrappy Muñoz was notorious for swinging at anything within reach of his bat, for better and for worse. The Tanner pitcher, from the stretch, alternated between reading his catcher's signals and looking back at second. Trammel nonchalantly eased off the bag, almost as an obligation, as though he had no other mind than to bide his time until a hit or a sacrifice compelled him to advance. Yet the instant the pitcher's raised left foot and momentum of his body were bound to follow through with a throw to home Trammel lit out for third, without any hesitation or glance towards the catcher, who was now springing to his feet to receive the throw, intentionally high and outside.

Anyone can throw a baseball faster than a man, or a youngster, can run. Two throws, from pitcher to home and from home to third; combined with the split second it takes the catcher to grab the ball from his mitt and put it back into the air; added to the split-second jump the runner already had while the pitcher still held the ball; and further strung out by the very brief moment it takes the third baseman to secure the ball in his glove and get it, when the throw is even slightly high, down to the runner who is sliding under the coming tag: all this constitutes precious seconds, just enough for the swiftest and savviest of base stealers to make it. There is this added advantage to the runner when the base in question is third, this major flaw in the minds more than the talents of the fielders: overconfidence. Watch any Little League team warming up before an inning. The routine is most always the same. The pitcher throws a few pitches. On the last one the catcher gets his practice against base stealers by throwing to . . . second base. It makes perfect sense that he do so. More runners get to first than to second. The throw from home to second is much longer, much harder, more common, and therefore the one that catchers try to hone to perfection. And third? "Anybody can throw a runner out at third," the young catcher assumes. "It's just right over there." And so the throw-out at third is, like so many other "easy" things in life, taken for granted. The catcher rarely practices it, and, what is more important, the third baseman rarely practices it.

Trammel, who had a feel for the game like no one his age, took full advantage of this oversight, this overconfidence. His sprint from second to third was "jack-rabbit fast," as his grandfather would say, but the slide was just as important. Without losing a step he launched himself into the prone position, headfirst, hands outstretched: Pete Rose rather than Lou Brock style in the day's lexicon. He slid to the right of the bag, catching the corner with his left hand as the throw came just inches too high. The third baseman knew as he brought the tag down it was a split second too late.

"Safe!" pronounced the base umpire, spreading his hands out wide, with no word of protest coming from the Tanner dugout.

"Yeah!" Trammel's dad shouted along with the rest of the Big Luke fans, and without thinking, he punched the chain-link fence he had been leaning against with enough force to draw blood. "Now 'at's what I call real *hustle!*"

Calling a brief "time" to the base umpire, Trammel, covered in orange sand, dusted himself off while the rookie announcer continued his saga. "He can pitch, he can hit, he can run. What can this kid not do?" As the "kid" grumbled that he could also give smart-aleck announcers "an old-fashioned butt-whoopin'," the expressionless base umpire held back a grin and pretended not to notice.

"It took ya long enough ta git here," joked Mr. Scott, the Big Luke assistant coach, who was now acting as the third-base coach.

"I won't be here fer long, neither, so don't worry none 'bout me," replied the runner.

"Yeah, 'bout 'at, Tram," Mr. Scott began, putting his arm around the boy and taking him to the side so the Tanner third baseman could not overhear them. "Here's 'a deal. Coach is gonna wont ya ta stay put 'til we git Muñoz on base over 'ere. So do whatcha have ta ta keep ol' Trent guessin', but don't risk gittin' th'own out, ya hear?"

"Yes, sir."

As Trammel got back on the base, Coach Steere called Muñoz to take this next pitch as well. This directive put the boy in a bind. Not only was his own forward temperament unsuited to such a patient policy, but his father, a hard-working man who had emigrated from Mexico in his teens, simply did not believe in walks. Mr. Muñoz could now be heard above the entire crowd either yelling at or encouraging his son, whom the father called curiously by his surname during ballgames (though he did not pronounce it as all the Texans did, moon yos´). What Mr. Muñoz was saying no one could make out—it sounded nothing like what was taught in the so-called Spanish classes in school—but no doubt the father was calling upon his son to disregard the coach's orders. The boy knew better than to look in the direction of his father. He just shook his head and stepped into the box, resigning himself to the fact he would have to wear himself out trying to explain things later that night.

Trammel knew that he was not going to try to take home, but the opposing pitcher did not know that. And Trammel made the most of that uncertainty. At third base he could look the pitcher straight in the eye and move down the base line just enough to threaten a steal but not enough to get thrown out. Twice the Tanner pitcher threw to third in a vain attempt to get the runner to stick more closely to the bag, but Trammel was not about to give an inch. It was not just the steal to worry about. Coach Roberts kept reminding his team of the circumstances in which they might make a play at home, but such a scenario required the runner not to have a very good jump to begin with.

Trammel's persistent fishing for a throw to third unnerved the young pitcher. Going back to his primary job, Trent saw his control badly impaired. He threw a second ball and then a third. With a count of 3 and 0, even Muñoz knew to take the pitch. When the pitcher, just to get one across the plate, served up a fairly fat pitch down the middle, the father's "Muñoz!" followed by a barrage of Spanish invective filled the stands. Trammel drew another throw to third, leading to another call from Coach Steere to take the pitch, which got Muñoz on base with a walk.

Runners on first and third put the pitcher and catcher in the most humiliating position. If they try to throw out the runner at first attempting to steal second, with no guarantees of accomplishing even that, a savvy runner at third might very well make it home. With Trammel on third, the Tanner coach did not want to try anything fancy, so Muñoz took second on the first pitch to the next batter, knowing that this boon for the team would not placate his father unless he scored on this outing and got at least two solid base hits.

Now the fruit was ripe for the picking. Two of the best base runners in the league were at second and third, with no outs. At the plate was Todd Raines. He was not the best pure hitter on the team by any means. Yet, unknown to Tanner Dodge, he was a competent bunter and batted in that place in the order for just this very contingency. Coach Roberts took a time-out to have a talk with his pitcher, no doubt encouraging the boy just to get the ball over the plate and worry less about the runners on base, which is precisely what Big Luke needed him to do at this moment. The Tanner coach might have called for an intentional walk to load up the bases and give the infield a force anywhere, but he knew the potential effect of having the bases loaded with no outs, though in one sense strategically sound, would prove psychologically devastating to the young pitcher whose nerves were already on edge. He was a good pitcher, too, and had gotten out of tough innings before unscathed.

Mr. Scott told Trammel what to look for in the first pitch, namely, that it would not be part of an intentional walk. Seeing the pitcher about to release the ball, Trammel took off like a shot towards home. The Tanner pitcher had no time to adjust his throw in order to allow his catcher to make the play at home. In any event, Big Luke's hitter was under instructions to get his bat on anything close just to get the ball in play. In fact, the pitch came in waist-high and a little inside, an ideal placement to allow Raines to put the bunt down the third-base line. Trammel raced past the ball on his way safely home while Muñoz easily advanced to third. The third baseman, seeing the play at home gone, just held on to the ball, knowing that a bad throw to first or an error there would allow yet another runner to score.

After this rocky beginning, the Tanner pitcher did manage to limp out of the inning, although not before Muñoz and Raines each put another run up on the scoreboard for Big Luke. Despite the close first inning, Big Luke now had a lot of momentum, and its star pitcher appeared to be in all but complete control of the game.

The rest of the outing went largely according to plan. Tanner desisted from the stunts of the first inning and tried desperately to hit Trammel's fastball, which he supplemented liberally with the knuckle and an occasional curve. One did manage to succeed: Blake Roberts. Blake, son of the manager and Tanner's cleanup hitter, hooked a hot grounder between third and short his second time at bat. Yet he was stranded on base, as Trammel struck out the next three batters while keeping Blake on first by demonstrating his aplomb in throwing both to first and second. After five innings of near perfect pitching, Coach Steere relieved his starter by sending Trammel to third and letting Banks take the mound for the rest of the game. Big Luke had another tough game later on that week in which the prudent coach would reverse the present order of pitching, using Trammel to put out the fire if the opposing team solved the older, though less versatile, fastballer. League rules and his own judgment caused Coach Steere to be economical in the use of his most precious resource.

Although Tanner's pitching recovered somewhat from the disastrous top of the second inning, Big Luke scored two more runs in the game, one coming when Muñoz knocked in Trammel from second on a line drive to right center. It was clear that this bit of action at the plate had obliterated the shame of the previous walk. Muñoz's father even called his son by his Christian name in his signature of praise, "Hey, hey, Rafi!" On the mound, Banks kept Trammel's one-hitter going with a shutout of his own, leaving the score at Big Luke's Sporting Goods 5, Tanner Dodge 0. That the league's defending champions could be beaten so soundly on Opening Day portended good things for the Big Luke team and a very ominous forecast for the rest of the league.

Only one other event deserves our attention from that particular ball game. Greg Peel, though he was not in the game for long, did have to make a trip to the plate. He walked reluctantly to the batter's box, hardly wanting to look at the tall boy on the mound who had beaten him so thoroughly. Nor was the chatter from the Big Luke side altogether inviting.

"Hey, is 'at a black eye I still see?"

"C'mone, Tram, peel eem up good jus' like ya done a while back!"

"Be careful, Tram. 'Is un might run off agin like 'e done b'fore."

Charlie, who had the umpire behind him, was a little more discreet. "C'mone up here, Peel. Y'ain't got nut'n' ta worry 'bout. You met Tram, b'fore, ain'tcha? 'E's a *real nice* guy."

The first pitch was a screamer high and inside, causing Peel to jump back a foot and a half and showing that Trammel still cared. Still, it was close enough to the strike zone to be considered just a somewhat wild pitch, as often thrown by fastballers. The next pitch was not even close. Had Peel not left his feet and fallen into the dust, it would have hit him right in the neck. Even knowing that it was coming Charlie had trouble catching it. At that point the home umpire had to intervene. He took off his mask and began to head out to the mound. Coach Steere started from the dugout, but the ump waved him off.

"Don't need you, Coach. Jus' gotta have a word witchur pitcher here."

Trammel came down off the mound, and, not having the ball, put his glove to his chest and crossed his right arm around it. He looked sheepishly at the veteran umpire, a man he knew from many games past and whom he respected.

"Havin' control pro'lems allva sudden, Tram?"

"Yes, sir, I reckon," the boy said, kicking his cleats into the dirt.

"Naw, Tram, y'ain't foolin' me. I know all 'boutchoo an' ol' Peel 'ere. 'At story run all over town. An' ya know what? Had 'at 'a' been my sister I'd 'a' done 'a same thang. Fact, you wanna gib'm a good whoopin' agin jus' ta make sure 'e figur'd it out, go right ahead. I ain't stoppin' ya. But 'at ain't got nut'n' ta do with 'is ball game here. When you're on 'is field, you play by *the rules* a' the game, or I'll th'ow ya outta here. Got it?"

"Yes, sir," the boy said, looking up. "I got it."

The umpire dropped the ball into the boy's glove and then concluded, "A'right, 'en."

Had he not been so humbled before, did he not recall with every inch of his flesh that Trammel would gladly seek him out and work him over again, Peel might have taunted Trammel with that same dastardly smile he had smiled the instant before being pounded into the ground only a few months ago. But at this moment he was merely thankful for the protection of the law and wanting to get out of the box in one piece. It was not clear, however, that Trammel had gotten the message when the very next pitch came blistering towards Peel's rib cage. The hitter landed on his back again, only this time to hear (his eyes being shut) the umpire call out a strike.

"What's 'a matter, Peel?" Charlie inquired in his long drawl. "Ain'tcha never seen a curve ball b'fore?"

Peel was now thoroughly humiliated, and this time there was an audience, a large one. He did not see the next two fastballs cross the plate. He was only too relieved to flee the righteous ire of the boy on the mound and get back to the safety of the dugout.

After the last out, the boys lined up with their respective teams, shook hands as two formations passing each other, and said, "Good game." Then the teams returned to their respective dugouts, grabbed their personal gear and bagged up the rest, and went to the far corners of the field, Tanner in left field, Big Luke in right, to listen to their coaches' brief commentary on the game. As the Big Luke boys sat Indian style in two rows of a semicircle, Coach Steere began his wrap-up.

"A'right, boys, y'all played tough out 'ere t'day. I didn't see nobody loafin' an' e'erbody had 'eir heads in 'a game. Mos' important thang straight off was y'all didn't lose your cool on 'ose bunts in 'at first innin'. Muñoz, 'at's 'a way ta cover first. Billy, it's a good thang you ducked er you'd 'a' got your head took off. 'At 'as a good snag on 'at line drive, by the way. I knew I had you over 'ere fer a reason. Tram, I got 'a sense 'ere's some kinda bad blood 'tween you an' 'at kid ya liked ta hit two er three times." The rest of the team snickered. "You'll have ta tell me 'at story over a sodee pop one a' 'ese days," said this astute leader of boys, who had heard the story from three different sources.

The all-seeing, all-remembering coach continued to run down the principal events of the game, offering praise where it was due, encouragement where it was needed. He said little, however, about Trammel's performance. That is, the attention given to the star player was not in proportion to its merits and was more often jocular than direct. He was not trying to cloud the brilliance of the thirteen-year-old or to spare the egos of the other players by implicit comparison. There was simply no need to rehearse what everyone already knew. Trammel was not "the franchise," as the saying goes. These same boys, particularly with Mr. Steere's coaching, would have been a good team without him. Yet, while being the most reserved boy on the team, he was the fiercest competitor, the best athlete, and the *animus* behind the shape, extent, and frequency of their victories. He was what his father called the "shootin' taw."

Though he was largely happy with his team's performance, Coach Steere was not all praise this hot afternoon. He never was, not even *mostly* praise except during these brief, shining moments after a win. He began the list of to-do's by bringing his assistant coach into the discussion, though it was, for all practical purposes, a one-coach show.

"Now jus' 'cause we pulled 'is'n th'ough don't mean we ain't gotta lot ta work on 'is week, 'specially 'cause we got another tough game comin' up on Thursdee. Mr. Scott, cou'd you remind me 'at we gotta work on . . .", whereupon were listed half a dozen of the boys' errors and inadequacies without mentioning any names in the flush of victory.

That was not the final word. "A'right boys. One last thang 'fore we git outta here. I reckon we oughta say a little prayer, 'specially since it's a Sundee an' all." The boys took off their ball caps and bowed their heads. Coach Steere, a devout Baptist from his childhood and a deacon in his church, prayed on behalf of his team.

"Dear Heavenly Father, we pray our thanks t'day: thanks not fer victory—'cause we know th'only real victory is th'ough your Son, Jesus Christ. But we pray thanks fer such a lovely day, an' fer the health a' these boys, an' fer lettin' 'em play the game a' baseball. It's a small thang, really, in 'a great scheme a' thangs. But 'ey show a lotta heart in it. An' we pray You'd watch over them an' 'eir families as 'ey live 'eir lives an' try ta do right in 'a world. Lord, let us always have You foremost in our hearts an' in our minds. In Your Son Christ's name we pray, Amen."

The post-game wrap-up time with the coach now done, the boys all returned to their respective families. Trammel was greeted with a hug from his mother, a coke with extra ice from his sister, and a pat on the shoulder and a couple of Slim Jims from his father. Although the family would be eating an early dinner soon, the boy was famished from not getting a proper lunch. Trammel loved Slim Jims, beef jerky, and any kind of meat really.

Since they had come in two cars, the family quite naturally branched out into the mother and daughter going home in one car, father and son in the other. That division of labor would allow "the men" to talk exclusively and purposefully about the game—or rather, the father to talk and the son to listen and absorb.

"Ya played a perty good game out 'ere, boy," the father began, drawling out the classic Texan understatement. "I 'as proud a' ya. 'At 'as a big game t'day with a lotta folks watchin'."

The father had just pulled out of the parking lot of the Little League fields and onto the long, winding road called Shady Brook Lane, whose shade-giving oaks, pecans, and elms created a singularly cavernous passage through one of the more established and affluent sections of the town. It was to this neighborhood, above all, more than to the homes out by the country club or to where the Joneses now lived, that the children of Dogwood loved to trick-or-treat on Halloween.   For while those latter two neighborhoods boasted of big houses (and therefore also generous offerings of candy) the looming trees, which appeared positively sinister when the homes were done up with the signs of ghouls and demons, shrouded the passage in darkness and mystery.

Trammel had been down this road with his father countless times: going *to* every game he had ever played and coming *from* every game. Since the Pee Wee football fields lay adjacent to the Little League fields, only a little farther down Shady Brook Lane on the East edge of town, Trammel had traveled this route in every fertile season—spring, summer, fall—since he had begun playing organized sports. He had looked out upon the abundant foliage— its blossoming and fullness and turning—throughout his childhood. Not until this coming football season, when he would play for the eighth-grade school team, would Trammel take a different route to a game, riding to a real stadium with the rest of the team on one of the school's buses.

On the way to these Little League and Pee Wee contests Trammel's father imparted last-minute instructions, going over things they had been discussing since the day after the previous game, doing his part to get his son's mind right for the game. The return trips, however, though still lessons of a kind, were more relaxed—except, of course, on those rare occasions when the son had not played up to the father's expectations and the tension could be cut with a knife. On this day of decisive victory over the previous year's first-place team, though, the father was all joy and pride.

"Yes, sir. Thanks."

"Yeah, you 'as perty relaxed out 'ere on 'at mound—looked like you 'as in charge 'a whole time. I tell ya, when 'at batter tried a bunt on 'at first pitch, 'e had your ol' man rattled, 'at's fer sure. Butcha took eem out without losin' a step. 'At 'as a game-maker right 'ere."

The father spit into his empty coke can.

"Yeah, well, I reckon we covered it a'right," the son replied laconically.

"Ya know, I tell ya 'nother way ta deal with a bunt like 'at. I saw ya th'owin' your knuckle an' perty good pitches, but in 'em cases ya gotta guess 'a bunt's comin'. Let's say you 'as already gonna th'ow a fastball. Whatcha do is send 'at ball as hard as ya can up high in 'a strike zone er maybe a little above it. Well 'a batter, see, 'll have ta brang 'is bat up at 'a last minute mos' likely, an' chances are 'e'll jus' pop up. Catcher'll be on 'a 'lert anyway an' be right 'ere ta grab it. An if 'a batter pulls off 'a pitch, th' ump might still call it a strike. Truth is, umps don't really like bunts. It messes with 'eir own rhythm an' what 'ey can see a' the plate. Least 'at's 'a way with any ump I ever known. See what I mean?"

"Yes, sir. I reckon I cou'd pull 'at off."

Their conversation continued in this same vein all the way home. On their arrival the father announced before the son could get out of the car, "'Ere's one more thang I wonta show ya." Trammel followed his father around to the back yard where the two of them had built a backstop in the far corner of the two acre lot and laid out a regulation-sized infield, complete with a pitching mound of hard sand. While Mrs. Jones had most looked forward to moving into a bigger house, her husband was more interested in what he could do with a back yard of the size offered in this new development. For the next half hour, until Trammel's mother had a decent-sized early dinner on the table, the father showed his son the tricks of pitching to the bunt, using his own arm as a surrogate to let the boy's begin to rest for a couple of days.

Chapter 5: Mom's Deal

The next morning, a Monday, Trammel downed his breakfast —four pieces of French toast and five slices of bacon, all covered in maple syrup—more hurriedly than usual. After gulping down the last of his juice and taking his plate to the sink, he returned the ball cap that had been hanging off the back of his chair (his mother would not allow him to wear it at the table) to its rightful place and went to his room to stuff a backpack with Slim Jims, bags of sunflower seeds, and Off!, all from his private stash. Trading out his team's baseball cap that he had on for his "lucky fishin' hat," the ball cap he had been wearing when he caught a five-pound bass on Lake Texoma, he headed for the garage and his bicycle. The instant after he turned the deadbolt, he heard his mother calling from the kitchen.

"Tra-am? Trammel David!"

"Ma'am?"

"Just where exactly are you headed, mister?"

"I'm fixin' ta go ta Lanny's. Me 'n' him's goin' fishin' 'is mornin'."

"At 'a pond," he continued as his mother appeared in the back entryway drying her hands on a dishtowel. "We been plannin' 'is fer a while since it's 'a first day a' summer an' all."

"Now you know I promised Mrs. Lorne that we were goin' over to visit them today. In fact, I confirmed it as you were hustlin' me out of church yesterday. Surely you remember me remindin' you half a dozen times?"

"Well, see, I figur'd everthang got pushed back since 'a game got rained out Sa'urdee. Me 'n' Lanny 'as s'posed ta go fishin' yesterdee, but a' course I had ta play ball. So see, I's figurin' we'd go ta Mrs. Lorne's, ya know, Joey's, t'morra ta git everthang back on track—ya know, the way we been plannin' it."

The mother was not falling for this specimen of adolescent casuistry. "No, son. We'll go to Joey's today, and you can go fishin' over at Lanny's tomorrow, and that'll put it all 'back on track.' Of course, you'll need to call Lanny to let him know."

Trammel quietly accepted the judgment of his mother: partly because his father had been more than persuasive on the impropriety of "back-sassin'," and partly because he knew his mother's will, once set, was immovable, but mostly because he instinctively accepted the chain of command in the Jones home. He returned to his room, tossed his backpack into a corner, changed out his caps again, and came back to the kitchen to call his friend with the bad news.

"Lanny?"

"Tram."

"Can't go fishin' t'day."

"Gotta go off 'n' do one a' my mom's deals."

"T'morra."

"Yep."

Then he slumped into a sofa in the "front room," a place in the house he rarely visited as it was his mother's retreat for playing the piano and entertaining guests. A print of one of Monet's *Water Lilies* hung above a baby grand piano Trammel's father had surprised his wife with on their tenth anniversary. On walls of pastel blue hung the family portraits taken around Easter. Though the pictures were perfectly lovely to the untrained observer, in each one Trammel bore the same expression of a thinly disguised exasperation at being in clothes he did not like wearing and having to wait on a picture that always took too long to take, while his sister's smile lit up with some silly remark she needled him with as her substitute for "cheese." At the moment, the disappointed adolescent sat crumpled in a pale blue and pink channel back "divan," as it was called by the great aunt who had given it to the family when her husband passed away, which, though an antique, was the most uncomfortable piece of furniture in the house in Trammel's mind. He rested his head on his hand, awaiting the events of the first day of summer break, events he had no part in planning. He heard his mother's voice coming from upstairs as she was fixing her hair.

"Tra-am, be sure to bring your glove and a bat and some baseballs. We'll go hit some. It'll be fun!"

Hit some. His mother's appropriation of his father's language in no way changed the score.

"Yes, ma'am," he responded slowly and solemnly. After a few minutes of brooding, Trammel called out to his sister, "Gitchur glove, too, Chris! Y'ain't gittin' out a' this."

Ceding the front seat to his sister, Trammel slumped into the back on the passenger's side, leaning against the car door. The drive from their house on the West edge of town where they had moved a couple of years ago to their old neighborhood was not far, but it revealed the recent history of North Texas. The town of Dogwood itself was a century old, having been settled by farmers moving from East Texas who chose the name based more on hope than arboreal reality. The once small town had been expanding rapidly for a decade. Trammel often tried to imagine what the town must have looked like when his father was growing up. His father had often pointed out the various strip malls that had once been fields where he and his friends had thrown up backstops made of two-by-fours and chicken wire, having no idea to whom the fields belonged and no sign on the owners' part that sprawling corner lots served any purpose other than allowing boys to play the game of baseball. One by one, these choice pieces of property had been gobbled up and put to use by the engine of commerce or more deliberate, adult civic action: "Drugstores and soccer fields," his father sneered, though he had financed much of this growth.

Passing by the church and turning into the old neighborhood, Trammel realized why his parents had decided to move, a change he and his sister had resisted for some time. All the houses were so *small*. They were all one story, and the garages took up most of the front façades. Trammel remembered that the doors to all the bedrooms in the old house were right there together—there was hardly a hall—and that when relatives came to town they had to sleep on the pullout couch in the family room. The house had no dining room—not that he cared where he ate—and no game room, either, a matter of far greater importance. The boy was convinced that the various elements to be overcome in the garage at the old house—the extreme heat or cold, the color of the walls, the wind from outside or a fan within—all worked to the father's advantage in their epic battles at ping-pong. In a more controlled indoor arena, the boy thought, he had a fighting chance. The fact that his father had ceased showboating by changing out his paddle for his shoe or a kitchen utensil or even a coke bottle (as he had done when the boy was eight) gave Trammel hope that victory would soon be his.

As soon as his mother pulled into the driveway Trammel remembered why visiting Mrs. Lorne and her son seemed such a dreary experience. That the house was much smaller even than his old house did not bother him. Rather the disorder of the place he instinctively found distasteful. There were always great heaps of clothes—some of the items he recognized as once his—piled up on a table or the threadbare couch. The faded wallpaper was peeling everywhere. A few large drinking glasses, their bottoms tainted with various dried liquids, sat without aid of coasters on the stained coffee table in the one small open room. Mrs. Lorne always made some cursory apology about the home being a mess, which Trammel considered a copout. He somehow knew, without having been told, that once his mother spent an entire day helping Mrs. Lorne clean and organize her house. There were no signs of that effort now. More than the disarray, Trammel suffered the smell of the place. Partly a mustiness from an aversion to cleaning, yet there was something more to it. It was, though not the same, similar to the smell of the nursing homes his mother used to drag him to when he was much younger. It was the odor of age or sickness, of a loss of hope, or imminent death. And that smell put Trammel even more on guard than he would ordinarily be in unfamiliar or unpleasant surroundings.

Entering the house and finding it just as he expected, Trammel assumed the impassive countenance that he had either inherited or picked up from his father in similar situations, a mix of resignation and forbearance, a look only his mother could read. Trammel was greeted cheerfully not only by Mrs. Lorne but also by the wan figure of a boy his own age, though far from his stature, pale but beaming at being host to such a distinguished guest. That Lorne was the woman's maiden name Trammel had learned from his mother some time ago. The boy had kept the surname of his birth—Fuller—although the source of that name had left his wife and son when the latter was just over a year old.

"Hey, Trammel! It's great to see ya," said the boy, not the least bit self-conscious in his enthusiastic admiration.

"Hey, man, how's it goin'?" responded Trammel in a nonchalant monotone.

"I bet you're glad school's out so you can spend a lot more time practicin' baseball," ventured the pale boy.

"'At 'n' fishin' 'n' other stuff." Trammel could not help thinking that he was doing none of those things now, things he liked to do.

After a moment's silence, Mrs. Lorne suggested that Joey show Trammel some of the new baseball cards her son had recently acquired. Trammel accompanied Joey to his room, actually the cleanest and most organized part of the house, and took a seat on the bed while the host carefully took out a cardboard box especially made for filing trading cards. Joey handed Trammel each player from the Rangers' starting roster. In response the latter would flip over the card to look at last season's average and offer various quips such as "boom er bust," "one-season wonder," or "got 'is game back las' season," things he had heard his father say at some point. Though bored, Trammel thought he was being polite in trying to carry on a conversation about baseball cards. He had collected his own during only one season when he was much younger and had stuffed them into a box long since forgotten. Although he did like going to the games with his father, who offered unceasing analysis on every player, pitch, hit, and out, Trammel did not otherwise keep up with the Rangers or any big-league team. The only person he had ever known to care about baseball cards was his father—and not about those recently printed. About twice a year when visiting Trammel's paternal grandparents, his father would ransack the lake house looking for his old baseball card collection, containing the likes of Stan "the Man" Musial and "Dizzy" Dean. "I hope we didn't th'ow 'em out when y'all moved. It'd be a gold mine!" he would exclaim, going to the attic to rummage through old boxes once again. Like any El Dorado, the collection was never found. Whenever Trammel went over to his real friends' houses, or vice versa, they might very well show each other their new acquisitions, such as fishing poles or knives or other forms of weaponry, but never baseball cards. But Joey did not have any of that stuff—no knives or fighting sticks or slingshots. His mother probably would not let him have such things for fear he would hurt himself, and he was not the kind of kid who would like such implements of defense anyway.

While explaining to Joey the mathematics of batting averages, something his father had taught him rather than anything he had learned in school, Trammel noticed the frailty of the smaller boy's frame. His limbs were more like sticks than arms or legs. Few of Trammel's friends had begun to acquire the muscle of the teen years, of course. For the most part, the boys his age were either lean or fat, nothing in between. Downing protein drinks twice daily, a regular regime of pushups, and starting to lift weights had made little difference even in the sinewy Trammel, the strongest kid in his grade, except for Fat Eddy, who didn't "count," and Jimmy Jenson, who had flunked a year. But Joey was not just skinny. He was hauntingly frail. At times he seemed almost transparent, as though you could turn on a flashlight behind him and actually see the light. Unlike anyone else he knew, except maybe for a few really old people, the poor kid appeared breakable.

Trying not to stare, Trammel noticed that a purplish flesh encircled the boy's eyes, giving him in that respect the appearance of an old person. For all his frailty, the boy radiated a strange, unearthly power from his eyes. Sky blue and always eager, Joey's eyes latched onto other people with a disarming, hopeful earnestness. For what seemed like minutes Joey would not blink at all, but when he did blink his lavender eyelids remained closed for a moment, as though he did not fully comprehend or sought some inner reassurance. In the back of his mind Trammel recalled what his mother had told him about Joey's illness, though it still did not make perfect sense to him. The short version of the story was that Joey Fuller suffered from Leukemia.

In the middle of his diatribe on why being a .290 hitter was like "kissin' your sister," Trammel heard his mother call from the other room, "Hey, Tra-am, think it's about time for you and Joey to play some ball?" That was the invitation, the order really, Trammel was dreading. It was one thing to go over to the kid's house on the first day of summer and suffer through a made-up conversation about baseball players and teams he cared little about. It was quite another actually to go out in broad daylight and make it look like he and this poor kid could or should ever play ball together. That really *was* kissing your sister, at least insofar as Trammel understood what his father meant by that oft-repeated phrase.

After a brief drive in Mrs. Jones's car, the whole crew arrived at the elementary school closest to Joey's house, the one Trammel had attended and his sister, too, until the family moved. Trammel, Joey, and Christie made their way out onto the baseball diamond. It was up to Trammel to figure out what to do. Joey's expectant, slow-blinking eyes looked to him for direction in a way suggesting that just throwing the ball around aimlessly for a while would not suffice.

"A'right, let's go ahead an' warm up a little. Let's get a triangle goin'. I'll th'ow it ta Chris; Chris, you th'ow it ta Joey here; Joey, you come back at me."

"I wanna throw it to you," objected his sister.

"Yeah, an' why's it matter?"

"'Cause I wanna burn ya."

"Look, stubborn, y'ain't gonna burn me; y'ain't capable a' burnin' me; so jus' git with 'a program."

Instantly the younger sister slung her glove into the dirt and put her hands on her hips defiantly. Trammel thought for a second and saw he was in no position to negotiate.

"A'right, look, have itchur way. Jus' stay closer ta Joey, an' y'all can both th'ow it ta me." The triangle moved from equilateral to acute isosceles.

Despite a few drops on Joey's part and Christie's intentionally throwing a ball over her brother's head once, which he made her chase down, warming up went as well as it could. The next step seemed natural enough.

"A'right, let's take a little infield. Joey, you go ta third, an' Chris, you take first."

"What're *you* gonna do?" his sister demanded.

"I'm gonna hit infield a' course."

"Why don't you pitch, and I'll hit? That's how we do it at home."

"'Cause we ain't practicin' *hittin'* right now; we're practicin' *fieldin'*, jus' like Dad does all 'a time. Where you been?"

"Yeah, but that's with Dad hittin' 'em."

"Well, Dad ain't here, is he? So it's up ta me."

"This I gotta see," laughed the iconoclast as she trotted off to first base.

Trammel took up his post at home after he retrieved from the car a big bucket of balls, some worn and some almost new, that he and his father had "scrounged" over the years. It did not help that, having never run an infield practice before, Trammel at first had difficulty placing the grounders where he wanted, much to his sister's delight. After a few attempts missed their mark, the natural athlete got the hang of it and began delivering reliable grounders and even an occasional pop-up to Joey down at third. Joey proved not so reliable in his fielding. In fact, he missed most anything hit to him.

Frustrated, Trammel looked to first base, only to see his sister sitting on the ground, her head buried in her glove. He could not hear what she was saying, or rather singing, to herself in a low voice but imagined it must have been along the lines of "This is boring" or "When can we go home?" Trammel could not have agreed with his sister's sentiment more, but at the same time could not have her embarrassing Joey like that, the implication being that he would never field the ball and thus never throw to first.

"Hey, look alive down 'ere! 'Is ain't no nap time." Trammel fired a hot grounder down the first-base line that missed his sister by a hair. Christie rose to her feet and had no time to answer him before another grounder sizzled her way. She bobbled it a little but threw the ball as hard as she could at her brother's head. Trammel caught it with his bare right hand.

"An' quit th'owin' like a girl!"

"You're a girl!" retorted the sister, whose anger turned to laughter as she licked her index finger and traced a mark in the air.

"'At ain't no chap! How many times I gotta tell ya? 'At ain't no chap! Ya don't even know the rules ta chaps."

Unreformed, the girl repeated herself in peals of laughter, "You're a girl!"

It was no use. Girls simply did not understand "chaps"—the contest of verbal insults that Trammel and his friends could play for hours on end—and his sister did not even try. She called things funny that were just plain stupid. For his part, Trammel, known widely as the "King of All Chaps," understood innately the difference between a clever barb and a childish, nonsensical, or desperate comeback. Inculcating such acute verbal awareness and discretion in his sister he would have given up on as a Quixotic enterprise, had he not such a high regard for the rules of this or any game.

But his sister was different. She did not play by his rules or the rules of anyone else. The tall, slender girl was actually a good athlete, the best softball player on her own team, though completely lacking in the keen discipline that made her older brother a star. Her reasons for playing the game were entirely social. Two summers ago her two best friends had invited her to play on their team. Wanting to spend time with them, Christie agreed to do so. Of course, she already knew how to play ball. The whole family took part in fielding for Trammel when his father threw to him—the sister mainly because she was allowed to chatter (i.e. hurl insults) at him, the mother only because the son promised not to hit screamers her way (Trammel's first lesson in placing the ball where he wanted it to go). Yet the father put no pressure on his daughter to perform. He was not inclined to do so, and it would not have worked on her free spirit anyway. At times Trammel found his father's laxity towards Christie mind-boggling. He had seen his father administering a stern lecture to his daughter, albeit halfheartedly and at the mother's behest, whereupon the girl, blowing bubbles the whole time, would pop a bubble in her face and then crack up laughing, soon to be joined by the father. Lecture over. In truth she was a sweet girl, loved her family and cared for her friends deeply, and would occasionally allow her true admiration of her brother to betray itself in small acts of kindness. Today, of all days, her caprice had resolved to nettle him.

Turning his attention from his sister to Joey, ready as he knew how to be for the next hit, Trammel realized that this "practice" was not working. Leaning on his bat, as an old man would a cane, he puzzled over Joey's performance. The kid did everything wrong. But why? Trammel knew that Joey's father had "run off," though he did not know that he had hardly made an appearance since then. Even if Joey did not have a dad, he had been playing baseball for years. Why had his coaches not taught him at least how to field an easy grounder? Trammel could not have realized that in every practice Joey had ever been to, he had been consigned to the outfield where few, if any, hits would come his way. With only one player to coach, Trammel did not have the luxury of strategically pigeonholing one in order to work with the others. He had to try something—anything.

"Okay, man, look here. We gotta change a couple a' thangs."

Trammel dropped the bat at home and began to move towards the boy.

"First off, ya can't jus' leave your hands on your knees like 'at. It's like you're restin' er sump'm'. Ya gotta be ready like 'a ball's comin' your way ever time. See, like 'is." Trammel assumed the stance of an infielder with his hands hanging loosely between his legs, almost to the ground. Joey tried to mirror him.

"'At's better, but look. Ya' gotta keep 'em hands down, close ta the ground, see. It's a lot easier ta go up 'n go down. See, like 'is."

Trammel demonstrated how a fielder would bring his hands up to catch a ball heading for his midsection.

"An' 'a other thang is, ya can't spread your feet out 'at wide. Ya know, the ball ain't comin' straight atcha. You're gonna have ta go ta the ball nearly all 'a time. So ya gotta be ready ta move. Put your legs, oh, 'bout 'is far apart."

Trammel crouched into his position again.

"Like this?" Joey asked intently.

"Yeah, 'at's better."

Joey still looked awkward.

"Ya know, I kinda rock back 'n' forth like 'is. Ya gotta be ready like you're fixin' ta pounce on it, see, like you're a tiger er sump'm. The main thang is jus' keep 'at ball in front a' ya. Don't let it git past ya."

Returning to home, Trammel had another thought and turned back to Joey.

"The main thang is, don't let 'a ball play *you*; *you* play the ball."

"I don't understand," Joey confessed.

Trammel, surprised, had never stopped to examine one of his father's basic axioms.

"Well . . . it's sorta like 'is. The ball's gonna do what 'a ball's gonna do. The deal is if you're gonna let it, er you're gonna do what *you* gotta do. See what I mean?"

"I think so."

"Yeah, you'll see."

Trammel resumed hitting grounders in Joey's direction, having now almost perfect control over how hard and where the balls traveled. Joey did not snag many but showed more ability in keeping the ball in front of him.

"A'right, 'at's good, see," Trammel encouraged him. "At least you're stoppin' 'a ball. But 'a ball's still playin' *you*. Ya gotta know where it's goin'. See, when ya get right down to it 'ere's jus' two kinds a' grounders: worm-burners an' 'a ones 'at hop: hoppers er choppers er whatever ya wonta call 'em. 'En agin, ya gotchur slow rollers, but we'll deal with 'em another time. Now with 'a worm-burners, 'ey come sizzlin' along, so ya gotta keep your glove down, like 'is, else it's goin' right under ya. Now sometimes 'a ball'll surprise ya an' jump up while ya gotchur glove down 'ere, an' 'at's when ya gotta take one in 'a gut fer the team. But 'at's better 'n losin' it. 'Ere's worse thangs in 'a world," Trammel stated, without a trace of irony, "'n gettin' hit in 'a gut with a baseball. An' 'en as far as 'a ones hoppin' like crazy, ya jus' gotta play the hop. I mean ya gotta figur' out whether ta charge 'a ball er go back a step. Nine times outta a' ten it's better ta charge it. A'right, 'en, keep your glove down an' play the hop. 'At's 'a deal."

While he saw infinitesimal improvements after offering various instructions, Trammel found that he had to break everything down into smaller tasks. Joey became so joyfully surprised when he began to scoop up a few that he made terrible throws to first. Nervous about the throw, he reverted back to missing the ball. Trammel decided to have Joey just act like he would throw to first and leave practicing the actual throw to some other time. That tactic also had the advantage of relieving his sister from her onerous duty and thus not having to worry about her increasingly vocal and somewhat valid complaints. It did not hurt either of their causes that Christie now alternated between doing cartwheels and asking their mother whether it was time to go.

Figuring that as much had been done in one day as could be with Joey's glove work, Trammel had them take a break and get a drink. Not knowing exactly what to say during this unscripted moment, Trammel resorted to planning the next step in the practice.

"Yeah, well, I reckon we oughta work on hittin' nex'. Yeah, it'll be good ta hit a few. 'Course, I don't wonta wear us out none. We pro'lly both got practice later on. Maybe you gotta game. I ain't sure."

"Yeah, Trammel, I've got a game," Joey smiled. "But I don't usually get to play that much—unless we're really winning or really losing. This is a lot more fun."

Trammel didn't know what to say. He felt bad for the kid.

As Joey swung ineffectually at a couple of easy warm-up pitches, Trammel realized as much work would be needed to remedy the boy's hitting as his fielding. His stance and swing amounted to a curious combination of natural awkwardness and poor imitation of professional players. The way he stepped into the ball was completely out of synch with his actual swing, the mark of a real beginner, while at the same time he waved the bat around before the pitch as much as some of the more idiosyncratic major league stars. He usually ended up chopping at the ball rather than coming into it with a really smooth stroke. Trammel figured the only way Joey might ever get a hit would be by pure luck or accident. After throwing a few more easy pitches, in which he slowed the ball down as much as he could without putting an arc on it, the puzzled young athlete again made his way in Joey's direction.

"A'right, man, look, we're gonna have ta do a few thangs with your swang here. The main thang is ya don't look real natural. Ya gotta look natural, see." Trammel took the bat from Joey and showed him a faultless swing at three-quarter time.

"Now a' course e'erbody's got 'eir own swang, see, so I don't wontcha jus' doin' what I do. The deal is we gotta find *your* swang. First thang is 'ey ain't no sense in wavin' 'at bat around like crazy. Ya know, I thank ya might be too worried 'bout 'a bat an' not thankin' 'bout 'at ball comin' your way. So jus' keep 'at bat steady. An' as far as your feet goes, 'ey need some work, too."

Trammel continued to offer detailed instruction in an effort to afford Joey some hope of hitting the ball. As with fielding, Joey's improvement was a slow march up hill. The most effective approach seemed to be to simplify the swing as much as possible. After trying small changes, Trammel finally had Joey just cock his bat straight back parallel to the ground so that all the novice had to do was bring it across his chest with no downward motion. At last, the unexpected happened. Joey hit one. It was not a great hit, just a slow grounder towards first that Christie had long since abandoned. But it was a hit.

"Hoorah! Good one!" Mrs. Jones applauded from the bleachers where she and Mrs. Lorne had been sitting the whole time, carrying on a conversation that Trammel's mother dominated and in which her son had no interest. Trammel rolled his eyes, sighed, and thought to himself that it would take a lot more than cheering to get this kid to hit a ball the right way. Watching the ball until it stopped in shallow right field, Joey smiled and then looked to Trammel to see what he would say.

"Hey, a'right man. 'At's a perty good one. Least ya put it in play. Let's see if we can't do that a couple more times."

It took a while before Joey got another solid hit, but he did manage to foul a few.

"'Least you're gettin' a piece a' the ball," encouraged Trammel. "But you're takin' too long ta make your mind up on most ob'm. Ya gotta be steppin' into it one way er th'other. When it's time ta swang, ya gotta swang like ya mean it—no beatin' 'round 'a bush. Not too jerky neither. Just a nice eb'm swang."

Trammel's coaching and Joey's persistence resulted in another two or three hits: nothing spectacular but, as Trammel put it, "nut'n' ta sneeze at." Each hit elicited a quick cheer and clapping from "the peanut gallery," as Trammel framed the mothers' enthusiasm in his own mind. When it was time to leave, the boys picked up all the balls, most of them gathered around the backstop. Tossing the last ball in the old bucket, Joey looked at Trammel with that same earnest expression he greeted everything in life.

"Thanks, Trammel, that was a lot of fun."

"Yeah, man, ya know, any time," replied Trammel, somewhat uncomfortably.

Dropping off Joey and his mother at their house, Mrs. Jones took up her son's halfhearted offer, which she had overheard at a mother's distance, and arranged for another such outing the following Monday.

"Bye, Trammel," Joey waved, as the car pulled out of the driveway.

"Yeah, man, we'll see ya 'round," nodded Trammel, now in the front seat with the window down, his right arm stretched toward the rear view mirror.

Without request, his mother took him to the new Braum's back on their side of town and treated him to a double cheeseburger, two orders of fries, a limeade, and an extra large strawberry shake, which Christie surreptitiously dipped a spoon into repeatedly, though she had insisted she did not want her own. The son was thankful that his mother had kept lunch to just the three of them, suspecting that she might have wished to invite Joey and his mother. Mrs. Jones, however, had a sharp sense of when her son had had enough of one of her "deals."

Chapter 6: Gone Fishin'

Trammel repeated the same steps he had taken the previous day. He was eager to get to the pond while it was still fairly cool. Yet having been wished good luck in fishing by his mother at breakfast, he had no need to slip out undetected. He had forgotten whether he was supposed to bring the bait or could rely on Lanny's supply, so he loaded up just in case. Into the same backpack containing the Slim Jims and sunflower seeds and a couple of other snacks he found around the kitchen he stuffed a Ziploc bag full of raw chicken hearts and gizzards and a couple of pieces of uncooked bacon for good measure. He did not think they would be using worms that day but dug up a handful from his worm farm in the back yard and put them into one of the plastic Whataburger cups he kept on hand for such purposes. Laden with such repast for himself, Lanny, and the fish, he switched out his team cap for his lucky fishing hat, as he had done the day before, and shouted out an "Ah-dee-os" as he opened the door to the garage.

Trammel's bike, as though waiting for him, leaned up against the wall in a spot known as "the place of honor." Owing to the water table levels, Texans do not have basements, so they must make the most out of their garages. Another advantage of the Joneses' new house was a garage twice the size as that of the older house: a four-car with an alcove running the length of the garage, save for a closet containing the water heater, on the door of which hung a dart board. It was in this alcove that Trammel and his father spent a fair amount of time when they were not playing catch in the back yard. On the left-hand side stood a sturdy wooden workbench, with an array of tools hanging up on a peg-board just above it. On the right-hand side of the alcove was mounted Trammel's speed bag, which encouraged him always to be ready for situations such as the Peel encounter. At the other house Trammel's father had to keep raising the bag as his son shot up like a weed but at this house had measured it to his own height. The six-foot stretch of wall between the workbench and the speed bag, each giving purpose and activity to a young man's hands, became the place of honor, so named because of the three signed pictures mounted there. The pictures belonged in the garage because there was no place in the house itself where Mr. Jones felt particularly at rest or that was exclusively his and his son's.

These three pictures, though in some sense gifts, had all been earned. The one on the left was a shot taken just as Roger Staubach was launching the "Hail Mary" pass to Drew Pearson in the playoff game against the Minnesota Vikings. The intensity of the moment was fully visible in the oncoming rush of the defensive linemen, the time ticking down on the game clock, and the concentration on the faces of those on the sidelines. In the midst of it all prevailed number twelve's undeterred, signature steadiness: the appearance not of being under unfathomable pressure but of the timeless assurance of an ancient Olympian statue hurling a javelin into the ages. Trammel and his father had watched that game on television. As important as that moment had been when all of Dallas had leaped to their feet in celebration and disbelief, perhaps more lasting had been the lessons imparted later, long after the flush of victory, in the father's characteristic way of deriving truth from the analogies latent in the contest and competition of sports. "Ya know, Tram," the father remarked one day out of the blue when they were working on a birdhouse Mrs. Jones had insisted on having for the back yard, "'ere's some men, not a whole lot, pro'lly not more'n a handful, 'at's jus' made fer pressure, like ol' Roger there. Ya know, 'a kind a' pressure 'at'd break another man. Maybe in football er baseball, maybe in sump'm else. I thank you may be one ob'm." On another occasion, the father imparted a maxim the boy could hardly forget. "Ya know, Tram, a man's known by what 'e does in 'a clutch. 'En agin, 'ere's some men 'at 're made fer the clutch."

The autograph of Roger Staubach, the epitome of all clutch players, was boldly signed across that unforgettable moment—that lesson—in sports history. Mr. Jones had gained it not by a chance encounter but because he had worked with some of the Cowboys, and eventually Roger, off the field. Soon after his parents had moved out to Lake Foster, after one of those unsuccessful ransackings of the attic in search of old baseball cards, Mr. Jones took Trammel on a long drive around the lake to look for places to fish from off the bank. A little reflecting on the advantages of living in a lake community so close to Dallas led him to a plan for using the branch bank of which he was then manager for developing the whole area. Such developments were sometimes slow in the making, but he reasoned that if he could secure a couple of "front office men" in the Dallas Cowboy organization, soon a good part of the team would be buying lake houses. And where the Cowboys went, the rest of Dallas would soon follow. In a couple of years, Mr. Jones had positioned himself as "loan man to the Cowboys." Not only was he a good loan officer, the men in the Cowboy organization instinctively liked the still athletic tobacco-chewer who could talk about the game not as a mere admirer or as a b.s.-er, but as someone who had clear insight. At last he brokered a deal on one of Roger Staubach's properties, the great quarterback having begun to establish himself as a major commercial real estate player. Shortly thereafter Mr. Jones was promoted to home office in Dallas as regional vice president of the growing Texas banking concern. As Mr. Jones and Mr. Staubach closed their deal, the former took out the famous picture and said, "'Ere's one other signature I'd like ta ask ya for, if it ain't too much trouble: partly fer my son and partly fer me." The hero obliged.

The second signed picture, raised higher than and in the middle of the other two, came to Mr. Jones as the result of his second of only two forays into politics. For as long as he had been aware of politics, he had thought of politicians—from either party—as double-dealing, self-promoting hucksters who could not make it in the business world or in some legitimate profession and therefore sold their souls and their votes to a gullible public for a sure salary and a modicum of notoriety. It was not a case of his not voting or his lack of interest in politics. He always voted, and he kept up with politics through the *Journal* and the Dallas paper, reading both every evening after taking a look at the sports page. His entire political philosophy he put forth in one maxim: "Any b'inessman 'at votes fer a Demo*r*at might as well slit his own throat." But he had no truck with politicians: never gave to their campaigns, never went to their rallies, never shook their hands if he could help it, though they often wanted to shake his. There had been two exceptions, both of whom he had supported with as much of his time and money as he was willing to give to outright politicking. The first was Barry Goldwater. In 1964, while in college, Mr. Jones had walked door to door in Fort Worth neighborhoods that voted Democrat and, on the weekends, throughout his own hometown, carrying his copy of *The Conscience of a Conservative*, explaining to skeptics that Goldwater was not only a safe candidate but the only man in either party who understood business, the economy, war, and true American principles. His job was made harder owing to Johnson's being a Texan. The election had been lost, but Mr. Jones never doubted that the principles had been right—as he reminded those who had argued with him for the next decade and a half. The book, incidentally, he would one day give to Trammel as the boy's primer in politics.

Mr. Jones did not have a picture of Goldwater, only a button from the campaign and a bumper sticker (the one he did not put on his car) with the chemical symbols AuH_2O. He did, however, have a picture of "ol' Barry's" most famous and die-hard supporter: Ronald Reagan. Three years before, while in the midst of his lake development deals, Mr. Jones had helped set up the Republican phone bank and train the party's campaign workers for the entire North Texas region. Afterwards, the party chairman of Texas asked whether there was anything he could do for the astute banker who had a gift for crafting complex political ideas into pithy, earthy sayings, imagining that the businessman and veteran and former local sports star might himself want to run for public office some day. Other than a retort about preferring to earn his own keep instead of "suckin' 'a hind tit a' gub'ment," the only request made to the party chairman (who would call on the banker again to help plan the '84 Convention in Dallas) was for a signed photograph of the president giving his inaugural address. That request was delivered a month after the inaugural. Mr. Jones immediately had the photograph framed and with embossing tape affixed at the bottom the memorable line, "We have every right to dream heroic dreams."

The third picture, hanging on the right at the same level as the Hail Mary pass, came as the result of a peculiar facet of the Texas Rangers' spring training. The occasion, of course, marked the professional team's effort to get the players ready for the season. One challenge for the manager was to keep his pitchers from throwing their arms out while at the same time giving his hitters the practice they needed in facing serious threats from the mound. It was easy enough to call up a few pitchers from the minor league farm teams, but the Rangers' organization also used the event for public relations. One way of doing so was by inviting in a few former baseball stars in the area to throw batting practice. A favorite of theirs had been Mr. Jones, who had actually played against a couple of the Rangers while in college and in his late twenties still threw a searing fastball. For four straight years, right after he got out of the Army, he took the mound for a week against the pros. These auxiliaries to the Rangers' squad, "ham 'n' eggers," as Mr. Jones called himself in mocking self-deprecation, were completely overshadowed by another addition to the Rangers' spring training who had been a baseball star in his youth: Charlie Pride, "the pride of Dallas." The son of sharecroppers who had given up a baseball career in the Negro leagues to see whether he could make it in the all-white world of country music, and was welcomed into that world, had a true fan in Trammel's father. Mr. Jones did not own or play on his own many records. On his way to work he listened to KRLD, the AM news station and radio home of the Dallas Cowboys. The only music, or poetry really, Mr. Jones ever sought out on his own was that of Willie and Waylon, the later songs of Elvis, and anything sung by his wife. But he liked Charlie Pride—a lot—and derived lessons for his son from that star's life and performances no less than from Roger's, the chief one being that any man who works hard and hones his talent can become anything he wants to become—in America. The team-signed baseball given to Mr. Jones for his pitching at Rangers' spring training was, without a thought, handed over to his son. The picture of Charlie Pride with an arm around him, both wearing Ranger baseball uniforms, was a prize Mr. Jones could never wholly give up. For this reason it hung in the shared space known as the place of honor.

The space below these three pictures was reserved for Trammel's bike according to family custom. There were many such customs in the Jones home: how to comport oneself in "the front room," the requirement of knocking before going into the mother and father's bedroom, the practice of the children keeping Saturday afternoon free to be with their father, who usually had to work even on Saturday morning, and the habit of the children answering their elders with "sir" and "ma'am." Each member of the family had, on the one hand, a certain number of specified duties and, on the other, was allowed a little of his own space and tolerated for a measure of idiosyncrasy. One of Trammel's spaces was the one under the three autographed pictures. And nothing else in the garage was worthy of such a hallowed space, nothing at all meant as much to the boy, as his bike that he spent considerable time riding and kept in pristine condition.

The bike Trammel rode was no ordinary bike. It was a Redline Proline, the top of its class in BMX bikes, a lot better than that Mongoose the kid who sold the most candy had been given. Not that Trammel had anything against Mongooses, upon more disinterested reflection, any more than Cadillac owners had anything against Chevies. At some point the proud owner of a Cadillac, like Trammel's grandfather, had probably driven a Chevy. But the initial sneer of the nouveau riche when looking upon the trappings of his origins is perhaps as unavoidable as it is an unseemly feature of human nature. Besides, Trammel had worked for his Redline a lot harder than Little Tommy had worked selling candy. At the beginning of last summer Trammel had in passing informed his parents that he meant to save enough to buy a certain kind of bike. Such thrift and resolution seemed like ideal traits in a son until the mother overheard from another mother that the particular bike her son had in mind cost in the neighborhood of five hundred dollars. Such a figure was two or three times what another, fairly good bike would cost. That seemed extravagant to her. The Joneses did not scrimp on things for their children. They were not nearly as "tight" ("tighter 'n Dick's hat band," as her father-in-law would say) as their Depression-era parents were. But neither did they spoil their children. And they had talked a lot about *not* doing that very thing despite their recently improved financial circumstances. Five hundred dollars! That could be part of his down payment on a car, the mother thought.

On the other hand, it was *Trammel's money*. He had earned it (we shall see) through the sweat of his brow. The Joneses were not parents who believed that their child could do whatever he wanted with his money any more than he could consider his room "off-limits" to his parents. But the prospect of *his* spending *his* money in the way *he* wanted seemed to gain for him the cause of justice if not of judgment. Before taking the case to her husband, Mrs. Jones decided to find out from Trammel a little more about his desire for this certain type of bike. It could be that a friend of his had such a bike and Trammel wanted one just as good, a case of his "trying to keep up with the Joneses." That impulse was forbidden since, as Trammel's father never failed to point out, "By God, we are the Joneses." Or there could be some other reason that Trammel could be coaxed out of. It just did not make any sense to the frugal mother that her son would spend so much on "a bicycle" he would only have for a couple of years before he would begin driving.

As it turned out, Trammel's choice in bikes was much more straightforward than his mother had imagined. There was only one reason for it: *speed*. The Redline Proline was apparently the fastest bike in production. Mrs. Jones tried to appeal to her son's pride by recalling to him something she had overheard, that he had beaten many boys in bike races all over town. He admitted that to be the case, relating to her that he had even beaten a couple of kids who had Redlines. But apparently this was due to the modifications he had been making to his own bike by changing out the components it had originally come with. These "components" he had been buying at a local bike shop where he spent much more time than the mother had realized. Then he launched into a lecture about different sprockets and cranks and torque that reminded her too much of her college physics class. She was impressed, however, that he seemed to be thinking of exercising economy in that he had considered selling his current, modified bike to one of the younger kids he knew, maybe in Christie's grade, who would love to brag about having Trammel's old bike.

At that point she knew she had lost her case. Should she take the initial information she had gleaned about cost to her husband, her son would respond, lawyer-like, with the argument, first, of speed; second, of the bike's being half paid for by the sale of his own bike; and third, of torque and all that other stuff she did not understand. Lurking in the background was the argument her son would never have the ill breeding to use against her, but one that her husband would definitely pick up on: that it was *the boy's own money*. So, without calling her son's interests or judgment into question, Mrs. Jones let the matter drop, and the son was glad to have enlightened his mother so much on the ins and outs of bicycle moto-cross. The mother could at least take comfort in the fact that her son spent so much time outdoors during the summers and did things that were clearly healthy for him, rather than playing those stupid (and expensive) video games just then sweeping the nation, to which her son had a natural aversion. Trammel did get the new bike. In fact, the day after Trammel threw a shutout—with nine strikeouts—in the state tournament the previous year his father offered to buy the whole thing, notwithstanding the boy's plan to spend his own money. In this instance the frugal mother managed to divert her husband's jubilation into renewed investment in their son's college savings and to set up a "car fund" for the future while allowing her son to buy the bike as promised.

Although speed was the most obvious virtue of Trammel's bike, which was known to boys his age all over town, it did have the more humble function of providing a means of transportation for the boy in his various rambles about the streets of Dogwood, thereby freeing the mother from her having to take him everywhere as has become the custom in the decades since. The boys of this small town spent countless hours going from one of their houses to another or from one side of town to the other in making it to their myriad of meetings at various ice cream shops, and, occasionally, though Trammel never did so, in going by a girl's house. This morning Trammel did not have speed and certainly not girls on his mind, barely putting force to the pedals (because of the torque) and spitting sunflower seed shells the whole way en route to his buddy Lanny's house.

Arriving at his destination, Trammel found the garage door open and Lanny's tackle box and rod and both the folding chairs already gone. He parked his bike in the garage, gathered up his own gear—one of his two tackle boxes and an old Zebco rod and reel that he kept at Lanny's house—and made his way down to the pond. "The Pond," as he and Lanny referred to it, having no other name that they knew of, occupied about three acres on a stretch of land less than a football field away from the heavily wooded Goose Creek, the same rivulet that ran directly through the town, from the Little League and Pee Wee fields on the East side, behind the houses of Shady Brook Lane, to the new developments on the Western edge of Dogwood where both Trammel's and Lanny's families now lived. The land around the pond—a low flood plain running from a twelve-foot drop-off behind Lanny's neighborhood —and the pond itself, hardly beautiful enough to build suburban houses on—constituted a developer's disappointing limits and a boy's last sanctuary.

"Tram! Where you been, man? I figur'd you'd be out here at 'a crack a' dawn after missin' all a' yesterdee."

"Wudn't gonna pass up on breakfast. Man can't fish on a empty stomach," Trammel explained as he baited his hook with a gizzard. "'Ey bitin' at all?"

"Jus' got down here m'self. Nut'n' yet. Where's you at yesterdee, anyhow?"

"Like I said, had ta do one a' my mom's deals."

"You mean, like shoppin'?"

"Naw, man, not *shoppin*! Ain't gonna miss 'a first day a' fishin' fer no shoppin'.'" Knowing that one way or another Lanny was going to get to the bottom of his friend's mysterious absence on the previous day, Trammel went ahead and disclosed the reason.

"Ya know 'at kid Joey, Joey Fuller?"

"Naw, can't say I do."

"Ya know, 'at albino-lookin' kid: 'a one's always missin' school an' havin' ta make up all 'is work. 'E's always on a baseball team but don't play much."

"I ain't never had eem in class, but I thank I know the one ya mean."

"Well, 'is kid's sick, sicker'n a dog, not all 'a time but a lot. Anyhow, my mom does stuff for eem an' 'is mom ever now an' 'en, an' brangs me along ta hang out with eem, I guess. Yesterdee she wonted me ta show eem how ta play some ball."

"Whatcha mean? Ain't he got no dad?"

"'Course 'e gotta dad. Ever kid's gotta dad. But I reckon you're right 'cause 'is ol' man run off when 'e 'as justa kid."

"Run off? Well, ain't 'at some shit?"

"Yeah, 'at *is* some sh— Hey, Lanny, wha'd I tell ya 'bout all 'at cussin' 'round me? How 'm I gonna stop cussin' if you're always 'shittin'' an' 'hellin'' up a storm?"

"I thought it 'as jus' 'round your sister."

"Naw, man. My dad overheard me cussin' th'other day. I 'as jus' workin' out in 'a garage, an' 'e come out an' said 'e didn't wont no cussin': not 'round my sister, not 'round my mom, not 'round nobody. Not 'at I ever did cuss 'round no women."

"Well, ain't 'at some shit?" laughed Lanny. "Like your dad ain't never cussed! Hell, yeah, 'e has. 'E's cussed with 'a best ob'm. But I see 'is point. You know *my* family, though. We ain't happy 'nless we're cussin' at sump'm. Anyhow, I can't blame ya fer missin' yesterdee if you 'as out helpin' some poor kid 'at ain't got no dad."

"What happened anyhow? D'you come down ta see if 'ey's bitin'?"

At that moment Trammel felt his rod bend downward, and he gave a quick jerk to his reel to set the hook but saw the line go slack again.

"Dad gummit! Bet 'at's a turtle."

"Naw, Tram, nut'n' much happened. I jus' come down here a couple a' times. I did catch 'at sorry ol' Van Strand snoopin' 'round, 'ough. I tol' eem 'e better watch eemself 'round 'is here pond."

"'E didn't set out no trot line, did 'e?" asked the concerned Trammel.

"You kiddin'? 'E knows I'd whoop 'is sorry ass if 'e did 'at agin. Yeah, my whoop-ass 'd be all over eem. Lyin' Yankee blue scumbelly," Lanny fulminated, quoting one of their favorite movies.

Miles Van Strand was a boy who had moved into Lanny's neighborhood about a year and a half ago. The family moved from the Midwest when the father lost his job, having soon found employment in the rapidly expanding Dallas-Fort Worth metroplex. Despite this good fortune, the wife and mother, Laura Van Strand, did not adjust well at all to her new surroundings. Within a month of moving to the town she began writing acid letters to the editor of the local paper complaining of how things were run in Dogwood and in the state of Texas in general. This tack did not prove the best means of acquiring new friends, and one of her countless gripes to her friends back home, or rather confidantes, became that the much vaunted "Southern hospitality" was pure myth.

Her son did not prove any more adept in acquiring companions. His place of origin did not constitute the primary obstacle. To be sure, the boys of Dogwood often displayed a natural aversion to the "Yankees" who moved into their town with growing frequency, but any initial ill will usually wore off when the newcomers proved that they could play sports, after all, and provided they did not insist on bad-mouthing the Cowboys while wearing their stupid Pittsburgh Steelers jerseys. Van Strand's unpopularity was wholly of his own making. It owed to his pretense of knowing everything and his not infrequent departures from the strict line of truth. The offense in question, which threatened to bring out Lanny's "whoop-ass," had occurred the summer before. Throughout the spring, not long after his arrival, Van Strand had come down to the pond on the weekends whenever Lanny and Trammel were fishing. He was full of lots of advice and of stories about the great fish he had caught back home. A few cutting quips from Trammel, and Lanny's assurance that they could do without "your Yankee lies," sent the boy packing. In the early part of the summer, they uncovered a scheme that brought shame on the Northern angler, to the extent he was capable of shame, and resulted in his semi-ostracism from the pond. Arriving at the pond one summer morning about an hour earlier than their normal time, owing to Trammel's having stayed over the previous night and their deciding to go fishing *before* breakfast, they caught Van Strand taking catfish off a trot line and loading them into a mesh basket. They instantly guessed that the new boy's plan was to make it appear like he had caught all those fish that morning and thus be able to pass himself off as the champion fisherman he had claimed to be. Lanny and Trammel did not, of course, allow any trot lines in their pond: "'cause 'ere ain't no sport in 'at an' we'd be all fished out in no time" (despite their other principal rule being that all fish were thrown back). Worse still was the outright deception. With clenched fists and outraged execration, the boys forced the fraud to dump all the fish back into the pond, told him that he could never fish at the pond while they were there, and further promised to string him up with his own trot line if he ever did anything like that again. From that day on Lanny assumed the duty of keeping a close watch on the pond during days he and Trammel were not fishing, just in case Van Strand was up to any of his old tricks.

As Lanny finished his report on the status of Van Strand and the sanctity of the pond, he felt a tug in his line and saw the tip of his rod bend towards the water.

"Salmon patties, comin' back," he exclaimed, reeling in what would be considered a disappointingly small catfish were the boys anywhere but the pond.

Their trademark phrase for every catch had been appropriated from an elderly man they had seen several times fishing off the banks of Lake Foster. The man always set up five or six long cane poles—never a rod and reel—and whenever pulling one in would cry out "Salmon patties, comin' back!" Without looking, he would fling the fish back over his head, a good fifteen feet behind him. In response, a couple of six- or seven-year-old boys, presumably the man's grandchildren, would rush to the flopping fish, one boy taking it off the line and throwing it into a big plastic bucket full of lake water, the other re-worming the hook in an instant and shouting back, "Salmon patties, comin' up!"—at which point the old man would fling the line back into the lake. The whole operation took less than a minute. Trammel and Lanny had tried to duplicate it using their younger siblings, neither of whom showed the dexterity of the two young boys or their eagerness to take part in such an exemplary division of labor.

"Go back an' gitchur older brother fer me," said Lanny, employing another stock phrase, while releasing the fish back into the pond. The boys always began with siblings or parents and worked their way up to older relatives or a more complicated genealogy, such as third cousin, twice removed.

"Hey, Tram, I been meanin' ta tell ya. 'At 'as some game you pitched 'a other day. I only seen 'a first part of it 'cause we had ta take off ta git t'a church picnic, but 'a part I seen 'as perty good. You 'as blowin' it by 'em poor saps like 'ey 'as 'em dummies at 'a mall, ya know."

"Ya mean manikins?"

"Yeah, manikins, 'xactly. It 'as like 'ey 'as jus' modelin' uniforms an' bats but didn't have no idea what ta do with 'em."

"I reckon so," acknowledged Trammel, laconically, spitting a mouthful of sunflower seed shells into the pond and watching them drift back to the bank.

The boys passed the morning this way, occasionally pulling in a fish and swapping stories, with Lanny doing most of the talking. Around eleven, though not knowing the time other than by the height of the sun, Trammel and Lanny felt a presence over their left shoulders. It was none other than Van Strand. He had approached cautiously, careful of how he might be received. Neither of the two fishermen did so much as glance his way or offer a word of acknowledgment.

"You guys catching any?" queried the interloper.

"'Course we are. We're fishin', ain't we?" returned Lanny.

"How big?"

"How big don't matter. 'Course nut'n' is big as 'a ones you tell us 'bout in your damn Yankee lies." Lanny was for once selective about whom he engaged in small talk.

"Whatcha wont, Strand?" broke in Trammel, exasperated, "'cause I gotta be honest an' say you're startin' ta walk on 'a fightin' side a' me." Lanny laughed when he heard his friend quote one of their favorite song lyrics to such good effect.

"What I wanted to show you guys was this," replied Van Strand, reaching both hands into the front pockets of his khaki shorts. He pulled out two store-bought items familiar enough to the two boys.

"Yeah, so?" returned Lanny, unimpressed.

"You guys see what I got? Dip and chewing tobacco. I've been dipping and chewing all morning. Here, you guys try some."

Not looking at the boy with the goods but turning to his friend, Lanny scoffed. "You b'lievin' 'at, Tram? 'At lyin' blue scumbelly. 'Ey ain't eb'm *got* chewin' tabacca up in New Jersey."

"I'm from Ohio," corrected Miles Van Strand.

"Same differ'nce. 'A point is you ain't never seen no chew 'fore you came down here ta God's country. An' you damn sure ain't been chewin' all mornin'. An' if we wudn't fairly peaceable, me 'n' Tram, we'd make you eat 'at chew fer tellin' more a' your lies."

"What's the matter, you can't handle chewing tobacco?"

"Look here, boy, I'm fixin' ta lose what little patience I got. Lemme hit eem, Tram, lemme hit eem jus' 'is once."

"Say Strand, ya say ya been chewin' an' dippin' all mornin' long?" broke in Trammel with a thought.

"That's right."

"'At's how we know you're lyin'. 'Course y'ain't got nut'n in your mouth right now. 'At's 'a first thang. But on top a' that, ya don't even know whatchur talkin' 'bout. Ain't nobody chews *an'* dips at 'a same time. An' mos' 'at does one don't do th'other. 'Ere's chewers an' 'ere's dippers, an' 'at's it; 'ey ain't no in-between. Sayin' you're doin' both ain't jus' a lie, like Lanny says. It's 'a mark of a amateur. But go on ahead an' th'ow me 'at chew, right after ya put some in your own dad-gum mouth, an' I'll tell ya a story. Ya wanna hear a story, Lanny?"

"Heck, yeah. I been waitin' on a good story all mornin' long."

Van Strand looked nervously at Trammel and realized the risky hand he had been playing had been called. He opened the packet and fingered the unfamiliar, dark brown, sticky leaves. Not knowing exactly what to do, and not wanting to appear squeamish, he pulled out a large wad of tobacco and put it in his mouth, trying to disguise his disgust at the strong taste and smell. Throwing the rest of the pack to Trammel, he began chewing all too rapidly, as though he had a piece of gum in his mouth, causing the juices to flow exorbitantly. He gagged, and his first attempt at spitting ended up more on him than on the ground. Meanwhile, Trammel calmly pulled out half as much tobacco, stuffed it into his cheek, and followed every soft bite into the "chaw" with brown stream of spit into the pond.

"Ya know, Lanny, I don't thank I ever tol' ya' what happened when my dad took me fishin' one time last summer. Maybe it 'as 'a spring; I can't remember. Anyway, we 'as sittin' in 'a boat out on Foster, not sayin' much, an' out a' the blue 'e says, "Say, Tram, wonta chew?" an' th'ew me a pack a Red Man—not 'is trainin' wheels Beech Nut crap Strand jus' gimme. Ya know, the real stuff. I didn't know what 'e 'as up to, ya know, maybe tryin' ta figur' out if I'd been chewin' on my own er what. So I looked at eem funny, an' 'e says, 'Go ahead, boy. By your age I 'as already chewin'.' So I took out a big wad a' chew, jus' like 'is kid behind us jus' done, an' started givin' it a good goin' over. An' my dad, 'e jus' sat 'ere, not sayin' nut'n' but kinda smilin', jus' smilin' with 'is eyes. 'Course I wudn't feelin' too good after a while."

"Hey Strand," paused Trammel in the middle of his narrative to address the amateur, "if you're fixin' ta puke, go off an' do it somewheres else, not right here where me an' Lanny's fishin'."

"So, d'ya puke, Tram?" interjected Lanny, "ya did, didn't ya?"

"C'mone, Lanny, you know me better 'n 'at. Man 'at can't handle 'is tabacca ain't much of a man. But I wudn't feelin' too good right 'en, 'at's fer sure. 'Course my dad says, 'Don't you th'ow up in 'is here bass boat, boy. If ya need ta toss up 'at breakfast, 'en do it over the side.' 'En 'e says, 'Boy, I bet 'ose donuts 're tastin' real good right about now, Mmm, Mmm,' an' stuff like 'at. But 'e 'as pro'lly jus' testin' me."

By now Van Strand had all but ended his romance with chewing tobacco. He fought with his stomach to keep down its contents, and he began swaying with lightheadedness.

Trammel continued, "So my dad says, 'Look here, boy, I been chewin' since I 'as, oh, twelve pro'lly, an' it ain't really a good habit ta get inta. 'Course I'd much ruther have ya chewin' 'n drinkin' 'n smokin' 'n' all 'at crap. But see your mom don't eb'm like *me* chewin'.' . . . Hey, Strand, I'm tellin' ya right now: don't you th'ow up here by my pond. You git yourself off a ways 'fore ya puke up your guts. . . . So 'e says, 'Your mom don't like me chewin', an' I ain't eb'm chewin' in 'a house much no more 'cause a' all 'em times I spilled my spit can on 'er nice carpet. So the last thang in 'a world she wonts is 'er prize boy ta start doin' what she's had ta put up with me doin' all 'ese years.'"

Trammel spit a couple of more times into the pond. "Hey, Strand, lemme give ya a tip. Don't ya know you're swallerin' too much? A amateur like you can't hardly keep swallerin' so much a' the juice. Now my ol' man, 'e cou'd pro'lly drink a whole cup a' tabacca juice, an' it wouldn't do nut'n' to eem. But you, you're likely ta puke any second now. Anyway, Lanny, my dad sorta made 'is deal with me. 'E says I can chew any time we're out fishin' er sump'm like 'at, but 'e don't wont me chewin' all 'a time, 'specially since my mom 'd pro'lly figure out what I 'as up to right quick. So 'at's why ya see me eatin' 'ese seeds all 'a time, ta try ta keep me off my chewin' habit."

Van Strand could not last any longer. He put his hands on his stomach and stumbled off. Needing to say something to cover for his hurried exit, he began to utter the words, "I gotta go, guys; my mom expects me for lunch," but did not even get to the "gotta" without starting to gag and cough up more saliva than he knew he had in him. He held it in for a while, but before making it halfway to the drop-off he fell to his hands and knees and did exactly what Trammel kept promising he would. Lanny broke into one of his interminable belly laughs while Trammel barely cracked a smile.

"Ya got eem good, Tram. Oh, man, ya got eem good!"

From his own mouth Trammel let sail the by now well-formed chaw a good fifteen feet out into the pond.

"I can't b'lieve it, Lanny. Some folks ain't got no sense. Wha'd 'at boy thank 'e 'as doin' by comin' out here 'n' tryin' ta chew with 'a big boys? 'E jus' didn't thank 'at'n th'ough, did he? Least he lef' us some chew, though," said Trammel, tossing the pack into his tackle box.

"Naw, 'e didn't thank 'at 'n th'ough," agreed Lanny, still laughing. "I'm jus' glad ya didn't make me chew none a' that stuff. I hate 'at crap."

"Well, man's gotta know 'is limitations," pronounced Trammel, quoting yet another of their favorite movies.

After a few moments passed, with Lanny still wiping the sweat from his brow owing to his laughing so hard, Trammel broke into the familiar refrain, "Salmon patties, comin' back."

Chapter 7: "Ain't No Differ'nce"

Early one Monday morning, a few weeks into the summer, Trammel set about his familiar routine. After breakfast, he pushed his lawnmower out of the garage and down the street to the Picketts' house. He had taken on five lawns that summer, the maximum number his father would allow, not counting the family's own lawn, which the boy did gratis. His father did not want him to be too tired out on game days from mowing lawns, or even during afternoon practices for that matter, so Trammel had to turn away plenty of business he could have had. These were giant yards, though; and, in addition to mowing, he did a lot of edging and other upkeep that added to his price and made this summer his most lucrative yet.

Although he hated selling things door-to-door, particularly when everybody else was selling the exact same thing at the same time and he got nothing out of it, Trammel had been interested in making money for quite a while. When he was in grade school and lived in the old neighborhood, he had done well at his lemonade stand, from which he had also sold blueberry muffins. The proximity of the family's house to his elementary school brought lots of traffic his way and allowed him to speed home to put out the refreshments his mother had prepared just in time to be ready for the crowds walking home at a more leisurely pace. At first Trammel had spent all his earnings—on knives and gun magazines mostly. But he began putting them to other uses when Mr. Jones told his son exactly what he did for a living. The boy learned that a person who had money could lend that money to those who had none, at least at the moment, and then charge a thing called interest on top of the original amount, thus making a tidy profit. As it turned out, every day different kids came to school without their lunch money and could use a small loan to avoid either starving or begging. Since Trammel never forgot his lunch money, and carried about ten times the amount of cash he needed, he was always happy to extend credit to his fellow schoolmates. His terms were simple: a quarter tomorrow on top of every dollar borrowed today; another quarter for the second day; and on the third, if it got that far, he would "come pay ya a visit." He had no idea what the going rate of interest was in the adult markets, but in his market the borrowers were free to choose either twenty-five percent per day on the principal or no lunch.

Like so many good enterprises, everything went smoothly until the government got involved. One day a fellow classmate let it slip to his mother that he needed more than his allotted dollar-fifty, and the dollar-fifty she had forgotten the day before, to "pay off Tram." After getting to the bottom of that problematic phrase, the mother called to complain to the principal, who in turn talked to the assistant principal, both unaware of Trammel's financial entrepreneurship until then, who then talked to the teacher. Despite the clear public benefits of this private system, the teacher required him to stop loaning money to people with interest. She said he was free to loan money without interest "out of friendship." Trammel responded that the first rule of the finance business was *not* to loan money to your friends because you would end up losing both your friends and your money (something his dad had taught him) and that "the laborer is worthy of his wages." The teacher replied that there was no labor involved in lending money, to which Trammel countered that there was "all kinda labor": first, the math behind percentages, which they had not even learned yet in school; next, the mental effort behind keeping up with all the loans a "finance man" had out at any given time; and finally, "on top a' all 'at, the whole b'iness a' collectin' off deadbeats." The young female teacher wanted to hear no more about "loansharking" and especially the business of collecting; that would be the end of his "exploiting kids" who had the misfortune of forgetting their lunch money. Trammel saw the writing on the wall but was determined not to leave her with the last word. An insight from his father's touting the virtues of his own industry flashed in the boy's mind.

"Yes, ma'am. . . . Say, Miss Dewey. Sump'm else I been meanin' ta ask ya. 'At's a perty nice car ya jus' got. Whatcha call it, a 280 er sump'm like 'at?"

"Oh, thanks, Trammel," the young teacher replied, caught off guard. "Yes, it's a 280 ZX."

"Boy, I bet 'at cost a perty penny."

"No, it wasn't cheap, that's for sure."

"D'you jus' buy 'a whole thang all at once? I mean with your own money?"

"Goodness no. A teacher could never afford a car like that out of their salary. Of course I financed it."

"You *financed* it? Well, *I'll* be," the boy mused in mock astonishment and walked off as the young woman felt a blush rise in her cheeks.

Once Trammel's financial services were shut down, the parents who forgot to give their children lunch money had to return to the school to drop off a lunch, according to the new policy. When that errand proved too inconvenient to the parents, the school, under the duress of further complaints, implemented a still newer policy of keeping some extra crackers and apples on hand for those without lunch money. The school could not keep any food the children would like, such as pudding or cookies, since then *too many* children would soon be forgetting their lunch money. None of the students was happy with the alternative meal, and several kept coming to Trammel for loans. He considered going underground for select customers but was just too much of a stickler for rules to do what his teacher had expressly forbidden him to do, however unjust the ruling might have been. This episode marked Trammel's first lesson in political economy.

Two reasons led Trammel to embark on his lawn mowing so early in the morning. The first was the simple desire to avoid the combination of the Texas sun and outside labor during the day when these two were least agreeable. The second was the not so simple problem of trying not to encounter Ashley Pickett "laying out" in her back yard. A couple of weeks earlier Trammel had opened the gate to the Picketts' back yard and found Ashley, an attractive peroxide blonde who was a junior in high school, luxuriating in her late morning tan while listening to the radio. He asked whether it would be okay for him to mow. The girl was completely unfazed by the intrusion and even stayed on her recliner a while longer as Trammel nervously scoured the back yard for any rocks or debris that he might not see while mowing: "policing," as his dad called it. After he had begun to mow and made a couple of passes around the perimeter of the yard, she looked at him lazily, smiled, waved, and then went inside, taking her radio with her.

As if this encounter was not unsettling enough for a pubescent boy, Trammel had to decide what to do the next week and the next. Just as Trammel followed his routine, so Ashley followed hers. If Ashley could be regarded as in any way typical, high-school girls were pretty simple creatures, especially during the summers. They got up late in the day, "laid out" in the late morning before it got too hot, then either went to or worked at the mall. The two latter efforts were really one and the same thing, since (as Trammel suspected rightly) any income earned from work was promptly spent in taking advantage of the employee discount offered by the department stores that employed mostly teenage girls. An hour or so after coming home from not too terribly taxing an afternoon at the mall—or at work rather—the teenage girl was then ready to receive any boys who might drive by in fast cars with designedly loud engines. The girl might get into such a car or oftentimes just lean into the window while talking to the boy or boys for half an hour or more, with the engine running the whole time.

The question became whether Trammel would intrude his schedule into the routine of one Ashley Pickett, high-school girl. He was not averse to happening upon Ashley in her bikini. Far from it. But he was determined not to do so too predictably lest she form the wrong opinion of him. He certainly did not want her to consider him a *pervert*, as though he might be waiting all week long to catch her lying out and thinking about it all the time! Even less so did he want her, insofar as he was younger and not a serious object of her attention, looking at his interest in her as "sweet" or "cute." Trammel did not want any girl thinking of him as sweet or cute. He was not a puppy. He was *neither* a pervert *nor* a puppy. Nor was he at that moment seventeen and thus a contender for her affections, one who could presumably rid her of the drive-by, big-engine boys. So he had to play it cool and interrupt Ashley's late morning worship of Helios only as if by happenstance, and this particular Monday was not one of those happenstances.

Trammel started on the back yard first so he could be well done with it before Ashley needed it for her purposes. As he was finishing up policing the yard and about to crank his mower, to his surprise the back door opened and out walked Ashley with something in her hand. She had clearly not been up long, as her abundant but normally coiffed hair was in a riotous state and she wore, as far as he could tell, only a tee shirt.

"He-ey, Tra-am, cou'd you do me a favor?" she yawned, not expecting an answer. "Cou'd you maybe open up this peanut butter? I 'as tryin' ta have some on my toast."

She handed Trammel an unopened jar of Jiffy, the old glass jar with the metallic top. Trammel knew the pressure was on. He couldn't *not* open the jar; he couldn't even look like he was struggling with it. Luckily, he thought, he had not already been mowing and gotten his hands all sweaty.

He regained his composure as he took the jar from Ashley. "Well, I'll see what I can do, but I ain't promisin' nut'n'." Trammel gave both top and jar a fierce wrench, using the force of each against the other, and the deed was done easily, to the girl's surprise and the boy's great relief.

"Here ya go," offered Trammel, trying to appear nonchalant and to stifle the crackle in his voice.

"Goh-lee, you're strong. I tried ten minutes and couldn't git the dang thang open."

"Well, see, my mom's always gettin' me ta open up jars an' stuff, ya know, when Dad ain't around. All ya had ta do 'as use a can op'ner an' crack 'a lid a little, ya know, ta let some air in. The whole deal's with 'a seal, ya know."

"Well, you're still my hero," she smiled, and began walking back toward the sliding glass door. Trammel, dumbfounded, tried to avert his eyes quickly when she suddenly turned back around.

"Sa-ay, Tra-am, I betcha gotta a lotta girlfriends at school an' all."

"Who, me? Naw. I mean *yeah*. I mean, it depen's on whatcha mean by girlfriends."

"Well, you'll have a lotta girlfriends in high school, anyway. You'll be real *pop'lar*."

With that prophecy, the sibyl disappeared through the door to her kitchen. A few moments later Ashley unexpectedly popped back out of her house again, motioning to Trammel not to stop the mower, which he held on to for safety, and put a corner of the warm toast with peanut butter into his mouth with her tanned hand, smiled one of those crinkly-nosed, squint-eyed girl smiles, then floated again back into the house, the verdict still out on what she had on besides a tee shirt.

Trammel's head went into a spin. He had no rational ability to process what had just happened; nor had he any vocabulary to describe it. Unlike Sharla Lewis, this older girl was not a friend of the family. Indeed, unlike Sharla Lewis, a.k.a. Miss Dogwood, whom the whole Jones family regarded as simply angelic, this girl his mother seemed not really to like. Whenever the family drove past her talking to one of her drive-by boyfriends, his father and mother would look at each other, the one with a wry smile, the other saying something under her breath. Trammel's father might offer some quip, such as, "Oh, babe, 'ey're jus' plannin' 'eir nex' Bible study," to which his wife might respond, "And she'll be happy to play the part of Delilah, Bathsheba, or Jezebel." Trammel was a great deal in the dark about girls. He considered telling Lanny about the whole thing, since Lanny was an interpreter of such matters, but quickly decided against it. If Trammel spilled the beans about Ashley's tanning sessions, Lanny would only start hounding him to help mow the Picketts' yard.

Still in a daze when he returned home, Trammel was startled by his mother when she happened upon him in the kitchen while he was eating a can of onion rings, pouring them straight from the can into his mouth.

"Back so soon?"

"Uh, yes ma'am, I jus' whipped th'ough it, ya know, wonted ta git it outta the way. Ain't no use in not gettin' it done," he responded with attempted composure.

"Well, good. Now you have a little time to hang out before we go over to Joey's."

"Oh, yeah, I been meanin' ta letcha know 'bout 'at." He saw his mother arch her eyebrow and hurried to reassure her.

"I mean, me 'n' Joey, we been doin' 'is a while, an' we got our own thang goin'. Me 'n' him 'as jus' gonna go up ta the school, ya know, without gettin' e'erbody involved. I 'as just fixin' ta take off on my bike an' stop by ta pick eem up."

"And so y'all planned this already?"

"Yes, ma'am."

Mrs. Jones paused a moment to think the whole thing through. "Well, how are y'all goin' to get up to the school with your equipment and all those baseballs?"

"Yeah, good point. See, I lef' a bunch a' balls over at his house las' time. We'll pro'lly jus' carry 'em in garbage bags er sump'm. It ain't no pro'lem."

"Well, okay then. If there's no need for Chris and I to go . . . Mmm. Maybe we can go out and have some fun on our own."

"A'right, 'en," said a relieved Trammel, pitching his onion ring can into the garbage bin. "Ah-dee-os."

"Oh, Tra-am," his mother called to him as he was heading to his room to get his glove.

"Yes, ma'am?"

"Why don't you see whether Joey would like to go fishin' with you and Lanny one of these days?" his mother asked in that way that was not asking so much as telling.

"Fishin'? You mean at 'a pond?" There was no mistaking her meaning, but the boy had to ask just to take in the full force of the idea.

"Of course at the pond. He might like that. Y'all'd have a good time together."

"Uh, well, I ain't really asked Lanny 'bout it, an', uh, I don't eb'm know if Joey likes fishin', ya know, but maybe we can figur' sump'm out. . . . I reckon I'll look into it."

"Good. Y'all'll have fun."

The whole ride over to Joey's house one of Trammel's father's phrases kept echoing through his mind: *roped into*. It seemed like whenever he had just taken care of one thing his mother wanted him to, he would get *roped into* another. He never knew exactly how it happened. He never saw it coming. But it always did.

While Trammel's weekly practices had not turned Joey into a first-rate ballplayer by any means, they had begun to show some results. Joey was throwing the ball a lot better; he was at least stopping, sometimes snagging, the easier grounders; and he was not turning his head from, and occasionally getting his glove on, the hot grounders that the better athlete had become an ace at hitting. Joey had also become a tolerable fielder of fly balls. Taking Joey through these paces rather quickly on this particular day, Trammel wanted to spend more time on hitting. For it was in the area of hitting that Joey needed the most help.

"Hol' on, I gotta go git sump'm," Trammel announced when it was time to begin batting practice.

Tossing his glove on the ground, Trammel trotted between two houses that backed up to the school grounds, disappeared for a few moments, and then reappeared carrying a contraption over his shoulder.

"Don't worry none; I didn't steal it. Robby, one a' my buddies, lives on th' other side a' the street 'ere. 'Is is his little brother's. I tol' eem I'd be gettin' it out 'is yard."

The device, which Joey did not recognize at first, was a "tee," a rubber cylinder that adjusted up and down a pipe, that was in turn affixed to a wood cutout of a home plate. These tees were commonly used in beginners', or tee-ball leagues, before most boys were old enough to hit a moving baseball. Trammel adjusted the rubber to a point that would bring the ball dead center into Joey's strike zone.

"You'll pro'lly thank 'is is stupid, but I ain't messin' witcha, man. My dad makes me do crap like 'is all 'a time. See, 'a deal is, you're worried 'bout two differ'nt thangs: gettin' down a good swang an' hittin' 'a ball. Whatcha need ta do is worry 'bout jus' one thang at a time. First, I wontcha ta know what it feels like ta hit 'a ball. 'En we'll work on 'a other thang."

Joey blinked significantly at Trammel, never doubting his methods or his motives for a moment.

"A'right, so what I'm gonna do here is set 'a balls up on 'a tee, an' you jus' thank 'boutchur swang. I don't wontcha swangin' *at* 'a ball but *th'ough* the ball. Got it?"

"Sure, Trammel, *through* the ball."

Joey took a couple of practice swings just to make sure. He stepped up to the plate to try it out. On the first couple of attempts he got more tee than ball, with the result being weak pop-ups that did not make it to the pitcher.

"You're gettin' a piece of it, a'right, but why you still choppin' down on it like you done th' other day? Remember: take your bat straight back an' jus' come th'ough with a nice, eb'm swang."

The next attempt resulting in a solid grounder between third and short, Joey looked to Trammel.

"See, 'at's better, but remember, if you gotta nice, eb'm swang, you'll pro'lly hit 'a ball straight level with 'a pitcher's gut—off 'a tee, at least. So jus' keep workin' at it an' thank t'yourself 'level swang.'"

Trammel kept placing baseballs on the tee, and Joey kept hitting them. When out of balls, they would go retrieve them and come back for another round. Save for occasional flubs, Joey managed to raise the trajectory of his hits from grounders to junior line drives just about chest high.

"See, 'at's what I'm talkin' 'bout. 'At's whatcha gotta do. Jus' swang th'ough the ball. Don't 'at feel differ'nt?"

"Yeah, Trammel, it feels a lot different. It feels like I'm really hittin' the ball."

"A'right 'en, watch 'is."

Trammel walked out to the spot where the pitching rubber would be, tossing a ball into the air with his hand, then stopped, turned, and drew himself into a pitcher's stance, his eyes staring with intensity at the strike zone. Joey instinctively backed away from the plate. Although he had been conducting a friendly batting practice with Joey for the last few weeks, Trammel's convincing pantomime now put him in the aggressive posture he would have had in a real game.

"Naw, man, jus' stay up 'ere. I ain't gonna th'ow it."

Joey stepped back towards home as Trammel went into a slow motion mock wind-up. Rather than releasing the ball, he carried it—as though it were moving through the air— as he walked back to the plate, and then he set the ball back on the tee.

"See."

"See what, Trammel?" Joey asked in wonder.

"'Ere ain't no differ'nce."

"No difference in what?"

"'Ere ain't no differ'nce in somebody th'owin' 'a ball an' hittin' it off 'a tee."

"But, Trammel, if the ball was coming this—"

"Yeah, a' course 'ere's a *differ'nce*. I ain't *stupid*. But 'ere ain't no *real* differ'nce. 'At guy on 'a mound—don't eb'm call eem a pitcher—'e's gotta git 'a ball right here, jus' like it sets on 'a tee. Jus' like it. 'At means 'e's gotta put 'a ball where you wont it: maybe a little higher, maybe a little lower, maybe a little inside er a little outside. But 'e's still gotta put it right here. An' 'en you can jus' smack it, jus' like you been doin' all day long."

Though he was trying to go along with what Trammel was telling him, Joey looked skittishly skeptical.

"Look, man, ya got it all wrong. *You* ain't gotchur mind right. An' if y'ain't gotchur mind right, ya might as well not eb'm be out here. Ya gotta gitchur swang down, an' 'at's what we been workin' on all day long. But once ya done 'at, 'en ya gotta start lookin' at real pitches. 'En ya keep your swang goin', an' it's jus' a matter a' decidin' which pitch ya wont. Ain'tcha never heard your coach sayin' 'Make it be your pitch'?"

"Yeah, sure, Trammel. He says that all the time."

"'At's what 'e's talkin' 'bout. 'E's basically sayin' ya gotta decide right. Ya gotta make it be the right pitch. Ya gotta take it here," Trammel demonstrated, thrusting the ball emphatically into the strike zone, "instead a' up here er down here. 'A 'course 'ere's also timin', but we can worry 'bout 'at some other time."

Trammel wondered whether he was getting through. "Lemme show ya one more time. Act like you're swangin' into it. Don't really swang; I don't wontcha hittin' me with 'a bat."

Trammel repeated his slow motion pitch, and this time Joey acted out his own part, ball and bat meeting right on top of the tee in the middle of the strike zone.

"See, 'ere ain't no differ'nce," pronounced Trammel with great conviction.

"Yeah, I think I see what you mean," ventured Joey, more hopefully.

"Look, it's like 'is. The pitcher's gonna th'ow the ball, but *you* ain't gotta take it. After the ball leaves 'is hand, it ain't eb'm 'is pitch no more. It's *your* pitch, but only if ya wont it. Sure, 'e's got a bunch a' differ'nt stuff 'e's gonna th'ow atcha, some of it good and some of it crap. When ya git right down to it, a pitcher ain't nut'n' but a waiter. Right as you're sittin' down an' ain't eb'm had a chance ta look at 'a menu, 'ey start in tellin' ya 'bout 'the special.' 'The special today is,' 'ey say. Who cares what 'a special is? 'Em sorry waiters been pitchin' 'a special all day long 'cause 'a manager's tellin' 'em to. But 'a special's crap. E'erbody knows 'a special's crap. Only a sucker orders 'a special er somebody 'at don't already know what 'e wonts. See, ya don't order no special. An' ya don't order 'at other crap ya don't wont off 'a menu, neither. *You* order what *you* wont. An' ya don't wont jus' some sorry ol' hamburger. An' ya don't eb'm wont jus' a reg'lar cheeseburger. You wont 'a bacon double cheeseburger with extra barbecue sauce. An' here's 'a best part. If 'e don't brang ya what ya wont, you can tell eem, 'I didn't order none a' that crap.' An' if 'e keeps brangin' it, 'en you tell 'a manager, an' you'll git ta eat fer free."

"I don't understand."

"See, 'at's my joke. You 'as s'posed ta laugh. Here's 'a deal. If you're in a rest'rant, an' 'a waiter keeps brangin' out crap ya didn't order, jus' tell 'a manager, an' 'e'll brang your stuff fer free. Same as when you're playin' baseball, an' 'a pitcher keeps th'owin' sorry pitches. 'En you git a walk. It's like gittin' a hit fer free. 'Course it don't do nut'n' fer your battin' average, which it why it's like kissin' your sister."

"Yeah, Trammel, I get it now. That's pretty funny."

"So the point is, you don't take nut'n' 'less you *ordered* it, 'less it's your pitch. 'At pitch is 'ere fer you; you ain't 'ere fer no pitch. Got it?"

"Sure, I got it. Thanks, Trammel, that helps a lot."

"A'right 'en. Let's try it out here with some real pitches an' see how thangs go."

Trammel returned to his post as batting practice pitcher in the hopes of putting theory into practice. Of course, there *was* a difference. Joey did not immediately learn to order only those things off the menu that he really wanted, and his timing still needed quite a bit of work, as Trammel suspected. Nonetheless, Joey's swing showed more consistency. He even began stepping out of the box on his own to practice the swing he wanted. With the aid of Trammel's constant refrains of "make it be your pitch," "keep your eye on 'a ball," "eb'm swang," and "quit orderin' crap," Joey's hitting did not rise percentage-wise, but the times he did make contact the ball actually went somewhere, in marked contrast to the rare squibs, pop-ups, and fouls which had been the only source of hope in previous weeks. As the practice was beginning to wear on Trammel and his plans for the rest of the day meandered through his mind, Joey sent one pitch straight back at him, shoulder high. Surprised, Trammel could still count on his faultless reflexes to snag the ball at the last second.

"Now look at 'at! Look at 'at! Tell me: what's wrong with 'at hit?"

The answer seemed obvious to Joey. "Well, you caught it, Trammel."

"Naw. 'At ain't it. I'm gonna ask ya agin. What's wrong with 'at hit?"

"It wasn't high enough?" Joey ventured again, not accustomed to the questioning of this young Socrates of the diamond.

"Naw. Nuh-uh. Answer is '*Nut'n*.' 'Ere ain't nut'n' wrong with 'at hit. Ain't a blame thang wrong with it."

"Yeah, Trammel, I mean it felt pretty good, but you caught it," insisted Joey, returning to his original conclusion.

"Yeah, a' course I caught it. But see, 'at ain't 'a point. First off, not ever joker on 'a mound's gonna catch a ball like 'at, not in Little League. An' on top a' that, look what happens if 'at ball goes just a couple a' feet 'is a way," said Trammel, holding the ball to his left, "er 'is a way," holding it to his right. "'En it's a clean base hit."

Joey was visibly pleased.

"Remember like I said at 'a beginnin'," reiterated Trammel as he walked toward home, "jus' remember . . . an' don't never fergit . . ." He put the tee back in front of Joey, put the ball for an instant on the top of it, and walked backwards out towards the mound, holding the ball out to his side. Stopping, he made a motion indicating that the ball was passing over the glove of a surprised pitcher. He then extended the ball behind his right shoulder. Upon this reenactment of a base hit, he pronounced, "'Ere ain't no differ'nce."

"There—ain't—no—difference," echoed Joey in agreement.

"A'right 'en, I reckon we oughta pick up all 'ese balls an' git on our way. Today 'as a perty good practice."

After they had retrieved all the baseballs and Trammel had returned the tee to Robby's back yard, the boys pounded some water, once icy, that had gotten warm in the noon sun. Trammel was puzzling over how he was going to do his mother's bidding.

"Hey, Trammel, I gotta question."

"Yeah, man, shoot."

"If there's really no difference, then how come nobody can get a hit off you?"

"Well, see, 'at's a good question," began Trammel as he considered how his theories of hitting contrasted with his theories of pitching and ruminated as well on the prospect of any hitter facing his formidable presence on the mound.

"First off, not e'erbody knows 'ere ain't no differ'nce. Fact, mos' folks ain't got no clue. So ya better keep all 'is ta yourself else e'erbody starts gettin' hits an' turns 'a game a' baseball into a old man, beer-guzzlin', slow-pitch softball league. . . . Th' other thang is, 'ough, 'at I ain't no waiter. I ain't gonna give ya whatcha wont, an' you don't wont what I'm gonna give ya."

Trammel reflected further. "See, 'a deal is, I'm meaner 'n Hell."

Joey looked astonished but dare not contradict.

"Ya come up ta the plate when *I'm* pitchin', an' I don't like ya—I ain't sayin' you in partic'lar, but anybody. I don't like ya. I can't eb'm stand 'a sight of ya. I don't wonta have nut'n' ta do witcha. You're basically my enemy. So I'm gonna git rid of ya. See, 'at's 'a deal. It's either you er me—an' it ain't gonna be me—at's fer damn sure. When my buddy Lanny comes up ta the plate, ya know, 'e ain't no friend a' mine. I got nut'n' ta say for eem. I jus' wonta git rid of eem. 'E's goin' down 'cause I ain't goin' down. 'At's 'a deal."

Trammel halted his diatribe and looked at Joey, whose innocent mind ranged back and forth between horror and disbelief.

"See, I know 'is might sound kinda crazy. I didn't use' ta thank like 'at. One time, I b'lieve it 'as a couple a' seasons ago, we 'as winnin' big—by seb'm er eight runs pro'lly. An' we 'as havin' a good ol' time out on 'a field. After an easy innin' I come back off 'a field—my dad 'as 'a coach—an' 'e didn't say 'is ta e'erbody, but 'e got me off a ways an' tol' me, 'e said, 'Whatcha doin' boy?' ya know, in one a' them ways like ya know you're in for it. I said, 'Whatcha mean?' 'En 'e said, 'Whatcha doin' out 'ere yuckin' it up?' An' I said, 'Dad, we're winnin' big.' 'En 'e looked right at me an' said, 'Butcha ain't won. An' y'ain't gonna win if you're gonna go out 'ere all carefree like your sister. She don't care 'bout 'a game. But I expec' more outta you. So quit horsin' 'round like a clown. Play angry!'

"Well, I played angry, a'right. I 'as mad at *him*. 'A next time up at bat I smashed 'a first pitch over the left-field fence. Well, 'e didn't say nut'n' else 'cept 'good game' after we'd won. But I thought about it 'a next couple a' days. At first I thought, 'what's 'e talkin' 'bout, "Play angry"?' I thought, 'ya know, my dad's a psychopath.' But 'en I got ta thankin' after our next game—'at 'as a lot closer—'ya know, 'e's dead right.' See, ya can't lose your concentration. Ya can't lose your edge. Ya can't lose your killer instinct. 'Cause if ya do, 'en you're gonna mess up, sure as 'a world. An' 'a other guy's gonna beatcha ever time. . . . So I guess 'at's 'a deal. Ya come up ta bat with me on 'a mound, an' we might be playin' baseball, but 'is ain't no game. See what I mean?"

"Yeah, I guess so, Trammel," replied Joey, somewhat enlightened, but still amazed.

"Hey, Trammel," Joey ventured, on further reflection, "are you ever happy, I mean, about baseball?"

"Well, I'm perty dad-gum happy when we win."

"No, I mean, are you happy like just when you're playing the game?"

"Well, I don't know. I ain't unhappy. It's more like, 'is is where I gotta be . . . 'is is what I do. An' I gotta do everthang right 'cause everthang's dependin' on me. See, I'm 'a one in charge a' the game. If I ain't in charge, ain't nobody in charge, an' 'at ain't right. So I'm thankin' 'a whole time 'bout what I gotta do ta win. I'm thankin' 'bout 'a whole game an' at 'a same time 'bout ever little piece of it. 'Cause ever little piece of it's gotta be perfect er the whole thang can't be perfect. 'Course it's never a hunerd percent perfect. But if ya do mos' everthang right, you'an git perty dad-gum close."

Happier with Trammel's second explanation, Joey wondered further, "Gee, Trammel, I guess you've thought about this stuff a lot."

"Yeah, ya know, me 'n' my dad, we just sit around an' thank up 'is kinda stuff. It drives my mom crazy sometimes. . . . Hey, ya know, I been meanin' ta ask ya sump'm."

"Really?"

"Yeah, ya know, I 'as wonderin' if you e'er go fishin'."

"No, I haven't been fishin' in a long time," replied Joey with a surprised hopefulness.

"Well, me 'n' my buddy Lanny, we go fishin' least once a week—down at 'a pond, o'er by where 'e lives. Anyway, I 'as kinda wonderin' if you'd wonta give it a shot some time er other."

"Wow, Trammel, that'd be great. Wow, I'd love to go fishin'. When's the next time you're going—if you don't mind me askin'?"

"Well, I reckon 'at'd be tomorra, ya know, if you're up to it."

"Yes, definitely. I'd love to come."

"Well, a'right 'en. I reckon I can draw ya a map back at your place. It ain't too hard ta figur' out. Anyway, I figur' we've had about enough fer today. I still gotta lotta stuff ta do."

Plans for the morrow made, the boys left the baseball field on their bicycles, Trammel having a bag of balls slung over his right shoulder, Joey holding his bat across his handle bars.

Chapter 8: Teach a Man to Fish

The next morning found Trammel down at the pond fishing next to his friend Lanny. On fishing days he did not do his lawns until the late morning, the idea being that fish, more temperamental than men, would mostly bite in the cool of the day and got too lazy to do much by the time the sun rose very high in the sky. He had told Joey to show up around 8:30 or 9, not so that Joey would miss out on any fish, but rather to prepare his friend for the arrival of a guest. In reality, Trammel, a powerfully secretive boy in many ways, was the one who needed the preparation. Lanny, to anyone with a name other than Van Strand, unfailingly proved to be a warm host in fishing or in any other endeavor.

"Hey, Lanny?" Trammel began. "You 'member 'at kid I tol' ya 'bout—Joey?"

"Ya mean 'a bowlegged kid?"

"Naw, 'e ain't bowlegged. You're pro'lly thankin' 'bout 'at kid Larry Sump'm, ya know, the red-haired kid. I'm talkin' 'bout 'is kid who's perty sick. He kinda looks like a albino—the one my mom likes me ta hang out with sometimes."

"Oh, yeah, now I know the one ya mean. 'At kid whose sorry-ass dad run off, I thank ya tol' me. So what of eem?"

"Well, my mom figur'd i'd be a good idea if 'e came fishin' down here at 'a pond, ya know, pro'lly 'cause like ya said, 'e ain't got no dad. So I went ahead an' invited eem ta come down here t'day. I shou'd 'a' pro'lly give ya a heads up."

"Naw, 'at don't matter. 'At ain't no pro'lem. 'E'll be showin' up perty soon, 'en?"

"Yeah, I 'magine. . . . As fer 'at Larry kid, 'e cou'dn't stop a hog in a narra alley."

Trammel's remark on Larry's ungainly stride sent his friend into an uncontrollable fit of laughter that caused him to drop his rod and reel and slide down the chair until he was lying in its seat. "Oh, man, 'cou'dn't stop a hog in a narra alley!'" he would say every time he could catch his breath, only to break out again. Trammel cracked a smile and spit sunflower seed shells into the pond.

"Whew, Tram, I ain't laughed like 'at in a long time," Lanny acknowledged, when his sense of mirth had finally subsided. "Where'd ya git 'at un'?"

"My grampaw. I been waitin' ta use it fer a while."

"*Your* grampaw . . . Boy, I bet 'e's got a million ob'm."

By "grampaw," Trammel referred to his paternal grandfather, Dr. Jones: other than Mr. Jackson, the war hero who had started the Little League, the only man Trammel had heard called by everyone important in town "a legend." That status owed not only to the many achievements in the small-town doctor's life but also to his unique, charming, and inimitable character and personality. Dr. Jones's given name was Roscoe—a name never heard save coming from the mouths of his wife or his wife's aunt: the same aunt who had given Trammel's mother the antique furniture on the death of the aunt's husband, known as Uncle Buck, and had then moved down from Oklahoma to be closer to the family. To everyone else in the town who did not call him "Grampaw" or "Daddy" he was Dr. Jones. The doctor's father had also been a small-town doctor in a nearby town and had farmed several hundred acres, but he died from a ruptured appendix when his son was less than a year old. That death prompted the widow to move with her son to Austin, her husband having said that if anything ever happened to him, she should take the boy to a town with a college so he could be assured of getting a good education. The boy had indeed gone to Austin High School, in a day when public schools in the state and the nation still taught things, and graduated salutatorian (just as Trammel's mother had from her high school). He then went on to the University of Texas and Baylor Medical School. Throughout high school and college he had worked in various capacities: as a short order cook, a soda jerk, a bicycle repairman, an elevator operator, and at last as a research assistant in a biological laboratory. Trammel had heard his grandfather claim that, as far as he knew, he had been the inventor of the cheeseburger, having started to put cheese on burgers before he saw anyone else do it. Whether a couple of brothers named McDonald ever stopped off for a bite at the East Austin Eat Shop is unknown to history. Having finished medical school in the early nineteen forties, he was drafted into the army medical corps. As the story went, he had been asked by his commander what his medical specialty was. The young doctor replied in a "smart-aleck" way, "obstetrics," thinking there would be no use for him in an army. That joke got him posted at a base hospital in South Carolina where for six months straight he delivered "war babies" G. I.'s had left their young brides with before shipping out for combat. After that, the young doctor served on a medical ship in the Pacific and attained the rank of major.

When the war was over, Dr. Jones returned to his roots by setting up a practice in the town of Dogwood, whose general practitioner had just retired. A few years later he, with another doctor from a nearby town, started a small hospital, a hospital that had continued to expand as the area grew in population and more doctors moved there. Aside from his medical expertise, Dr. Jones was known for his bedside manner, having a joke for every patient based upon the patient's age, sex, and temper. He acquired many of those jokes from the different pharmaceutical salesmen who frequented his office but also wielded his own storied muse. Until the early seventies, this small-town doctor had made house calls. He ceased doing so only when he scaled back his practice over the last few years. Trammel enjoyed walking down the old main street of town with his grandfather because there was no one the man did not know. After a brief encounter with these folks, always accompanied by a joke or piece of gossip, Dr. Jones would reveal to his grandson, "Yep, I delivered all her kids," or "Yep, I sewed him up." There did not seem to be anyone in the town whom his grandfather had not "sewed up" or "patched up" or whose children he had not brought into the world. His grandfather's patients evidently thought a great deal of him or sometimes had to pay him with currencies other than money since the patients were always bringing the doctor huge baskets of peas, freshly carved steaks, loaves of homemade bread, and more pies than anyone could eat. The pies in particular usually ended up in Trammel's house and on Trammel's plate.

Now in his early seventies, Dr. Jones had not retired and intended never to retire, but he had consented to his wife's desire of moving out to the lake and coming to town only three days per week. Rather than to his actual practice, the doctor now diverted a large amount of his attention to his service in the AMA and TMA. Trammel did not exactly know what his grandfather did with these medical associations, only that he went to a fair number of conventions and conferences around the country and that these efforts were devoted to "stoppin' socialized medicine," whose realization would turn out to be just as bad as "what wou'd 'a' happened if we'd 'a' lost the war." "The gub'ment's got no way a' knowin' what my patients need and can afford better'n I do," was the experienced doctor's diagnosis on the matter. It had been one of these medical conventions that had caused Trammel's grandfather to miss the opening day game. Otherwise, Trammel's grandfather and grandmother, a memorable character in her own right (who—not her husband—had given Trammel's father his first lessons in baseball), tried to make it to most all the boy's sporting events.

Later that morning Mrs. Lorne dropped off Joey on Lanny's street, and the boy came, gear in hand, down to the pond. Trammel had already thought to get a chair for him out of Lanny's garage on a trip back to use the bathroom. Trammel also showed the good graces of introducing the two boys, who did not know each other formally.

"Uh, Joey, 'is here's Lanny."

"Hey, Lance," enthused the newcomer with a polite wave.

"Hey, man. I seen ya 'round," returned his host. "Jus' take a seat, man, an' we'll see if ya brang us any luck. 'Ey ain't been payin' us no mind all mornin'."

"Thanks for havin' me," returned the grateful boy, who opened up his brand spanking new tackle box tentatively and began, presumably, looking for the right lure. Trammel and Lanny did not notice the boy's confusion for a while, but the rattling of the contents of the tackle box and the time it was taking him to get his line in the water at last caught their attention. Finally, Joey decided upon a large, unwieldy frog with mechanical legs and attached it with some difficulty to the swivel at the end of his line. Holding his rod directly in front of him, he pushed the button to his closed-face reel, only to have his lure drop to the ground. Puzzled, he wound it back up and pushed the button again. Trammel and Lanny watched their guest for a while, glanced at each other in tacit disbelief, then looked back to Joey, not without compassion.

"Say, uh, Joey, whatcha up to over there?" Lanny asked.

"Oh, I'm sorry. I was just trying to figure out what, uh, what thing to use."

"Whatcha mean *thang*?"

"Yeah, I mean what lure to use."

"Lure! Hell! I mean Heck, man. Ain't Trammel tol' you *nut'n'*? We don't use no fancy lures down here at *the pond*. 'Is here's catfish country! 'At means nut'n' but chicken hearts, gizzards, bacon, worms from time ta time, an' some stank bait if ya got it, the stankier the better. What's 'a deal, Tram? Did ya give your boy here th' impression we 'as some kinda high fallutin' fishermen. Whatcha call 'em?"

"Anglers," replied Trammel, drawing on an ongoing conversation about what kind of fishermen these two assuredly were *not*, at least when down at the pond.

"Yeah, we ain't no anglers: no lures, no fancy spinnin' reels, no fly fishin'. 'Ey ain't no trout in 'is here pond. 'Ey ain't eb'm no bass in 'is here pond. None a' that crap. Down here it's Zebcos an' chicken hearts all 'a way. Ya better help eem out, Tram."

Joey was indeed in need of such help: in the simple arts of catching catfish and in the means of fishing in general. Absent any instruction on what actually went on down at the pond, something Trammel had never thought to impart—the word "pond" being to him a self-evident proposition—Joey and his mother had gone to the sporting goods section of the local Wal-Mart the previous night and loaded up on the oddest assortment of fishing tackle imaginable. Searching the contents of the tackle box, Trammel found monstrous hooks and weights meant for deep sea fishing down in the gulf, fancy but impractical lures that would not have enticed the biggest bass in Lake Texoma, tiny jigs that might catch bream but would no doubt prove vastly inferior to worms, a roll of forty-pound test line, along with other irrelevant accoutrement.

It dawned on Trammel that not only had Joey gotten the wrong things to fish with, but all this new equipment must have set him back a pretty penny.

"Ya know, man, I ain't one ta criticize a man's choice in fishin' tackle, but you been had. Didn't nobody help ya where ya bought all 'is stuff."

"No, me and my mom just bought a bunch of stuff that looked good. We didn't really know what kind of fish we'd be catchin'."

"We ain't goin' after Jaws, 'at's fer sure. Where 'd'ya git it all? Wal-Mart?"

The boy nodded.

"Yeah, you'n git some perty cheap stuff at Wal-Mart, but 'ey ain't gonna help ya none. Findin' help in Wal-Mart's like waitin' on rain in Lubbock. Nex' time ya oughta go ta Big Luke's. Tell 'em Tram sentcha. 'Ey'll gitcha all fixed up. If I 'as you, I'd take all 'is stuff back an' gitchur money back er trade it in fer sump'm 'at'll work 'round here. See, Lanny's right. All ya wont's a hook about 'is size an' a sinker like 'is," he indicated, holding up items from his own tackle, "an' sump'm a catfish is gonna smell from a mile away. . . . Hey, but at least ya got 'a right kind a' reel. Look here, Lanny: a Zebco. 'E's a man after our own heart. . . . A'right, 'en, let's start by doin' 'at knot over agin."

In the latter instance, Trammel referred to Joey's and his mother's attempt at tying the fishing line to an excessively large swivel. It had taken Joey and his mother the better part of an hour to get that far, the bulk of their time being spent reading the directions that came with the rod and reel set.

In a few moments, Trammel had shown Joey how to tie a knot that would not unravel with nylon line, fasten on a couple of sinkers with needle-nose pliers, and worm a hook, every fisherman needing to know how to work with live bait.

"A'right 'en, I'm gonna put a cork on 'a line so you'n see what's goin' on if ya git a hit. Me an' Lanny don't use corks much no more, but 'at's pro'lly the best way 'til ya git used ta what a good bite's gonna feel like. . . . Now, I reckon I oughta show ya sump'm 'bout castin'. See, I don't know whatchoo 'as doin' a wholla go, but all ya gotta do 's push down on 'is button an' hol' it. Don't let 'er go 'til ya wonta th'ow it out 'ere. See what I mean?"

"Sure. Yeah, thanks, Trammel."

"A'right 'en, give it a shot."

The first cast Joey plunked straight down into the water ten feet in front of him.

"Yeah, see, ya let 'er go, a'right," encouraged Trammel, "butcha waited too long 'at time. Whatchur tryin' ta do is jus whip it out 'ere, jus' cast it, real easy like. Like 'is." Trammel demonstrated in the air a nice easy flip of the wrist.

Joey's second try got his line only a little farther out.

"Okay, I see whatchur doin' now. It's like you 'as whackin' sump'm, like you 'as tryin' ta hammer a nail. It ain't like 'at. Don't worry 'bout tryin' ta get it down in 'a water. The sinker'll take 'er down. Whatcha gotta do 's cast 'er out 'ere, way ouch yonder. It's almos' like you 'as pushin' it out 'ere, not so much as th'owin' it. Like 'is." Trammel showed him one more time. "Jus' look way out over the pond an' let 'er rip."

The third attempt proved a charm. Joey's cast was not the longest in fishing history, but hook, line, and sinker took flight well enough to settle in a spot eligible for the notice of a small catfish.

"Now, see. 'At's what I'm talkin' 'bout."

Returning to his own place Trammel saw his own rod, which he had leaned against the back of his chair, bend violently toward the pond.

"Geez, Lanny! I thoughtcha had my back."

"Oh, yeah, I's jus' fixin' ta tell ya. 'Ere's a fish on your line," the friend replied, in mock earnestness.

"Just fixin' ta tell me!" Trammel retorted as he quickly seized the line and gave it a tug to see if the fish was still on, then set to work reeling it in. "If I lose' is'n I'll be th'owin' you out 'ere ta git eem back."

Lanny guffawed and reassured his friend, "Ya still got eem, Tram. Salmon patties, comin' back!"

Trammel did manage to pull in only their second fish of the morning, a small catfish that could very well have been the same one Lanny had caught earlier.

"Dad gummit. All 'at work fer 'is little pip squeak," Trammel lamented as he easily removed the hook with his needle-nose pliers. "Go back an' gitchur daddy fer me." The fish splashed and instantly disappeared into the brackish water.

The boys sat without speaking for a good ten minutes. Often that was the way with Trammel. He was not one for small talk. Whether alone or with others, he could sit brooding in his own thoughts for untold amounts of time. Not that he was ever at a loss for words. Once invested in a topic he could declaim on it better than anyone. But as long as somebody else was willing to take up the burden of conversation, or if no one chose to speak at all, he remained perfectly content with that rarest of treasures in the modern world: silence.

The presence of a newcomer made Trammel, if anything, even more laconic. Lanny usually took it upon himself to initiate the conversation, anyway. Lanny was a natural raconteur blessed with a nearly perfect memory. He could recall the lyrics of a song he had heard only once or twice. Better still, he could recount an entire movie, scene by scene, a feat that could last as long as the movie itself. This was no unimportant service to Trammel, who was kept from certain R-rated movies that Lanny's family was likely to be first in line to see. To be sure, Trammel did not boast the steel-trap memory that his friend had, but for his own part he possessed a merciless logic that allowed him to figure out the plots of movies long before any resolution was apparent to the average spectator. His mother refused to sit next to him at the theatre while watching a murder mystery, since the boy was quite likely to say thirty minutes into the film, "He done it," and then leave to get some popcorn. More daunting, this thirteen-year-old could almost always tell you whenever the writers and directors had failed to catch some gap or error in the plot. As Lanny had not seen a movie that weekend, though, there was less to talk about.

The silence was broken by the unexpected disappearance of Joey's cork. Trammel and Joey noticed it go under at the same time.

"Oh, my gosh! Trammel, look, my thing went under! What do I do?"

"Well, start reelin' eem in, dad gummit! Don't let eem git away!"

Trammel instinctively put his rod behind his chair once again and leaped to the edge of the water and pulled on the line to make sure it was still taut. Meanwhile, Joey, in a jerky fashion, reeled in the line, surprised by the resistance he was feeling.

"He's fighting back. I can tell he's still on."

"'At means y'ain't lost eem. Jus' keep reelin'.'"

At last, when the line was drawn only a couple of feet from the bank, Trammel yanked it up to reveal a small, colorful fish fighting desperately for life. Joey was elated with the catch yet looked to Trammel with some hesitancy since the present fish was smaller than the one Trammel had caught earlier.

"Well, I'll be dad-gummed. Look at 'at, Lanny, can ya b'lieve it?"

"You gotta be kiddin' me!" Lanny slapped his knee. "Whadya bring out here witcha, man, some kinda magic?"

Initially elated, Joey nonetheless found the excitement of the other two incongruous with the size of the fish.

"I don't understand."

"Look at eem. Don'tcha see the differ'nce b'tween your fish an' 'a one I caught a wholla go?"

"Well, yeah. Your fish had whiskers and was gray, and this fish has a lot a' colors and, you know, is kinda flat."

"Yeah, 'xactly. 'At's 'a whole point. 'Is here fish is a bream. Bream's small but 'e's a fightin' fish. An' ain't nobody caught a bream in 'a pond since . . . How long we been fishin' down here, Lanny?"

"Since I moved out here. Three years, pro'lly."

"Three years," Trammel confirmed. "Pro'lly never, far as we know."

"Really?" Joey asked, beaming.

"'At's a fact. 'Is here's a first."

After the initial astonishment had subsided, Trammel cued Joey as to the next step.

"Well, I reckon y'oughta unhook eem an' th'ow eem back. I'll let you do th' honors 'nless ya wont me ta help."

"We have to throw him back?"

"'Course. Despite 'a fact 'at 'e's a bream, 'e's perty small, an' b'sides 'at, 'em's 'a rules."

"The rules?"

"Yeah, ya know, we can't have our pond all fished out, an' b'sides 'at, 'ese fish 'a' gotta grow."

"Oh, I see. Sure, those are the rules," assented Joey, obviously disappointed.

"What 'as ya hopin' ta do with eem, anyhow?" asked Trammel, seeing the boy's joy fade. "You cou'dn't git two bites out of eem if you 'as thankin' 'bout eatin' eem."

"No, no, I knew he wasn't big enough to eat. It's just my mom. She always wants to take pictures of stuff like this, and she told me to save any fish I caught for a picture."

"Ya mean when she comes back ta pick ya up?"

"Yeah."

"Well, huh. Yeah, I see whatcha mean. I reckon we cou'd keep eem on a strainger 'til your mom showed up an' 'en th'ow eem back afterwards. 'At be a'right, Lanny?"

"Course. 'At's what we do at 'a lake mos' 'a time, anyway."

"Yeah, good point. A'right, 'en. We need us a strainger, Lanny."

"I'm on it." Lanny was already fishing a stringer out of his cluttered tackle box and then tossed it to Trammel, offering a "heads up" just in time for Trammel's reflexes to kick in. Now that keeping the fish had become important, Trammel took upon himself the office of getting it off the hook and onto the stringer, showing Joey how to go about it. That settled, Joey looked to Trammel for the next step.

"Do you think I should use a worm again?"

"Heck, yeah, man. Ya gotta learn ta dance with 'a one what brung ya."

Missing the idiom entirely, Joey was glad to see that his instincts had proven correct, and he labored for some time, and finally with result, at getting a worm on his hook. His cast went a little farther than the previous, successful one.

The next half hour, save for the moments when Lanny or Trammel were bringing in the standard fare of small-fry catfish, were given to speculation over how a bream could have gotten into the pond. They considered and dismissed the possibility that Van Strand and his dad could have put it there, the former having told the neighborhood that he had caught a lot of bass out at Lake Lewisville and then stocked the pond with them. There could be no truth in that story given Van Strand was its author and since that interloping family from the North did not even have a bass boat.

Hardly anyone caught bass off the bank anymore. They owned that Van Strand was ignorant enough to mistake a bream for a bass, but their theory that using a worm as bait was far more plausible. They had not used worms since, well, at least since The Flood.

As the day grew longer, and the fish became less and less interested in what the three boys were throwing at them; as Joey's second catch ended up being just another catfish, Lanny got to wondering.

"Ya thank I oughta tell eem, Tram?"

"Tell eem what?"

"'Bout 'a Head, a' course."

"C'mone, Lanny, e'erbody already knows 'bout 'a Head."

"Naw, e'erbody *don't* know, an' 'at's what scares me, Tram. I run inta folks all 'a dad-gum time 'at ain't never heard nut'n' 'bout 'a Head. You might say 'ere's wide spread ign'rance out 'ere 'bout 'a Head. An' I ain't scareder a' nut'n' 'n ign'rance."

"Well, go ahead. Ain't nobody stoppin' ya."

"What's the Head?" Joey asked innocently.

"What's 'a Head! What's 'a Head!" Lanny repeated for emphasis. "*The Head*'s your worst nightmare. *The Head*'s whatcha gotta worry 'bout ever time ya come down ta 'is here pond. *The Head*'s whatcha gotta be lookin' out for ever time ya go explorin' up an' down 'a creek over yonder like me an' Tram use' ta. 'Member that, Zebulon?"

"Yep. I 'member."

The name Zebulon, for Zebulon Pike, the discoverer the famous peak that bears his name, had been Trammel's pseudonym while exploring Goose Creek when Lanny first moved to this neighborhood. That Trammel did not answer his friend with the latter's choice exploring name, Meriwether, for Meriwether Lewis, was telling.

"*The Head*'s whatcha gotta protec' yourself agint ever time ya fall asleep at night. An' *The Head*'s whatcha always gotta be watchin' for, 'cause jus' when y'ain't, 'e'll be comin' aft'ya. An' you can take 'at ta the bank."

"Wow," marveled Joey, looking out over the pond and to the crowd of trees beyond the pond, obscuring the banks of Goose Creek.

"See, it happened like 'is," continued Lanny. "Ya 'member in 'a sprang, more 'n a year ago, when we had all 'at rain, an' parts a' the town 'as floodin'?"

"Yeah, I think so."

"Well, it came down sump'm awful out here. Water from 'a pond come plum up ta, I'd say, pro'lly three-quarters 'a way up 'at drop-off back'ere, pro'lly higher," recalled Lanny, pointing behind him. "Me 'n' my brothers come out an' watched it fer a long while, an' 'a water jus' kep' a comin'. Well, 'a main thang is 'at 'a pond an' 'a creek spilled inta each other. An' whene'er 'at happens, ya don't know wha' t'expect: strange thangs pro'lly. Anyhow, it took a couple a' days b'fore the water went back down, an' another couple a' days ta dry out. 'At whole time we 'as jus' waitin' ta git back down here ta the pond. . . . Th'ow me some 'em seeds 'ere, Tram."

Trammel obliged the young Homer with a full bag of sunflower seeds.

"Ya wont some?" offered Lanny to the guest.

"No, thank you," replied an intent Joey, who did take a drink from his Gatorade bottle.

"Well, see, at first we 'as thankin' 'bout comin' down here an' seein' what kinda fish 'a flood might 'a' brung up from 'a creek. But 'en ol' Tram said, ''Em fish ain't goin' nowheres. We can git at 'em fish any time. 'Ey're ours now. What we gotta worry 'bout is what else 'a flood might 'a' brung up.' So we all figur'd we might oughta come down here an' check thangs out, ta make sure 'ere wudn't no big snakes er nut'n' jus' hangin' 'round, waitin' on us." Lanny raised his eyebrows suggestively and Joey nodded.

"Well, we wudn't 'bout ta come down here unarmed, a' course. Tram brung 'is Benjamin pump. I wonted ta bring my .410, but my mom wouldn't let me, so I got my slingshot instead: ya know, one a' them fancy ones with 'a thang 'at goes across 'a top your arm, ya know, ta keep it steady. An' Billy Ray, 'e's my older brother, e's got 'is CO2 powered BB pistol 'at 'e can make shoot rapid-fire, like a machine gun. An' Shane, my little brother, 'e had 'is little pea shooter. B'sides, we made eem carry all 'a ammo. An' we had a bunch a' knives an' th'owin stars an' other stuff like 'at. So we 'as perty ready, I guess, fer jus' 'bout anythang. But not hardly fer what we 'as fixin' ta see."

After taking a drink from his own Gatorade bottle, Lanny loaded another handful of seeds into his mouth.

"So we come down here, an' Tram says we need ta make a couple a' passes 'round 'a pond b'fore we know it's safe fer fishin'. So 'en we started off headin' in 'at direction," motioned Lanny, pointing counterclockwise. "We 'as checkin' thangs out ta make sure 'ere wudn't no snakes er nut'n' like 'at. We seen a couple a' frogs, an' 'a whole place smelled kinda funny, ya know, like a jungle er sump'm. But we wudn't too bothered 'bout nut'n' 'til we got right over yonder, 'cross from where we're sittin' right now. An' 'at's when we seen eem."

"Saw what?"

"The Head. 'E jus' popped out a' the water, pro'lly fi'ty, maybe seb'mty-five feet from where we 'as at. An' it jus' sat 'ere lookin' at us."

"What kind of a head?"

"Whatcha mean, what kind a' head? It was *a head*, man!"

"I thank 'e means," interjected Trammel, "like was it a human head er some kind a' animal's head er what. I get 'at question a lot."

"Naw, man, it wudn't no human head. It 'as some kind a' *creature*'s head, sump'm I ain't never seen b'fore an', ta tell 'a truth, don't wonta never see agin. It 'as 'bout as big as, wha'd ya say, Tram, a tether ball?"

"Yeah, 'bout 'at. Pro'lly a little bigger."

"Yeah, it 'as bigger 'n a softball, fer sure, but nowhere's big as a basketball. But 'at's still a perty big head comin' up out a' the pond. An' 'e 'as jus' sittin' 'ere, lookin' at us, like 'e's sizin' us up fer dinner. Well, at first we jus' kinda stood 'ere in shock. An' 'at 'as our biggest mistake. *Hesitation kills* when it's life er death. Ain't 'at right, Tram?"

"Yep, 'at's a fact." The rhetorical question hardly needed answering, Lanny drawing on one of the fundamental maxims he had gleaned from the pages of *Guns & Ammo*.

"We shou'd 'a' jus' startin' blastin' eem right 'en an' 'ere 'cause 'at's 'a closest we got to eem all day long. 'En, after a while, Tram says, 'Whatchoo clowns waitin' on?' an' aimed 'is Benjamin pump right at eem an' fired. 'En I says ta my brother,

'Machine-gun eem, Billy Ray!' an' Billy Ray started machine-gunnin' eem, but 'a Head 'as long gone by that time."

Lanny reeled in his line to see whether his bait was still on and, satisfied, cast his line back out. Then he continued his epic.

"Now, lemme tell ya sump'm 'bout Tram here. See, when it comes ta shootin' 'is Benjamin pump er any other gun fer 'at matter, 'e don't miss. We call eem Sure Shot fer 'at reason, er sometimes Eagle Eye. Fact, ever gun 'e owns is jus' single-shot, 'cause like 'e says, 'It only takes one.' Ain't 'at right, Tram?"

"Yep. Least *I* only need one."

"So my point here is 'at Tram hit eem. Tram shot 'a Head, sure as 'a world. An' 'e had 'at pellet pumped up perty good, so *you know* it had ta hurt. But all 'at didn't stop 'a Head none. Now 'e kep' 'is distance, a'right. But 'e jus' kep' comin' up ta see what we 'as all about, 'cause, see, the Head's a powerful curious creature. Butcha know, what kep' happenin' is 'at we'd be at one side a' the pond, an' 'e'd come up at th'other. An' we'd shoot at eem; we'd give eem everthang we got, but we 'as pretty much outta range. Me 'n' Tram 'd shoot first an' 'en we'd say, 'Machine-gun eem, Billy Ray,' an' Billy Ray'd machine-gun eem. But it didn't do no good, seein' as how the Head ain't dumb enough ta sit aroun' an' git shot at all day long."

"How 'bout a little help here, Tram." Lanny had a fish on the line but was far too preoccupied with his narrative to pay it any heed, so he passed off the catch to Trammel and turned toward his audience.

"So it took us a while a' runnin' up an' down 'a pond b'fore we got smart an' decided ta split up. See, 'at way, one of us 'd always be closer ta the Head when 'e come up. But 'en Tram said we gotta 'void shootin' each other in a crossfire 'cause 'a Head might jus' be smart enough ta git us ta kill each other one by one an' 'en come up out a' the water fer the last one, an' 'at'd pro'lly be my little brother. Ya know, animals can figur' 'ese thangs out. 'Ey gotta sense 'bout which one's 'a weakest a' the bunch an' ain't got no survival skills. So we figur'd out 'is plan where Tram'd be on one side a' the pond an' Billy Ray'd be on 'a other, an' whichever one 'as closest to eem 'd take a shot. An' I'd be 'bout twenty feet behind Tram takin' ever shot I cou'd 'cause I's at a angle. My little brother jus' stuck with me, 'cause 'a last thang we 'as gonna do 'as take eem home ta my mom all shot up er ate up. Anyhow, we started off down at 'at end a' the pond headin' back 'is way. An' when we got, oh, perty much ta where we're sittin' right now, whatcha reckon 'a Head done?"

"I don't know," responded the mystified and still rapt Joey.

"'E come up right in 'a middle: smack dab b'tween Tram an' my brother. It 'as like the Head 'as readin' our minds er sump'm! A' course 'ey hesitated agin—we all did—fer a minute, 'cause nobody knew who s'posed ta shoot. The Head had us in a crossfire. 'En Tram figur'd out a new plan right 'ere on 'a spot. He shot at 'a Head, 'en dove outta the way so Billy Ray cou'd start 'is rapid fire. I shot at eem, too, but sling shots ain't got no acc'racy. I pro'lly shot eight ainches from where the Head was, but it 'as too late by then. He'd already gone back under."

"Gimme 'at rod back, Tram. You done stole enough a' my fish t'day without me havin' ta give ya any fer free." Trammel had already unhooked the catfish, thrown it back in, and re-wormed his friend's hook, all three of the boys now using live bait in the hope of bringing in another bream. Lanny cast his line back out and resumed his normal post facing the pond.

Joey, hardly blinking, waited expectantly for further light or some kind of conclusion to the story. None forthcoming, he asked of Lanny, "Well, what happened then?"

Lanny raised his eyebrows and stared directly at Joey for a moment. "What happened 'en? What happened 'en? 'At's just it. Nut'n'. Ain't nut'n' happened. 'At 'as all she wrote. . . . Hey Tram, why don't ya give us some them Slim Jims you're always carryin' 'round an' ain't never offerin' ta nobody."

Trammel took three Slim Jims from his backpack and distributed them. "All ya had ta do was ask."

Lanny bit off a good piece of his and then continued as he was chewing. "Like I said, nut'n' happened. We sent my little brother up ta git us lunch. We set out a, whatcha call it, Tram?"

"A perimeter."

"Yeah, a perimeter. We set up in three differ'nt points 'round 'a pond. We had my little brother go up an' brang us back some chairs. We eb'm set *him* up in one 'cause 'e kep' askin' why 'e didn't get no chance ta kill 'a Head eemself. An' 'e said 'e wou'dn't git us nut'n' else 'nless 'e cou'd be a equal partner. So we set eem up an' 'en we had 'a Head completely boxed in. An' we sat 'ere fer a coon's age with our guns an' knives an' th'owin' stars, jus' waitin', jus' waitin' fer the Head ta make a move. We eb'm started th'owin' some bread an' stuff inta the pond, hopin' 'e'd git hungry. But 'e didn't never come up agin. An' 'e ain't never gonna come up, not in 'is here pond."

"Do you think you killed him?"

"'Is boy's askin' if we killed 'a Head, Tram. Did we kill *the* Head?"

"Naw. We didn't kill no Head," pronounced Trammel, spitting into the murky water. "We might 'a' rattled eem a little, gib'm sump'm ta thank about. But I doubt we eb'm scared eem. He solved us. 'At's all."

The boys sat in silent wonder for a spell while the immensity of the mystery sank in.

After some time, Lanny resumed the tale. "Now, you may hear 'at 'a Head 'as caught. But, 'at's jus' a dad-gum lie started like mos' lies 'round here by 'at Yankee blue scumbelly Van Strand. 'At's a differ'nt story. Back in 'a Fall, see, 'at sorry ass come down here fishin' on 'is own when ain't nobody lookin'. An' 'e caught some little ol' snappin' turtle. An' 'en ya know what 'e done? 'E goes an' gits ever little ign'rant kid in 'a neighborhood ta come down here an' look at it an' tells 'em it's 'a Head. 'Course 'e don't dare come ta my house 'cause 'e knows me an' my brothers 're the only ones on 'a whole block 'at eb'm seen 'a Head. But my little brother 'as at some other kid's house, an' 'e come runnin' over, sayin' 'Strand's tellin' e'erbody 'e caught 'a Head, but it ain't no Head, Lanny.' So I called Tram right quick an' 'en come down here with Billy Ray ta set thangs straight. An' ya know all 'em little kids 'as b'lievin' eem, like 'e eb'm spoke 'a truth once in 'is sorry life an' like we'd 'a' got all worked up 'bout some crappy little ol' snappin' turtle."

"Ya can't hardly blame 'em little kids, Lanny. 'Ey don't know no better."

"Naw, ya can't blame 'em fer bein' ign'rant, Tram. But kids nowadays'll b'lieve any ol' dad-gum thang. 'Ey can't see th'ough a liar like I cou'd when I's a kid. Anyway, we 'as yellin' at eem an' sayin', ''At ain't no damn Head! Stop lyin' ya damn Yankee!' By the time Tram got over here Billy Ray's about ta whoop

Strand's ass fer persistin' in his lies. But 'en Tram rode down here on 'is bike. An' 'en 'e walks straight up ta Strand an' says, real quiet like, 'What's 'a deal?'

"An' Strand says, 'Well, uh, I caught 'a Head.'

"'En Tram says, 'Who tol' ya 'bout 'a Head in 'a first place?'

"An' Strand says, 'Well, I heard about eem.'

"'En Tram says, 'Was you out here 'at day when we 'as huntin' 'a Head five er six hours straight in 'a hot sun an' seen eem pro'lly eight er ten times? 'Cause if I 'member rightly, 'at 'as right aroun' sprang break when you 'as back up in New Jersey er whatever rock you crawled out from under. An' you didn't know nut'n' 'bout 'a Head 'til 'ese kids 'round here tol' ya. Ain't 'at right?'

"An' Strand says, 'Well, I guess so.'

"'En Tram says, 'So you're kinda a Johnny Come Lately when it comes ta the Head, ain'tcha, Strand?'

"An' Strand says, 'Yeah, but—'

"But 'en Tram says, '*But nut'n'*. Show me 'is head a' yours.' An' Strand pointed at 'a turtle. 'En Tram says, ''At's it? 'At little ol' thang? You tellin' me I don't know the differ'nce 'tween a crappy little snappin' turtle, 'a kind me an' Lanny been catchin' down here long 'fore you showed up, an' '*a Head*? You mus' take me fer some kinda fool er some kinda liar.'

"'En Tram stepped back an' took out 'is Buck knife, an' you can b'lieve ol' Strand 'as shakin' like a dog shittin' peach seeds 'cause Tram'd already said 'e's gonna gut eem an' strang eem up one a' these days after we caught eem down here with a trot line. An' ya might 'member, 'at 'as right after Tram here whooped Peel's ass, an' e'erbody 'as scared shi—"

"Lanny, wha'd I done tol' ya 'bout all 'at cussin'? We gotta gues' here t'day, so ya gotta be on your bes' behavior. What'll happen if I brang my sister down here agin?"

"She'll catch all 'a fish like she always does an' make you madder 'n a wet hen, 'at's what'll happen. Butcha ain't gotta worry 'bout me 'n' your sister. I'll pro'lly marry your sister, like I done tol' ya.

"So anyway, Tram backs up, lookin' straight at Strand, an' whips out 'is Buck knife, an' nobody said nut'n', 'cause ain't nobody wontin' ta mess with Tram at 'at point. An' you cou'd hear the click a' the knife, ya know, when 'a blade locks inta place." Lanny demonstrated with his own lockback knife and sprang up to act out the rest of the scene.

"'En Tram walks over ta the turtle. 'At turtle 'as still on 'a line, see, an' Strand 'ad stuck some sticks in 'a ground 'round eem so 'e cou'dn't go nowheres. An' so Tram walks over to eem an' puts his foot on 'a back a' the turtle an' stretches out 'is neck an' cuts 'is head clean off. 'En Tram takes 'at turtle's head off 'a hook, steps up nexta the pond, an' th'ows 'at dad-gum head halfway 'cross 'a pond. 'En 'e looks back at Strand, closes up 'is knife, an' says, ''At's what I thank a' your head.' 'En 'e got back up on 'is bike an' jus' rode off. Heck, man, 'e took 'at drop-off back 'ere like 'e's jumpin' a curb." Lanny sat back down in his chair and took another bite of Slim Jim.

"A couple a' little kids started cryin' 'cause a' the turtle, but nobody else said nut'n'. Billy Ray jus' said, 'Damn! 'At 'as cold.' An' 'en 'e went over an' took 'a rest a' the turtle an' th'ew eem inta the pond like a discus er sump'm. 'En we all took off, leavin' Strand jus' standin' 'ere, still shakin', like 'a lowdown liar he is."

Joey looked at Trammel—who sat expressionless, occasionally spitting sunflower seeds, his fierce and penetrating eyes fixed upon the pond—with a mixture of horror, admiration, and awe. Joey knew less than the other boys in the school about the Peel beating. Despite being the butt of Peel's stupid insults on more than one occasion, Joey nonetheless had taken no pleasure in hearing about the fight. And he had not yet made the connection in his mind between the boy he had gotten to know a little, and whom he admired so much, and the figure in Lanny's tale who was capable of such ruthless action.

"Now, we done a lotta thankin' after discoverin' 'a Head," the bard picked up again after a while. First off, we had ta arm ourselves better'n what we had been. I kep' askin' my mom ta let me brang my .410 down here, but she said 'at ain't gonna happen."

"Ain't no .410 gonna kill 'a Head nohow, Lanny, 'cause 'e ain't gonna letcha git in range no more. We done had our chance."

"See, Tram's right, but it ain't gonna hurt none ta have it down here. So I bought me a crossbow, but my mom don't eb'm let me shoot 'at neither 'nless my dad's around. I figur' she thanks I'm stupid enough ta shoot my little brother by accident er sump'm.

An' Tram got eem a blowgun. We figur'd 'at wou'dn't kill 'a Head neither 'nless we poisoned 'a darts, like 'ey do in Africa, but we ain't figur'd out how. But a blowgun's still a good weapon ta have around."

"Yeah, but all 'at don't matter, Lanny, 'cause 'a Head's done gone."

"You may be right, Tram. But 'a Head also knows 'at we're the only ones 'at gotta good look at eem. So 'e might come back here ta cover 'is tracks. On top a that, y'ain't gotta live down here close to eem like I do."

"What kind of animal do you think the Head is?" wondered Joey.

"Well, see, 'at's 'a other thang. I started doin' a lot a' research after seein' 'a Head ta figur' out what we 'as up aginst. An' ya know 'ere's all kindsa beasts an' monsters out 'ere 'at most folks don't know nut'n' about. Ferget aliens. Who cares about aliens when we got Bigfoot an' Sasquatch ta deal with? Jus' look at 'a Loch Ness Monster. 'E's been aroun' fer centuries, an' only a few people ever eb'm seen eem. See, I figur' the Head's a lot like ol' Nessie 'cept 'a Head's . . . Whatcha call it, Tram?"

"Amphibious."

"Yeah, 'e's amphibious, a'right, meanin' 'e lives in water mos' 'a time but can come up on land whenever he da—, I mean when he dad-gum well wonts to. Tell me agin, Tram, if he's amphibious 'at makes eem a what?"

"A amphibian. How can you ask me 'at? You sat right 'ere in Mr. Honneycut's class with me an' listened ta th' exact same stuff."

"Like I tol' ya Tram, I didn't hear none a' that 'cause I 'as sittin' nexta Jana the whole time, an' she looked a whole lot better'n all 'em rats an' frogs 'at I cou'd see on my own any time. An' it didn't help none 'at 'a tests 'as always on Thursdees, the very same day she 'as wearin' her cheerleadin' outfit."

"If 'at ain't 'a sorriest excuse I ever heard!"

"What can I say? You know me, Tram. 'I'm a Cowboy fan, not a soccer man, and I live to love Texas wi-i-men,'" sung out Lanny, altering the lyrics as he saw fit, country and western lyrics being a rhetorical proof in all cases decisive.

"An' b'sides bein' amphibious," Lanny continued, picking up the thread of his story, "'e's a meat eater."

"A *carnivore*, dad-gummit!" expostulated Trammel.

" A carnivore, 'course I knew that. An' 'at's what scares me eb'm more, 'cause what's 'at Head gonna be eatin' if 'e's a carnivore?"

"I don't know, like fish, maybe?" guessed Joey.

"Yeah, fish fer sure. Butcha gotta remember. The Head's *amphibious*. Durin' 'a day 'e's pro'lly snackin' on fish an' turtles an' whatnot, jus' like I'm eatin' 'is Slim Jim here. But 'en at night, 'at's when 'e gits real hungry. An' 'e'll come up out a' the pond when ain't nobody lookin' an' 'en go after 'is supper. An' see, 'at's 'a other thang. We don't eb'm know whether the Head we seen was a baby Head er a full-growed momma Head. See, if he 'as jus', say, kinda a kid-sized head, 'en 'e'd pro'lly start off on dogs an' cats an' reg'lar ol' pets. Ya know, 'So long, Fido.' But 'en what'd happen by the time he got up ta be maybe, I don't know, like 'a same as a high-school kid? 'En wha'd 'e be eatin'? Well, 'e'd pro'lly start off on 'a little kids first."

Lanny took another bite of Slim Jim. "An' 'en I got ta thankin'. What about all 'em kids on 'a news ever night: 'em kids ever show back up? 'Ey's s'posed ta be lost er run off er sump'm. But how many them kids did 'a Head git?"

"Do you think—?"

"I don't know. I can't prove nut'n'. But 'at's 'a whole point. How many them dogs you read about on signs all over town 'at s'pose'ly run off: how many them did 'a Head git? We don't know. 'At's 'cause 'a Head ain't stupid. We done seen 'at. A reg'lar human criminal's always gonna leave a trace er clue er sump'm. But 'a Head, 'e don't leave nut'n', not eb'm *the bones*."

"Well, did you call the police? I mean, maybe they could help," offered the concerned young man.

"Did we call 'a p'lice? Did we call 'a p'lice? 'Is boy wonts ta know if we called 'a p'lice, Tram."

"P'lice is law enforcement."

"Yeah, Tram's right. P'lice is *law enforcement*. What kind a' charge 'ey gonna bring agins' 'a Head? Jaywalkin'? An' how're they gonna git eem out a' the pond in 'a first place? Lure eem out with a donut?"

That last remark sent both Lanny and Trammel into one of their fits of laughter that Joey joined in, not altogether knowing its source.

"Lure eem out with a donut! I'll have ta remember 'at 'un, Tram. I tol' ya I still got it. Anyway, the deal is 'a p'lice ain't got nut'n' ta do with 'a Head. 'Ey ain't eb'm got no . . . Whatcha call it, Tram?"

"Jurisdiction."

"Yeah, 'ey ain't got no jurisdiction. See, the Head's a matter fer the gub'ment. Ya know, like one a' them special agencies 'at follows U.F.O.'s eb'm though the gub'ment says 'ey don't exist. But once you git 'a gub'ment involved, 'en all Hell 'd break loose. See, 'cause 'a gub'ment's gonna overreact. 'Ey always do. 'Ey'll send pro'lly fi'ty guys in suits out here ta take pictures, an' 'en 'a next thang ya know, 'ey'll pro'lly be drainin' 'a whole pond. An' not jus' 'is pond but ever pond an' lake an' creek 'round here, jus' lookin' fer the Head an' comin' up empty-handed, like 'a gub'ment always does. An' all we'd be left with is a bunch a' empty lakes an' ponds an' no fishin'. Nex' thang ya know people'd starve, what with no fish ta eat. So 'a best thang ta do's just leave the gub'ment out of it an' take care a' your own damn self. An' try ta keep from bein' ign'rant,'cause ign'rance kills more 'n anythang. . . . So if I's you, I'd git me a weapon er two, just ta protec' yourself an' your mom. You'd pro'lly wonta start out light, with jus' maybe a Swiss Army knife an' a Buck knife like 'is'n. Don't start askin' your mom fer big stuff b'fore she sees ya ain't gonna cut yourself all ta pieces."

Lanny handed his Buck knife to Trammel to hand to Joey so he could take a look at it. With big eyes, Joey opened it and started a little at the click of the blade into place. He did not successfully close the blade until Trammel showed him how. This rudimentary lesson in weapons training was interrupted by the honking of a horn. Joey's mother had arrived, not entirely to the boy's satisfaction, though he was eager to show her his fish. He hurriedly got his gear together, took the stringer of fish up for a quick picture, and returned to throw his day's catch back into the pond.

"Thanks a lot, Trammel. Thanks, Lance. This was great!" he said with a broad smile on his face.

"Good luck, man," said Trammel.

"Yeah, man, we'll see ya 'round," said Lanny.

Once the boy had left, the two friends returned for the short while they were out there to their previous silence, save for a brief commentary on their guest.

"'E ain't half bad, Tram. 'E's jus' gotta lot ta learn."

"Yeah. Kid kinda grows on ya. . . . 'E'd make perty good sausage, I reckon."

"Make good sausage! Whatcha mean by that?"

"I don't know. Jus' sump'm my grampaw says."

"You mean like 'e cou'd make *us* some sausage er like 'e'd be *in* 'a sausage?"

"Like I said, it's jus' sump'm my grampaw says. I ain't figur'd it out yet. Ya know, 'e's gotta million ob'm."

Chapter 9: Open Season on Tram

That Sunday found Trammel and his family in church. There was no game that day, nor the following, so he could actually concentrate on what Pastor McGuffey would have to say in his sermon. Before the service started, while members of the congregation were still chatting to each other, Trammel sat silently in the pew as he always did. He figured folks came to church to pray and to listen to the choir, to read the Bible and to hear what the preacher had to say, rather than to practice their "chin music," as his father might call it. As was his custom, the boy read the passages of scripture from his Bible on which the pastor would base his sermon. One was very familiar to Trammel, his favorite part of the whole Bible: the story of David and Goliath. Another was Jesus' parable about building your house on rock, not sand. Trammel had no idea what these two texts had to do with each other. Pastor McGuffey, however, had not failed him yet in bringing things together that seemed completely different.

Much of today's service was in fact very familiar to Trammel. The opening hymn brought a smile of recognition to everyone's face: "Amazing Grace." Trammel liked the hymns he knew better than the unfamiliar ones the pastor would sneak in to make the whole service fit with the sermon. That trick never fooled him. "Amazing Grace," on the other hand, he enjoyed immensely, especially when his mother sat with the congregation as she did today, the choir still not off summer break. His mother knew it by heart and could send her rich soprano to the rafters. Trammel knew it, too, at least the first verse:

Amazing Grace, how sweet the sound,

That saved a wretch like me.
I once was lost and now am found,
Was blind, but now I see.

The confession of sin he knew pretty much by heart, but he always thought about the words afresh every time he recited them in church. Trammel had done some "stuff" that he was not too proud of that week, mostly arguing with his sister, who drove him nuts. He was also pretty sure there was some other stuff that he should have done but had left undone, although he could not think of anything right off hand. He had probably not loved his neighbors as himself—though he thought he helped them out whenever they needed it. After the second reading came the offering. Trammel had made a hundred dollars that week, so he put ten in the plate. He had once heard Pastor McGuffey preach a sermon on what "tithe" actually meant, and the dutiful boy was not one to shortchange the Lord. Trammel liked the way his church passed the offering plate right off the bat as opposed to other churches that did so after the sermon, making it seem that the preacher was "singin' fer 'is supper." And thank God his church dispensed with the pretense of the children's sermon, which he found insufferable, since it broke up the momentum of the service and provided unnecessary comic relief. As for little children, they should be off in their own Sunday School—listening to Bible stories or coloring Jesus—rather than fidgeting and staring off into space and predictably guessing only the wrong answers in front of their parents and the whole congregation, all of whom pretended the spectacle was somehow cute.

Everything seemed in order until the attendance pad reached his hands. Trammel had no interest in whomever sat on his same pew, unlike the older ladies who would make a study of the attendance pad and invariably smile at the people who marked "visitor" as the roster made its way slowly down the aisle. He was in fact content to have his mother sign up the whole family. He had no need to make his mark in church. But that day a big loopy handwriting with hearts serving as the dots over the *i*'s could hardly fail to draw his attention. Then he saw the name: Cindy Bristol. What was she doing here! He froze as he considered this unforeseen menace. In his peripheral vision he saw a blond head lean forward and a heavily lipsticked smile, too much so for church, that could only have been meant for him. He was careful to look straight ahead and pass the wretched pad off to his father as though he had noticed nothing.

Trammel's normally keen interest in the sermon was befuddled that day. He followed the pastor through the story of David. His favorite part was not actually the slinging of the rock or the cutting off of Goliath's head, though of course that was where the action was, but rather when David said to Goliath,

> Thou comest to me with a sword, and with a spear,
> and with a shield: but I come to thee in the name
> of the Lord of hosts, the God of the armies of
> Israel, whom thou has defied. This day will the
> Lord deliver thee into mine hand; and I will smite
> thee, and take thine head from thee; and I will give
> the carcasses of the host of the Philistines this day
> unto the fowls of the air, and to the wild beasts of
> the earth; that all the earth may know that there is
> a God in Israel.

What Trammel admired most was David's having no doubt, no hesitation, no lack of faith in his challenge to the giant warlord. He simply did what had to be done, counting on all his practice with bears and lions to see him through. As long as David took the field, no one, not even a marvel of nature, would dare defy the armies of the Living God. David's confidence in himself seemed to be the best example of the kind of "Christian courage" Pastor McGuffey talked about frequently, though not normally in reference to real wars. Somewhere in the middle of the pastor's explanation of the parable from the Sermon on the Mount, though, which Trammel would have liked to understand, the boy got lost.

What was *she* doing in *his* church? Pretty much everybody knew that Trammel was one of the few kids in his class who went to Dogwood Presbyterian. Most of the other kids went to either First Baptist or First Methodist. He did not actually know which one of them Cindy went to, but it had to be one of the two. Since another kid moved, he and Jill Dixon were the only kids from the same grade in his school who went to this church. And Joey. Yet there was Cindy: sitting right next to Jill. But those two had never been close friends. Jill was not even a cheerleader. And Cindy normally hung out only with other cheerleaders. The only explanation that made sense was that Cindy had decided to "use" Jill to get to him.

Trammel had known Cindy only since the sixth grade, the moment when the three elementary schools on the west side of town all merged to form Dogwood West Middle School. Cindy had gone to Bowie, whereas he had gone to Travis. He did see her once, before a football game between the two archrivals. The two fifth-grade cheerleading squads were talking to each other at the corner of one of the end zones: why, he could not figure out since they cheered for opposite sides. He was not paying them any attention but rather working through a few plays with the offense, until a couple of the girls started calling out his name. "Tra-aam! Tra-aam! Hey! Trammel D. Jones!" He ignored them at first, until finally the coach told him to answer them lest no one be able to concentrate on the game plan. Trammel motioned to them with his hands as if to say "What is it?" Then one of the girls yelled back, "Take off your helmet!" That seemed a stupid request to Trammel, but he obliged them anyway. He removed his helmet to reveal a dazzlingly blond, almost white, shock of hair, at which point they began giggling and kind of falling into each other in the way girls often do. Trammel, mystified, flipped his helmet back on his head, stuck his mouthpiece in his mouth, though the game had not yet started, and got back to work. One of the girls in that group of cheerleaders, the one who had goaded the girls from his school to call over to him, was none other than Cindy Bristol.

Cindy had renewed her interest in Trammel from the first day of sixth grade when they ended up having two classes together. The interest was not reciprocated, especially when Trammel somehow picked up from the other girls that Cindy was not usually very nice. In the notes that got passed back and forth between girls, whether during class or while in the halls, Cindy had written some mean things. She also set up a sort of court around her. Those who liked the people she liked, who disliked the people she disliked, who were cheerleaders or at least popular in some other way, and who wore the same lip gloss, all got to become a part of her network. The others had to carry on their lives with the knowledge that they were not a part of that network. She was extremely imperious even with her own friends. One rumor circulating was that she would not play "Charlie's Angels" with her friends unless given the part of the Farah Fawcett character. As she was clearly the blondest girl in the sixth grade she could only play the blonde angel. It would make no sense for her to play the parts of Kelly or Sabrina—especially Sabrina. Another blonde who wished to put forward her credentials for Farah, i.e. Jill, would be presented with the stubborn fact of Cindy's blondest-ness combined with her resolution not to play the game on any terms other than her own. Her logic was impeccable, her humanity more in doubt. Trammel cared little for the details of Cindy's machinations. He simply heard that she was mean to other girls, girls he thought were pretty nice, girls he had known for a while. He also observed that she brushed her hair too much.

Throughout their sixth-grade year Cindy had pursued Trammel, but he was a tough nut to crack. He had a natural presence, owing to his gravity rather than to any conceit, that made him almost unapproachable to those who did not know him. To those who did approach he felt no obligation to talk, as seen during a sixth-grade dance in the gym that Lanny had tricked him into attending, at which he said no more than twenty words to anyone. Trammel did not talk on the phone at home, never chatted with his classmates during class, passed no notes, and did not hang out at his locker. At any parties Trammel went to—those mixed-sex parties sponsored by parents that begin in the sixth grade—he spent the whole time either eating or dominating at some game of skill such as ping-pong. If the home had no such game, he would take out a deck of cards and round up a group of boys to play poker in a corner. So completely elusive was he, even in the few moments she did get to talk to him, that the willful Cindy finally gave up. In their seventh-grade year Cindy "went with" an eighth-grader and therefore left Trammel pretty much alone. That boy was now in high school. This coming year Trammel and Cindy would be in the eighth grade together, the highest grade in the school, and there was just no other boy Cindy could imagine going with. And she could not imagine *not* going with someone, not as the most popular, or at least the prettiest, girl in the school. Her design was fixed.

The entire game plan had not at that point become clear to Trammel, but he knew something was afoot. As the pastor pronounced the blessing, charged the congregation, and passed down the center aisle, Trammel yearned to go in peace to love and serve the Lord, on this occasion with more dispatch than usual. The boy followed close on the heels of his father, only slightly less eager to get out of there than his son was since the Rangers would start a double-header at noon. The father had been sitting right on the aisle, so things looked good until Trammel's mother caught up to them.

"Hey, Tra-am, did you see that Jill brought Cindy with her to church today? . . . There they are, right there."

His mother smiled at the two girls, who had made their way down the outside aisle and were turning along the rear pews to intercept him at the doors to the sanctuary, which was anything but that to him at this moment. His mother, *his own mother*, had *blown it*, he thought: unless, of course, she did these things on purpose.

As the girls' and Trammel's paths crossed, he saw his sister head off to talk to some of her friends and his mother begin a conversation with some lady in charge of church stuff. That meant he would be there a while longer. His father had slipped away.

"He-ey, Tra-am," the girls chimed.

"Hidee."

"Whatcha been up to all summer?" Cindy began, innocently enough.

"Jus' doin' what I gotta do. A lotta stuff."

"We saw ya ride by the pool a couple a' times on your bike. We waved, butcha mus' not 'a' seen us."

"Naw, I reckon not."

"Wa-ell, why don'tcha come ta the pool some day ta visit us?"

"Can't. Baseball."

"Don'tcha play in the evenin'?"

"'At don't matter. Coach says I can't go swimmin'." Trammel was referring to the time-honored custom of not going swimming on the day of a baseball game. In the Jones home, this injunction was extended to practice days as well. As a result, whole summers would pass with Trammel swimming no more than five times. He had also quit going to the water park when the officious lifeguards began stopping boys from crashing into each other and surfing their way down the slides on their mats.

"O-oh. That's weird."

"B'sides, like I said, I gotta lotta stuff goin' on."

"We see your little sis up at the pool sometimes. She's gettin' *so-o* tall an' she's *so-o* pretty." Coming from a self-adulatory tall and pretty girl, this was a high compliment.

"Yep. She's a reg'lar bean pole."

"Won't she be comin' ta Wa-est next year?"

"Yep."

"Awww," cooed Cindy, looking at Jill, who smiled back, "that's so-o *sweet*." There was that word again. "She'll have big brother ta protect her."

"Ain't 'at what brothers is s'pose' ta do?"

"Yea-ah, an' that's why it's *so-o cute*." And that word. The two girls looked at each other again and giggled.

"So-o is Christie goin' ta try out for cheerleader?" Cindy inquired.

"I don't know. Hope not. I'll pro'lly try ta talk 'er out of it." In fact, Trammel had no idea what his sister's plans were for the coming year. She probably did not either.

"Aww, that's so-o me-ean. Don'tcha want her to be *pop'lar?*" Cindy seemed wholly insensitive to the fact that Jill had tried out this past year and not made it. Then again, Jill hardly seemed slighted by Cindy's comment and would probably try out for cheerleader again in high school.

"She already got more friends 'n I'll ever have. Bein' a cheerleader ain't gonna make no differ'nce."

"Wa-ell, be sure ta tell her if she needs help ta let me know. I'd be happy ta help her."

"Whatcha mean?"

"I mean helpin' her ta practice her cheers an' routines, silly. The older girls always help out the younger ones. I could come over ta y'all's house for a week or so, and she'd learn all the cheers in no time. Tryouts for sixth grade are in a month or so."

Trammel did not like the direction this conversation was going. He had noticed Joey, who was about to exit the sanctuary, looking in his direction, probably wondering if he should confirm the plans regarding their weekly baseball practice. With a subtle nod of his head, Trammel motioned for Joey to come over, which he did with some hesitation.

"Hey, man. 'Is here's Cindy."

"Oh, hi," he said, starting to extend his hand until, thinking better of it, he pulled it back awkwardly and put it in his pocket.

The look on Cindy's face said everything. Her carefully cultivated charm—carefully cultivated by her mother, that is—could at the moment barely keep her lip from curling and thereby revealing her contempt for anything or anyone outside the privileged realm of the "popular."

To add to Cindy's discomfort, Trammel offered some details about his summer. "Me 'n' Joey here been playin' a little ball an' doin' a little fishin' 'is summer."

"Really?" she responded in shock. This revelation was beyond her comprehension.

No one picking up the thread of conversation, Joey tried earnestly to join in. "So, will you be a cheerleader again next year?"

"Yea-uh," replied Cindy, astonished at his ignorance of current events. "Weren't you there the day of cheerleader tryouts?"

"Oh, that's right. I remember now. People clapped for you more than anybody else. Wow, you must have been really happy."

Cindy managed a polite grimace for such faint praise and turned back to Trammel, who was sorry to have brought the poor boy over only to be slighted. Attempting to put the ball back in her court, he asked Cindy, "When d'y'all start hangin' out?"

The two girls looked at each other.

"I guess at the start of the summer," answered Cindy.

"Yeah, since then," Jill affirmed.

"We came ta church together once before, but you weren't he-ere," Cindy noted.

"'At musta been 'a weekend I's over at my grampaw's. We didn't have no game 'at Sa'urdee."

Just as Trammel was about to say, "I reckon we gotta get a move on," the pastor, who had finished shaking hands with all his exiting congregants but these four, headed over to the group. He could hardly allow this younger part of his flock to remain unshepherded for long.

"Well, this looks like a troublesome group," began the jovial pastor, putting a strong hand on Trammel's shoulder.

"Hidee, Pastor. We 'as almos' outta here."

"No cause to rush off, Trammel. Let's see, I can't remember whether we've met. I'm Pastor McGuffey," announced the pastor, extending his hand to Cindy.

"Ya-es, sir. I'm Cindy. I was here a couple a' weeks ago. I came with Jill," offered the girl with a kind hand and her best smile.

"Oh, that's right. Sure, I remember now. So are you just visiting for the summer, or are you from in town here?"

"Ya-es. I grew up here."

"And, so do you go to a church in town, then?" That was one thing Trammel noticed about preachers, even Pastor McGuffey. They always wanted to know whether you had a church to go to, which they often referred to as "a church home." He figured it must have been a kind of occupational requirement to check up on people's Sunday doings. Then again, he could never remember meeting a doctor out in public and being asked the last time he had been sick.

"Ya-es, sir. I go ta First Baptist."

"Oh yes, Pastor Bob. I've known him a long time. A fine man. They even say he can carry a tune." Pastor Bob was widely known to have a deep baritone and to love leading his congregation in song.

"Ya-es, sir," Cindy smiled.

"So Tram, what's on the schedule for this week? Do you have some games? Oh, and Joey, I imagine you might have some games, too?"

"Yes, sir. I gotta couple," replied Trammel.

"And will you be pitching?"

"Yes, sir. In one ob'm."

"And do you expect to win, or does that go without saying?"

"Yes, sir. We'll pro'lly kill 'em."

"Well, I hope you don't *kill* them."

"I reckon 'ey're hopin' 'at, too. But 'at ain't gonna make no differ'nce."

Pastor McGuffey wondered whether he should, but then decided not to, explain the meaning of his joke. Trammel understood the pastor's joke but thought his own much cleverer.

Then the pastor inquired what should have been the obvious, "So are y'all all in the same grade at school?"

"We are *now*," replied Trammel quickly.

"Oh?"

"Well, Cindy flunked a couple a' years, so we caught up to her."

A look of horror momentarily crossed the pastor's face until the barb registered with Cindy and she denied the accusation, gently hitting Trammel with her Bible and smiling gratefully for the first real attention he had paid her that day.

"I did no-ot. That's so-o me-ean."

Pastor McGuffey thought it an opportune time to make his exit. "All I know is, you need to watch this one," remarked the pastor, pointing to Trammel. "And, Cindy, you are welcome to come back any time."

"Great," Trammel thought, "open season on Tram. Eb'm my own pastor's aginst me."

After a moment of silence, Cindy divined that the exchange could not go much further and preferred to leave things on an upbeat note.

"Wa-ell, Tra-am, I guess we better take off. Don't forget ta tell your little sister about me comin' over ta help her. An' jus' call us if ya wanna hang out," she invited.

"Yeah, jus' call," echoed Jill, who normally had more to say to Trammel at church.

"Ah-dee-os," returned Trammel.

"Bye, Joey," Jill said, turning to follow Cindy out of church.

Joey took his hand out of his pocket to wave good-bye.

Once the girls had disappeared from sight and the boys were alone in the sanctuary, Trammel shook his head and looked at Joey.

"Thanks, man—fer savin' me."

"What do you mean? From Cindy? I thought she was the prettiest girl in the school."

"Yeah, well, 'at's what e'erbody thanks. But I've had dealin's with 'er. She ain't all 'at nice, 'nless she wonts sump'm. I don't trust 'er no futher 'n I cou'd spit. Not *as* far, pro'lly."

"Wow. Well, I guess you would know. I've never really talked to her before."

"Y'ain't missin' much. 'At I can guarantee. So, anyhow, we meetin' tomorra?"

"Sure. If you can make it."

"Well, I figur' we oughta make it a early one. Say 'round eight if 'at ain't too early. I got a lawn I gotta mow later on."

"Sure. That would be great."

"A'right 'en," affirmed Trammel as they began to walk towards the door.

"Say, uh," he ventured further, after a moment's reflection, "ya know, me 'n' Lanny's been thankin'. An' if ya wonta come out fishin' agin, 'at ain't no pro'lem. Me 'n' him's gotta do sump'm 'is comin' week, but after that i'd be a'right."

"Oh, wow, thanks, Trammel. You bet I'll come fishin' again."

"A'right 'en. . . . Man's better off fishin' 'n at some dumb pool, at's fer sure."

Chapter 10: The Pitch

Like all good things, the summer was passing quickly. As baseball season drew to a close and before August football practices began, fathers were taking off work so they could go somewhere with the family: down to the Gulf or perhaps up to the mountains of Colorado, where it was a good twenty degrees cooler. Mothers, aside from planning for vacations, were keeping an eye open for good back-to-school sales, whether in clothing or school supplies. For the vast majority of school children, the routine had not yet changed; there were still three or four good weeks of summer left. But the recent high-school graduates, amid a series of parties with their friends since childhood, were busily buying things for their dorm rooms—some useful, most entirely useless—before leaving home and taking the first step on the road toward adulthood. And their successors took on a new pride— some would call it cockiness—in calling themselves *seniors*.

No part of this summer was passing more quickly, though it did not seem so to those involved, than the present baseball game in which Trammel found himself—the game in which he was pitching—the last game of the season for the Dogwood Little League. It was an excruciatingly hot Saturday afternoon in late July, but the Texas heat was far less relentless, far more merciful, than Trammel's arm. From the thirteen-year-old's fastball, there was no shade.

Trammel had grown another inch or two that summer. The speed he had picked up on his fastball led to some control problems at first. Yet the trouble with the pitch bore fruit because he was forced to perfect his other pitches more than he would have otherwise. When his fastball was working, Trammel was untouchable. For the innings he pitched, all but one of his games that season had been shutouts, three of those no-hitters. He had by far the lowest earned run average of any pitcher in the league. Today, with a much bigger crowd watching than normal due to its being the last game, no one had yet gotten to first base on the opposing team: no runs, no hits, no walks, no errors. Only a handful of batters had even gotten a piece of the ball, usually a foul, and only three had put it in play. "Three up, three down" had become such an ingrained habit that the players facing Trammel that day almost feared doing anything different.

Trammel was "hot" more than metaphorically. In fact, he was suffering from a fever. He had come down with it the previous evening, his temperature ranging between 102.5 and 103.0. When he woke up that morning he was still at 101. He should not have even been in the game, much less been pitching. No doctor would have agreed to let him play. But Trammel always played.

At the moment, one boy was leaving the batter's box after a last-ditch swing following two called strikes proved utterly unavailing. The boy—his head downcast, still holding the bat in front of him with both hands, staring at it as though *it* was at fault—barely noticed from under his helmet the next batter up as he passed the on-deck circle without offering any word of encouragement. The new hitter, having put two "donut" weights onto his bat in order to anticipate the speed of the pitches he would face, was now having trouble getting them off. So he kept beating the handle into the ground, sweating beads, knowing that everyone was waiting on him. Finally removing the weights by hammering them with another bat, he trotted almost apologetically to the plate, making the fateful mistake of looking towards the mound, thus catching a glance of Trammel's menacing scowl: the pitiless glare that said, "What makes you think it'll be any different for you?"

Trammel went into his windup—he had not pitched from the stretch all day—and then sent a smoking fastball just off the inside corner of the plate. The batter swung, or rather flailed at it, in part not to let the first pitch go by as had the previous batter, in part to fend off a pitch that came in far too close and too fast for him to feel safe.

"'At's woooone!" the ump sang out, pointing toward the first-base dugout.

Not moving out of his crouch, Charlie flicked the ball back to the mound and yelled out, "C'mone, Tram, th'ow another screamer like 'at 'un right in 'at same spot!" As Charlie shifted his mitt to the inside corner, he signaled for the curve, which Trammel approved with a slight nod.

Despite his coach's warning to "Stay in 'a box," the boy naturally flinched backward, ever so slightly. A relatively slow-moving pitch—at least you could see it—headed in for that same spot, only to break sharply just as the batter set into his swing, leaving him swatting at air.

"'At's two!"

"C'mone, Tram, ya got eem guessin' now! 'E don't know which way's up!" yelled Charlie. Then the catcher, as if to himself, pleaded, "I hope it ain't 'a knuckle. Man, do I hate 'a knuckle."

Trammel rifled a fastball across the outside corner of the plate, just above the batter's knees, eliciting a tentative check swing that was simply a guess.

"'At's threeeee, an' you're ooouuuttta here!" the ump growled as he took two slow steps rightward, assumed the umpire's straddle, and waved his fist back and forth for dramatic effect.

Charlie sent the ball around the horn and trotted toward the star pitcher, making fists with his left hand. "Dad-gummit, Tram. I'm gonna have ta soak my poor ol' hand after 'is game." Trammel took off his glove by pinning it under the opposite arm, retrieved a handful of sunflower seeds from his left back pocket, tossed them into his mouth, and walked slowly back to the dugout. The other boys filed in before him. His right arm, still holding the glove, hung harmlessly by his side.

"'Nother great innin', Tram. Y'ain't wastin' any pitches. How ya feelin'?" Coach Steere inquired for the umpteenth time that day as Trammel entered the dugout.

"Jus' fine, Coach. No pro'lems."

"Ya got another innin' like 'at 'un in ya?" The coach did not dare say the word on everyone's mind lest he jinx the star player and scotch his as yet flawless game.

"I reckon. 'Ey ain't figur'd nut'n' out yet."

"A'right 'en, git a little more water, have a seat, an' take a rest."

The coach began instructing his hitters as Trammel filled another Dixie cup from the cooler and had a seat on the bench. Out of another cooler he took an ice bag that his father had insisted the boy use while in the dugout. Trammel put the bag to his forehead and closed his eyes, resting his elbows on his knees as though praying, blocking out everything but the relief brought by the ice. He had been stranded on base in the last inning and most likely would not be up to the plate again unless the team finally got a rally going. In spite of his effort on the mound, Big Luke's bats had been cold that day. Trammel had gone two for four, knocking in one run and scoring another. While Big Luke had already secured first place, a win for John L.'s Auto Parts would move them from third to a tie for second with Tanner Dodge, the team Big Luke beat on Opening Day. Tanner had managed to squeak out a win against Big Luke later in the season and was thus the only team able to win a game against Trammel's team. The boys of John L. were thus playing for pride, while those of Big Luke had nothing at stake: a sure recipe for a complacent last-game loss.

Trammel's father had just returned to his seat in the stands on the front row. He thought about seeing how his son felt: to make sure he was drinking enough water and knew to keep bringing the fastball interrupted by an occasional knuckle or breaking pitch. Given that his son had thrown a flawless game so far, though, he did not want to do anything to jinx the boy or to break his concentration. He thought it better just to stay put and not change a thing.

Meanwhile, there were other eyes on the dugout, eyes that eluded both the coach and Trammel's father. Otherwise, one of them would have intervened to prevent the pitcher's mind from wandering. And those two older men knew just how an adolescent male mind could wander. Among the other uncustomary spectators who had come out for the last game of the season, Cindy Bristol had just shown up with Jill, and they were making their way behind the bleachers on the visitor's side, stopping to talk to people they knew.

"Oh, man. I can't b'lieve 'at. 'Ere's Cindy. An' Jill with 'er," reported one of the boys of Big Luke. "What're they doin' out here?"

"Who cares? What's it matter when she's wearin' shorts like 'at?" asked another boy rhetorically, referring to Cindy's choice of ultrashort and provocatively tight shorts.

"It ain't 'a shorts I'm lookin' at," commented a third.

"Jill don't look too bad, neither. She musta been out in 'a sun all summer," noticed the original spotter.

"Tram, you goin' with Cindy agin?" asked Charlie with more than passing curiosity.

"No, I ain't goin' with 'er. An' I ain't never did go with 'er," replied Trammel, keeping his head on the ice, alone in not turning in the girls' direction.

"'En you won't mind if I asked 'er out."

"Knock yourself out, man. Jus' try ta keep your mind on 'a dad-gum game fer the nex' innin'. I need a catcher out 'ere, not no skirt chaser."

"Yep. Here they come. An' 'ey're def'nitely lookin' your way, Tram."

"I reckon I'm right pop'lar by now," remarked Trammel, quoting one of his favorite movie lines.

"He-ey, Traa-aam," Cindy's voice called out, a few yards from her reaching the back of the chain-linked dugout.

"Hi, Tra-am," echoed Jill, who waved to the other boys looking in her direction.

"Hidee," replied Trammel, not turning his head, but looking up to see the game.

"You're really pitchin' a great ga-ame," cooed Cindy, who had not seen a lick of it.

"Man does what a man's gotta do."

Some of the boys laughed.

Having no idea why that remark would be considered funny nor whether it was meant as a barb aimed at her, Cindy decided not to take offense and to allow them their mirth. She then arrived at her main purpose.

"Now that this is your last game, me an' Jill was thankin' you might finally come swimmin' with us at the pool," Cindy coaxed, glancing at Jill, who smiled back.

"Can't. All-Stars."

Trammel, leaning on his knees, spit sunflower seed shells unceremoniously through the fence in front of him. Technically,

Trammel could make no such statement. The coaches of the Dogwood Little League would not vote on the All-Star Team until the coming Monday, and the team would be announced the following evening in a special ceremony at the field. There was no doubt, however, that Trammel would not only make the team but that his selection would be unanimous, something that might be true of only three or four other players in the league and no other thirteen-year-old.

Cindy had clearly not taken the post-season into account and had not expected such an abrupt, three-syllable rejection. She remained undaunted in her realizing her end, though.

"A-aww," she pined in that fake hurt voice girls sometimes use to get their way. "You can't at least come by ta visit us even o-once?" she purred, leaning into the fence behind Trammel.

Without turning, Trammel felt the disbelieving eyes of his teammates on him, their mouths agape at the prospect of Cindy Bristol at the pool. He had to relent—a little.

"I reckon I might pass by on my bike if you 'as ta make me a sandwich."

"A sandwich?" Cindy turned up her lip.

"Yep. Man's gotta eat."

"Why would I make you a sandwich?" asked the astonished girl, whose mother had imparted to her daughter most every feminine art, save the one Trammel found useful.

"Y'ain't gotta. An' I ain't gotta come by no pool, neither."

Though not having a mind as quick as Trammel's, Cindy yet realized in a flash that the boy's visit would be on his terms or not at all.

"Wa-ell, what kind of a sandwich?"

"A big sandwich, with a lotta meat on it. An' not no baloney neither. With some a' that real hot mustard. An' some p'tata chips: 'a really hot kind, if ya don't mind. An' maybe some ice' tea, ya know, in a thermos."

"Okaaaay," agreed Cindy, in a tone of disbelief. "So when are ya comin' by-y?"

"I ain't figur'd 'at one out yet. I reckon I'll give Jill a call ta give y'all a warnin'."

Jill smiled, happy for the attention and the chance of being an intermediary on so important a mission.

"C'mone, Billy! Swang like ya mean it! We gotta git some ducks on 'a pond out 'ere!" Trammel's shouted non sequitur, as he jumped to his feet and reached high up on the opposite side of the cage, indicated that the social planning was over. Cindy, mission somewhat accomplished, realized it to be the appropriate moment to retreat back into the crowd.

"Wa-ell, you fellas keep playin' goo-ood. Bye, Tra-am," concluded Cindy.

"Byyye," waved Jill.

"Ah-dee-os," replied Trammel, without looking around.

When the girls were out of earshot, Trammel's teammates upbraided him for his complete want of courtesy.

"Man, you gotta be kiddin' me, Tram! Why'on'tcha jus' go up ta the pool?"

"Heck, I'd live up 'ere, Tram, if I knew Cindy's gonna come by, 'specially lookin' like 'at."

"Man, are you crazy? Are you blind? Was you eb'm lookin'?"

"I say we *all* start goin' ta the pool—ever day."

Trammel would have none of it. "You clowns better gitchur eyes off 'em tan legs an' gitchur minds back on 'a dad-gum game. We ain't won nut'n yet, an' 'is ain't hardly the time fer y'all ta be engagin' in no perverted fantasies."

Logan, the team jokester, had to get in on the act. "Hey, Tram, will you come visit *me* at 'a pool if *I* make ya a sandwich? I'll be sure ta brang your special p'tata chips."

"Naw," replied Trammel, spitting out the remains of his sunflower seeds and picking up his glove. "But I will come visitcha in 'a hospital when I give ya the beatin' you been askin' for your whole sorry life."

The boys on the bench cracked up laughing at this exchange, but the time for jokes was now over. The players, following Trammel's cue, put on their gloves and waited, apprehensively, to take it to John L. for one more inning.

Trammel, glove again tucked under his right arm, waited at the opening of the cage. A few feet away Coach Steere leaned against the fence at his usual perch outside the dugout, too intent on what his players were doing at the plate—or not doing—to have noticed the unexpected guests. As Todd Raines, now batting lower in the order than he had in the opening game, hit into the third ground-out that inning, both Trammel and the coach shook their heads. The top of the inning was over, and Big Luke had failed to put any runs on the board again. The score remained two to zip. Trammel had wanted a more decisive win in the last game of the season, and the coach had hoped that another run or two in the last inning for Big Luke would dash any remaining hopes John L. had for this ball game.

"Hol' up a sec, Tram," the coach said and then exhorted his players scattering out onto the field on what kind of inning they would need to have to make this game theirs.

The team having cleared the dugout, save for the few remaining players on the bench, Trammel looked to the coach.

"Yes, sir?"

"Look here, Tram," the mentor began, resting a beefy forearm on Trammel's shoulder, "you pro'lly got 'is all figur'd out, but I need ta tell ya anyhow. 'Em boys over 'ere," he motioned with an inconspicuous right thumb, "'ey don't wont none. 'Ey don't wont no more a' what you been givin' 'em. All 'ey wanna do is git outta this innin', an' finish 'is game, an' go home—an fergit about 'is game like it never happened. It'd be diffren't if 'ey thought 'ey had a chance, but right now 'ey don't thank no such of a thang. An' you can't let 'em thank 'ey do. 'At's why you gotta keep brangin' 'a heat, Tram. You gotta brang 'a heat like y'ain't never brung it."

"Yes, sir," replied Trammel, eager to get on with it.

"Right now 'ey've had a belly full a' Trammel D. Jones an' 'is fas'ball. If you git out 'ere an' jus' take it to 'em, it won't take but nine, ten, eleb'm pitches maybe—no more 'n 'at. An' 'en 'a game's all yours, Tram. Now look, you're at 'a bottom a' the order. You done all 'a work already. Jus' brang it home."

"Yes, sir," agreed Trammel, glancing out towards the mound.

"An' Tram . . ."

"Yes, sir?"

"'Is un's one fer the history books, young man. An' you've earned it." Removing the weight of his arm, the coach gave the young pitcher a slap on the back of the shoulder to bid him take the field and wish him luck.

At this moment it was the part of a player from John L.'s to wait on Trammel rather than the reverse. Yet the young athlete did

138

not quicken his step one iota or even seem to care that the whole game was waiting on him as he strode towards the mound. Even the umpire, normally a stickler for pace and punctuality, seemed to understand that he did not control the tempo of this game. Seeing that Charlie had the ball, Trammel nodded. The catcher tossed the ball, which Trammel snatched from the air with his bare left hand. He imperceptibly dropped the ball into his right hand and put his left into the glove under his arm. Taking the mound with a natural authority, Trammel stood for a moment, picturing the strike zone as an artist would look at an almost completed canvas that only required a few more finishing touches before becoming a masterpiece. Charlie crouched behind the plate.

The voice coming over the P.A. system, that of the same high-school student whose brashness on Opening Day had offended so many—players and fans alike—now offered a quick, hushed commentary, as unobtrusive as that of the polite announcer covering a golf tournament.

"Ladies and gentlemen, as Big Luke takes the field for this last inning, I remind you that none of the John L. players have made it to first base: no hits, no errors, no walks. And Mr. Jones has thrown fifteen strikeouts."

With that introduction, Trammel took one warm-up pitch—one only. The crack of the glove echoed for a nervous opposing team and a silent crowd to ponder. After the single, intimidating throw, Trammel nodded to the umpire, who in turn waved the skittish batter to the plate.

From around the field, the chatter started up.

From Billy at first base, "C'mone now, Tram! Three up, three down. Jus' like 'a last few innin's."

Russ Howell at shortstop seconded that motion. "C'mone Tram, you're at 'a bottom a' th'order now. 'Is is gonna be a cakewalk."

Logan Dwyer from way out in left chimed in with, "C'mone, Tram, 'ese boys couldn't hit a piñata on 'eir birthday, much less a fas'ball comin' from Tram the Man."

And finally, Jeff Banks at third offered the closing remarks: "C'mone Tram, let's git 'is un over quick so's 'ey can put 'er in 'a history books."

Only Muñoz at second, a brooder like Trammel, was silent.

The first batter presented no difficulties for Trammel. The boy might have shown a faint glimmer of resolution in facing the first pitch. But when that pitch proved to be an unassailable fastball, the batter, as Coach Steere had suggested, wilted. He clearly would have preferred the safe obscurity of the dugout, or of home, to the conspicuous post of a hopeless enterprise. A second fastball, followed by a curve that left the batter swinging at a phantom, brought Trammel one step closer to perfection.

The next hitter was, if anything, more cooperative. After taking a tentative stab at the first pitch, he froze up on the next two, not seeing them as they blazed by, only hearing the smack of the leather and the call of the umpire. There was no longer any need for the umpire to be demonstrative. The third strike had become as routine as quitting time at a factory: the whistle blows, and the workers file out mechanically, released from the sweat and labor of Adam, hoping to find some joy in the repose of a bar or of home. Just so, the boys of John L.'s Auto Parts, one by one, had served their turn at the plate that day, each waiting for his time of toil to be over and his moment of deliverance to begin.

As his second player struck out that inning and hope dwindled to a thread, John L.'s Coach Cobbs called for a time out. "Ump, give us a minute here."

If the pause in the action was meant to rattle Trammel, it was of little avail. Standing on the mound, a full head above all the other players, he surveyed all things around him. Nearly six feet tall, possessing the slim, sinewy body of the adolescent athlete, he stood in a supremely confident *contreposto*, his weight leaning to his right. His right hand, in a crook at the wrist, held the ball against his thigh, fingering the various pitches he might bring against his adversary. His left arm he had tucked into his side, like an eagle's wing, resting his glove just over his shoulder, in the manner pitchers do. He eyed the familiar strike zone—in front of him sixty feet away—and, just to the side, the batter's box where would stand his opponent, wearing a shiny helmet and wielding a metal club.

All day long the young thrower of baseballs had been in complete control. Every pitch followed his orders. Fastballs flew by the opposing hitters. Curveballs broke like fighter jets in a dive. Knuckleballs danced as he wanted them to dance. Arguably, he could have relied exclusively on the power of the fastball. But the other pitches brought a beauty and diversity to his game while they kept their author himself from getting bored. The hitters, like puppets on a string, were no less under his command. They swung wildly or timidly—well behind or far ahead of the pitch—as he wanted them to. They went out looking when he did not intend them to swing. His infielders acted out their bit parts in the game on cue. His outfielders were afforded a day of rest. Even the umpire—the strike zone having been established so imperiously at the beginning of the game—seemed to follow his instructions. It was now Trammel's strike zone; he owned it. Any close pitch was given the benefit of the doubt. Few had not been close. He had worked with impressive economy throughout the game, throwing just enough "junk" to keep the poor opponents guessing. And guessing was really the best they could do. For while the combined outcome of their individual attempts was predetermined, the details of their fates they knew not.

For the past two innings the spectators and bystanders had put their whole minds on the game. The mothers had stopped talking about what plans they had for the rest of the summer, now that the season was over. The fathers had stopped swapping stories about how things had been in their day and had less interest even in the particulars of their own sons' performances than in the work that was unfolding before them. The younger kids had stopped running to and from the concession stand. The regular "cup ball" game, fifty feet behind the first-base dugout, that served as a miniature of the game on the main field for players of all ages without a game that day, had no participants. The ladies working in the back of the concession stand had come out of the hot kitchen and were standing in a row, their arms folded, intent upon the scene. More surprisingly, Christie sat anxiously by her mother, with no friends around, cheering on her older brother. Trammel D. Jones, a thirteen-year-old boy, was schooling them all in the reality of human excellence.

John L.'s coach looked down his bench to see if there had been any players he had forgotten to put in that day. There was one.

"Joe, I need you to pinch-hit for Johnny." The latter, relieved, removed the batting helmet from his head and returned to the dugout.

"Who, me?" questioned the startled boy, not thinking it was his time.

As the boy picked out a bat he thought worked better for him than any of the others and set off to meet his doom, the older man held him up for a moment, resting a heavy arm on his shoulder.

"Look here, Joe. 'Is kid's good. I ain't gonna lie ta ya. But 'a only thang 'e's doin' is th'owin' a baseball. Maybe a little faster 'n what y'all are use'ta. But 'e's usually puttin' it right where ya wont it. All I need ya ta do is go up ta the plate, take a deep breath, an' take a good swang, ahead a' where you're used ta swangin', way ahead. 'E only wonts ta th'ow three more pitches, so they're gonna be up in 'at strike zone. Ya just gotta find one ob'm. Ya see what I'm sayin'?"

"Yes, sir," replied the boy, looking intently into the coach's eyes.

"Now, Joe, you been hittin' perty good in practices lately, an' ya got a couple a good licks in 'a last few games. So you can do this. I b'lieve in ya."

"Yes, sir."

"Go git 'em 'en," the coach charged, with a pat on the boy's bony shoulder.

The batter did not make the mistake of looking in the direction of the mound as he made his way deliberately towards home. Instead, he glanced quickly to the right at his nervous mother in the stands and then returned to thinking about having an even swing and making it be his pitch and what his coach had just told him and all the things he had learned that summer.

As the boy passed the on-deck circle, Trammel rolled his eyes to the right to see who his next and last victim would be. It was Joey! This was a turn he had not expected. His game plan called for some nameless kid to make the final out, not the boy he had worked with all summer, not the boy he had gotten to know a little. His heart burned within. Yet he gritted his teeth and gripped the ball even more fiercely, bringing his forearm muscles into play as the taut wires of a piano.

The young man atop the concession stand announced the new player. "Batting for Johnny Rivers, number two, Joey Fuller." This revelation brought mocking chatter from the Big Luke side. Dwyer out in left began the barrage.

"What a gift, Tram! My *sister* cou'd out-hit 'is kid."

Banks at third asked rhetorically, "Is 'is all 'ey got?"

Billy at first laughed out, "Aw, c'mone, Tram. Easy out, man. Easy out. 'Is kid ain't nut'n'!"

Trammel looked to his left. His nostrils flared. *Of course* this was an easy out. But he didn't have to rub it in like that. There was no call for making a joke out of the poor kid. How would *he* like to be at the plate this minute? It wouldn't be so funny then. The joke would be on *him*, not on this kid with all kinds of problems, who never said a cruel word to anyone. Trammel remembered how in practice the coach had to get him to slow down his throws to first so Billy could handle them. Yet that plain fact did not keep him from having a good old laugh now at Joey's expense.

Trammel returned his sights towards home. He saw Joey testing the bat evenly across the plate, drawing it straight back parallel to the ground rather than pointing it skyward as the pros do, in the way *he* had taught him that summer. Joey's expectant eyes were fixed on *him*, unblinking. Trammel's brow furrowed in torment as he tried to figure out why it had to be this way, why it had to be Joey at the plate and not any other kid in the whole dad-gum league. But Joey it was and no other. The young man was, for once, at a loss as to what he should do.

In an instant his mind set upon a flurry of calculations of the most desirable outcome: of what he wanted, of what he thought was right, of what others would notice or believe, of what was best for everyone involved. He looked to Charlie who was signaling for the fastball. Trammel brushed it off. Charlie called for the fastball even more emphatically. Trammel brushed it off again. Then Charlie, not entirely happy with his judgment being questioned so, particularly since he had been practicing his own brand of gregarious gamesmanship—"Ya know, I'm jus' tellin' ya, 'at ball comes fast, a lot faster 'n people thank it's gonna"— extended two fingers downward, just under the umbrella of his mitt: the sign for the curve. Trammel gave his consent. Inching his thumb back and shifting his fore and middle fingers together, the young man muttered under his breath, "Okay, man, ain't no differ'nce."

As Trammel set into his wind-up, all eyes were upon him: the step back with the left leg, the hands held together—ball in glove —lifted skyward, the unnoticed pivot of the right foot, the shift of all weight onto the right leg, the twist of the torso as the left leg now cocks back along the perimeter of the waist, the hands brought downward behind the right side; that same leg, from its cocked position then moving downward in the direction all things tend, followed by a sweeping fanfare of the gloved hand; meanwhile the ball, having lurked from behind the ribs, the shoulder, the head of its launcher, now becoming visible, the highest point on the field, as the hurler brings all his weight and strength down the slope of the mound and further adds a searing snap of the sinewy arm, like the shot of a missile from a leather sling: every note of the rhythm composed, orchestrated, and practiced to convey maximum force into the hard mass of cork, string, and leather that now takes flight, adding its own twists and turns and varying speeds to avoid the assault of the stick: the darting, ducking, elusive projectile which on the best of days is only occasionally struck by the naturally defensive batter, standing woefully armed in a chalked box. Just so Trammel offered another textbook launch, and the pitch he put forth looked no different from any of the others he had thrown that day—even to a trained eye.

Then the unimaginable happened. No one had been watching the other boy. He posed no threat. The spectators and parents and other players that day did not see the batter's left leg lift slightly and his own weight begin to shift. They did not see his hands bring the bat forward across his chest, perfectly parallel to the ground. They did not see and could not have seen his unblinking eyes follow the ball from Trammel's hand on its short course into the meat of his bat, which he presented full force at the precise moment the ball crossed dead center of the plate, the only juncture at which anyone could have gotten a hit on that day. They did not see any of this; only the boy's mother did. But they could not avoid hearing—rather than the customary crack of leather—an unexpected yet undeniable clank of aluminum hitting a hard object. And they could only gasp when the ball took on a new and different flight.

Events unfolded pretty much as Trammel had expected they would, as he now took on the role of spectator rather than of active agent in this affair. The hit was not a screaming line drive by any means but a floater—a true Texas Leaguer—into shallow left center. It could not be reached by the shortstop who was playing up. Bradley in center was not a starter, and Logan Dwyer in left was the worst player on the team. The two placements owed to Coach Steere's understandable, though perhaps too charitable decision to use Trammel's command on the mound to give the weaker players significant playing time during the last game of the season. The coach had left Todd in right, figuring that if any of the right-handers up that inning could hit one out of the infield, he would only be able to get the bat around in time to slice one down the right-field line. There would then still be a chance of throwing the runner out at first. But fate took advantage of the less skilled players. Had either Andy Dan, the regular center fielder, or Trammel been in center, the blooper would have been caught.

Though he paused for an instant, no one more surprised than he at such unexpected good fortune, Joey dropped his bat and began to run towards first as fast as his thin legs would carry him. The same surprise and indecision that stalled the hitter himself affected the fielders doubly. Bradley in center finally snapped to and ran towards the line of the ball's trajectory. Hoping that he could still salvage Trammel's perfect game by throwing the runner out, rather than squaring up his body and fielding the ball in front of him as he normally would have, he took a quick backhanded stab at the ball as it bounced a second time and died in the grass. Thus the center fielder came up with nothing, his momentum instead carrying him a few feet past the ball. Meanwhile, Joey, on receiving the go-ahead from the first-base coach, rounded the corner with economy as Trammel had taught him that summer, neither having any idea that the knowledge of the student might one day be turned against the master. Dwyer finally got his act together but not until Joey was safe at second with a stand-up double, a look of surprise and disbelief plain on his face.

Though still in shock, the crowd was beginning to accept what had just happened as truth rather than the hot sun playing tricks on their fancy. The mighty warrior on the mound had lost his perfect game, only three pitches away from its consummation, and they all felt bad for him, even the fans on the John L. side. But whether the Big Tram had thrown a bad pitch or, on the other hand, some fluke or accident or miracle had taken place: that was impossible to tell. Trammel's own verdict on the case became plain for all to see. When Russ threw the ball towards the mound, shaking his head in sympathy and with a grim look on his face, Trammel stabbed the ball out of the air with his right hand, then turned his back to second base, where stood Joey, whom Trammel could not look at in that moment, glued to the bag and not going anywhere. At the base of the mound Trammel paused for a moment, head down, his wrists resting on his hips, in the way pitchers stand whenever sullen or thinking. Still holding the ball with his right hand, he took the cap from his head and used the back of his wrist to wipe the sweat pouring from his fevered brow. He then placed the cap back on his head, the bill low across his eyes. Those eyes still set on the ground in front of him, he issued a sudden jerk of the head. The bill of his cap obscured what his mouth might have uttered, but it was clear he was not happy with himself. This crowd knew that this was not the way of Trammel D. Jones. He often glared at opposing players who managed to squeak out a hit against him and sometimes shook his head in silent disgust at the errors of his own teammates, but he never lost his composure, never got angry at himself, and never cursed. He must be mad, really, really mad. It was a perfect piece of theatre that removed any possible doubt.

In the Tanner stands attention began to be directed to Joey's mother, whose face was streaming with tears. The other mothers turned to her, congratulated her, leaned over to extend an accepting hand to her shoulder, her wrist, her knee. She could hardly believe it. Her boy—her son alone—out of all the players on his team, out of all the players in the league who would have faltered in the batter's box facing the best pitcher on his best day, out of all of them, her little Joey got the hit. He would be so very happy.

On the Big Luke side, Trammel's own mother saw not and heard not the sympathetic gestures and words of the other mothers, though they were not slow in coming. Her own tears came, though not many. It was her heart that pounded, sorrowful for her son, joyful for the only boy she could *ever* want to get a hit off of her own. She looked past her tears, past the crowd, past her own husband leaning against the fence to the right of the stands, to fix her eyes on her son: the boy she had conceived and borne and nursed and brought up, the boy who was becoming increasingly a man—with his own thoughts and heartaches and goodness and purposes, with his own stubborn sense of right and wrong. The mother saw only her son, the rest of the world lost in a bright blaze around him, with newfound love and awe.

The pitch Trammel had thrown was not a bad pitch. Technically, it was a curve ball, only one from which some of the break had been taken out. From his vantage, Coach Steere could not see the difference, though he regretted Trammel's changing the original call. Charlie, having been overruled, saw nothing the matter with the pitch Trammel had thrown, though he wanted to know more about it from its author. Everyone watching was convinced because it had been a decent enough pitch. Most of the other hitters facing Trammel that day, so intimidated as the John L. players now were, would have swung and missed. It simply was not Trammel's pitch. In fact, it was a pitch Joey had hit before, and more than once, when Trammel was explaining the curve ball to him that summer, teaching him how to "wait for the break." Trammel could not have given Joey the full-blown, dive-bomber curve, as the pitcher had branded it, any more than he could have thrown his untrammeled fastball. With only one summer, and with Joey's obvious physical limitations, there was no way in heaven the boy could ever be made to hit one of Trammel's pitches. So, without exegesis on the goal, Trammel had resolved to make Joey into a fair hitter of what other pitchers would be throwing at him. And the two had worked as persistently and as hopefully towards that end as two boys ever worked at anything, as true brothers— older and younger—would have. And it was one of those pitches Trammel had decided to throw that day: just one. After that, the fire-thrower would return to his old self, and the pale boy would be on his own. Trammel considered that chance more than fair: a fifty-fifty shot. Actually, it was more like thirty-seventy. In baseball, however, three hundred is nothing to sneeze at. And so no one knew. Joey had, in fact, never seen one of Trammel's true pitches, so little playing time had he gotten over the years—never, as fate would have it, when Trammel was pitching. Otherwise, he, too, might have succumbed to fear or awe.

Only Trammel's father, who knew his son's talents as well as he knew his own, who knew his son to be *better* than he had been at that age, was not entirely convinced by the performance. Leaning against the fence, far too agitated to sit, Trammel's father hardly moved a muscle—did not yell, did not blink when the ailing boy sent the ball into the outfield. He merely cocked his head a little and spit a stream of tobacco juice through the fence as the ball made its way back to the mound, studying his son's face and movements carefully, wondering whether such an incredible thing could have happened if it had not been according to his son's own design and will.

The unexpected turn of events sent the two coaches into high gear. Joey's improbable hit afforded John L.'s Auto a glimmer of hope. Coach Cobbs knew that he had one slim chance of still winning this game. If Trammel were burned up enough about blowing his perfect game, he might lose his control for just one batter. That would have to be Ricky, batting ninth and now up, who was not a bad base runner. With two men on base, then, Tanner would be back to the top of the order. His best hitters would just have to put the ball in play by hook or by crook. Each step would bring a little more momentum to the John L. cause.

"Ricky, c'mere. . . . Look here," the coach said, putting his left hand on the boy's shoulder and turning him towards the fence, as though the Big Luke side could read lips. "You 'member the sign fer takin' a pitch, don'tcha?"

"'Course, Coach. You say 'big swang.'"

"'At's right. I wontcha ta keep takin' pitches 'til I tell ya differ'nt. We're gonna see if ol' Tram's rattled enough ta pull a walk out of eem. Now if 'at don't work I wontcha watchin' 'is first pitch like you's gonna hit it. I wontcha ta watch it real close. Draw a bead on it 'cause 'at's how the next one's comin'. 'Is kid's got y'all psyched out, but all 'e's doin' is th'owin' a baseball. Joe showed us 'at sure 'nough. You jus' listen ta me."

The third-base coach shouted instructions to Joey. "Look here, Joe, 'ere's two down. Run on anything! But if it's a grounder ta this side, don't run 'til 'a ball's left his hand. Got it?"

Joey blinked, uncomprehendingly, having very little experience at running the bases.

"Okay, look, fergit 'at. Fergit what I said. Jus' watch me. Jus' watch me an' do what I tell ya."

Meanwhile, Coach Steere issued his own orders. "A'right, look! 'Ere's two down! The play is at first! The play is at first! Billy, you be on 'at bag, boy, and make sure ya use both hands ta brang 'at ball in. You stay at first. If 'e tries ta bunt 'is a way, Tram's got it. Banks, watch fer the bunt! 'Ey're gonna try anythang 'ey can ta git on base! Brad, back up jus' a little! We can't have anythang gittin' past ya! Keep the dad-blame ball in front of ya, ya hear me?"

As the fielders prepared for come what may, Coach Steere looked to his ace. "Tram, you got 'is'n?"

Trammel's dark, fierce, brooding eyes fixed on the mentor. The young man gave an ever so slight nod of the head—the faintest yet unmistakable whisper of an unwavering purpose, whose strength revealed itself in decisive, awe-inspiring action.

The next batter reached the plate with some little confidence, planted in his mind by the logic of improbabilities: "If Joey can get a hit, why can't I?" He heard his coach's reminder in the background, "Okay, Ricky, big swang, now!" But as he tried to "draw a bead" on the pitch he was instructed to let pass by, the winged fastball shattered the glass house of his flawed logic and his coach's desperate hope.

"'At's oooone!" rang out the familiar refrain.

Now that the doubt about the pitcher's control was put to rest, Coach Cobbs had to make a decision, which was really no decision. Would he cling to the illusion of a walk, or would he give his hitter two chances at these devitalizing fastballs?

"Let's go, Ricky B. Show eem whatchur made of!" came Coach Cobbs's voice, the distinctive appellation followed by the idiom being the sign to swing at anything.

The second pitch screamed across the inside corner of the plate, right above the knees. The batter's feeble swing seemed awkward and out of place.

"'At's two!" came the umpire's call, followed by the disabling clicking sound of his counter. That left the coach with one final decision, the only one he could really make.

"C'mone, Ricky Tiki, jus' git a piece of it," yelled the coach, signaling for the bunt.

As Trammel, pitching now from the stretch, lifted his left leg, the batter swung into a bunter's stance—too soon; they always did too soon—causing a chain reaction. Banks rushed down the third-base line as he had been instructed. Howell scrambled from short to third. Billy held his place, not moving to the bag in case of a hard bunt, but readying himself mentally for the throw to first. Charlie, already in a half-standing crouch because of the base runner, moved his feet to be sure to pounce on anything close. Trammel, still in control of the game, in a split second shifted his aim from the knee area he had been working to keep any hit on the ground to high up in the strike zone. He fired the ball with relish and conviction. Having the bat around ahead of time in order to intercept the coming pitch was no guarantee of getting a piece of one of Trammel's fastballs. Bringing the bat upward as he saw the shot coming in high, Ricky did manage to graze the bottom of the ball, sending it upward a few feet in a frantic backspin. The hitter was only just dropping his bat and heading for first when Charlie, the best catcher in the league, sprung to his feet, held out his glove underhanded, caught the pop-up, and cradled the ball in his chest protector to make sure it did not spin out of his grasp.

The umpire called the batter out with great flourish, the game was over, and, to the secret relief of everyone, order was restored. Trammel had flown from the mound after releasing the ball. Upon seeing Charlie's quick grab, he stopped in his tracks, eased himself up, and stood motionless between the mound and home. It was all over. There was nothing more he could do, nothing more he had to do. At that moment he did not know exactly which direction to walk. Charlie tossed the ball to the ump, took off his catcher's mask, and jogged out to meet his friend.

"Tram, man, what happened with 'at pitch?"

"I don't know. I had 'is gut feelin' 'at 'a kid mighta got lucky an' hit my fas'ball since 'e knew it 'as comin'. I didn't figur' 'ere 'as no way 'e could hit 'a curve. But 'a ball didn't break enough, er maybe 'e jus' swung right where 'e needed to. I can't figur' it out. Maybe I jus' got too cocky er sump'm."

"Well, man, shake it off. You th'ew a great game. 'At's 'a greatest game *I* ever seen pitched."

"Yeah, man, thanks."

Soon this conversation—the special understanding, unique in sports, between a pitcher and his catcher—was opened to the other players coming in from the field to rally around their champion and to those who had ended up the game in the dugout.

"Great game, Tram."

"Man, you 'as hot t'day."

"Too bad 'a season's over. You 'as jus' gettin' started."

"We couldn't 'a' done it without ya, Tram. I mean it," chimed in Logan Dwyer, the team jokester, referring to the entire season and to their first-place finish.

Every Big Luke player patted him on the back or on the shoulder and offered a word of praise. Every boy put a hand on the tall, gutsy, strong-willed athlete, who, his fever now breaking, had somehow been healed that hot summer day by throwing a baseball.

Meanwhile, the players of John L.'s Auto Parts, their spirits needing to eke out some kind of comparable moral victory, however small, looked to Joey.

"Good hit, Joey!"

"You did what we cou'dn't do, man."

"We shou'da had you up 'ere at 'a beginnin'."

And so they each extended a hand to their momentary savior, their single source of hope on a day with precious little hope.

The young announcer, who had gained over the season a becoming insight into the thoughts and passions of the boys and the expectations and needs of the crowd, ratified what the players themselves were demonstrating on the diamond:

"Ladies and gentlemen, let's all give a hand to Trammel and Joey and all the fine young men who've been showin' us today a thang or two about the game of baseball. It's been a great season for everybody."

The fans, who had been dazed by the abrupt ending, and were still contemplating the almost perfect performance and its one surprising flaw, stood in one sweeping motion to offer their ovation to the toils of adolescent triumph.

As if on cue, the two teams lined up just to the side of the mound to shake hands. Each player extended a right hand to slap the hands of the other players passing by.

"Good game. Good game. Good game."

The only variation of the theme came when Trammel, last in the queue as was his custom, stopped Joey, also last, as all the others walked out of earshot. The pitcher sent a slow motion punch into the smaller boy's spindly arm and said in mock anger, "I didn't say nut'n' 'bout gettin' a hit off *me*, man. What 'as you *thankin'*?" Then, grasping the boy's hand in his own, he presented his authoritative word of approval. "Naw, man, 'at 'as a great hit. Way ta put it out 'ere, Joey."

"Thanks, Trammel," Joey beamed, still surprised at his good fortune. "I owe it all to you."

"No, man. 'At 'as you all 'a way."

The boy's pale face blushed with pride. As Trammel turned back to the dugout, his eyes were full.

Coach Steere offered his own condolence, putting two strong hands on the boy's shoulders. "Ya ain't got nut'n' ta hang your head about, Tram. 'At 'as as good a game as I ever seen pitched—by *anybody*." Trammel realized the implication of the final word, since Coach Steere, who grew up in a town not far from Dogwood, had played against Trammel's father in high school.

"Yes, sir. Thanks, Coach. . . . Thanks fer bein' a great coach. I 'preciate it."

"You're the one I need ta be thankin', boy. 'Is team's built around you. An' we got a whole 'nother season of it. We'll take it to 'em next year, 'at's fer sure."

Big Luke had no postgame huddle that day. The season was over. There were no reflections to make, no mistakes to recall, no more victories to plan. The players had already been invited to the team party at Tony's Pizza Parlor, where Mrs. Jones had reserved the upper room. It was big enough to accommodate all the players and their families, replete with arcade games, which Trammel despised, and a ping-pong table, where he would be in command until his father brought his hand to bear. As the other players scattered—most jumping over the outfield fence, as had become tradition on the last game of the season—Trammel drifted out the narrow gate off the first-base dugout that had just been opened. His mother stood waiting for him with an embrace that the exhausted son did not bristle at but seemed rather to expect and want.

"Oh, son, I am so proud of you." She held him fast until, remembering his illness, she put her hand to his forehead to check his temperature, which had gone down.

"You're just so wonderful," the mother continued, looking into her young man's eyes. "I'm blest to have you."

"Thanks, mom," the son replied. "Well, I reckon I'll see ya back at 'a house."

"Of course," said the mother, wiping her eyes. "I'll make you a big steak for dinner." She and Christie, who likewise gave her brother a hug, left for home, having come in the family's other car for some reason or other.

Trammel now made his way to his father, who stood waiting with the last Gatorade sold at the concession stand that year.

"Here, boy. Ya better drink 'is down, the whole thang," the father prescribed as the two ballplayers ambled out to the parking lot. The boy lumbered into his father's car, resting his glove on his right knee.

The ballpark's immense crowd soon dwindled down to a few. The women's auxiliary shut down the concession stand for the last time that season while a couple of players on the home team gathered up the bases. As the home-plate umpire was returning his chest protector and the game balls to a supply room built onto the back of the concession stand, Joey, sent on an errand by his mother, appeared at the door. The umpire heard a tentative knock and turned around.

"Excuse me, ump, I mean sir. I was wonderin' if you had the game ball. You know, the one I got a hit with."

The umpire, a gentle man in his mid-forties who taught geometry and statistics at the high school, thought about the fact of the request and its impossibility of delivering. He had circulated half a dozen baseballs during the game, all of which he had just dumped into a bucket of used balls that got distributed to the teams whenever it filled up. The spirit of the request, however, he understood.

"Yeah, sure, uh, Joey, right?"

"Yes, sir."

"Yeah, this is the one. In fact this smudge right here might be the mark you made with that hit of yours."

"Oh, wow, that's great. Thanks a lot, sir."

"Don't mention it. . . . I guess you must be really proud of getting a hit off such a great pitcher."

"Yes, sir. I can hardly believe it."

"You know, it's kinda funny," Joey reflected further, "Trammel's the one who really taught me how to hit a baseball this summer. We practiced every week. No way would I want to mess up his perfect game. But, you know, he seemed really happy about it, like he was proud of me. I guess what I mean is that he's more than just a great ballplayer. He's like the best kid I ever met."

"I think you're right, Joey. I 'magine deep down Trammel is pretty proud you got that hit off him," agreed the ump, his own questions being now answered.

Father and son were silent during the long ride down Shady Brook Lane. Not only was the father better at either praising or criticizing his son's performance than consoling the boy, who hardly grasped for affection anyway, he had no idea what Trammel must be thinking at the moment. Indeed, his son's frequent moments of brooding silence—his intense bouts of introspection broken up only by cryptic phrases introduced by the words "I reckon,"—were utterly mysterious to the father, who typically said whatever was on his mind, though he had gotten used to his son's ways. Besides that, what could he say? The boy, suffering from a fever, had taken the mound against one of the best teams in the league, playing for pride, and shut them down—silenced their bats completely but for one pitch. And on that issue the father could add nothing. If it had been simply a bad pitch, no one regretted it more than the boy. Saying anything, even making an excuse for him, would only be to rub it in further. And if it had been, as the father strongly suspected, a pitch meant for Joey to hit, then not a word could be said. Such a thing would have to remain hidden, not just for now, but forever.

What made Trammel's father and mother proudest about their son were not the many sports victories, though those did make the father exceedingly proud, was not their boy's impressive stature and good looks, and was not even his uncommon sense and cleverness, well beyond his age. Rather, what most impressed them was his fierce, uncompromising will to do what was right — on every occasion. They both suspected that these brooding silences, this "stewing," resulted from his internalizing a moral resolution, at times his suffering for it, prior to doing what must be done. Only on this occasion he had acted first—as he had to—and was now agonizing over the propriety of the action afterwards. And it could not be easy because it had cost him something; it had cost him something that he had wanted very badly. For Trammel it was not just a matter of a baseball game. That is, baseball was no different from anything else he did, whether school or fishing or fixing things or thinking through difficult problems. He was not just a "winner," a fierce competitor, in the way his father had been when he had played sports. He was the true perfectionist. That was the way he lived his life. And the closer he came to perfection, the nearer he came to tasting the glory of true mastery, the less satisfied he was with any performance short of perfect. Trammel did not just want to be the best in the ordinary sense: the best in the league, the best in his school, the best in the town. He was already that. He wanted to be the best *ever*. He wanted his name to be the answer to that age-old question of men, young and old alike: "who is the greatest?" Trammel did not then know whether he would make his mark in sports or in some other endeavor. But until he found his calling, his true love, he would give it all he had in everything he did. Had he thrown an ordinary shutout or even a no-hitter with a couple of walks, he would have been in a very different state of mind. In that case he would have had a half-dozen pitches to think about and regret. Such a game would call for his renewed resolve to work even harder in practice and to think more clearly while on the mound, but he could still be moderately happy with it. In this game he had done everything right. He had been in control every moment of the game. He had thrown a single bad pitch: just *one*—on purpose—because the fates and something inside of him seemed to want it that way. As a consequence, he had given up the thing *he* most wanted for an elusive prize he did not then understand. And what was worse, everyone had gone home from that game not knowing the *truth*, the truth of his perfection, the truth that *no one*, no thirteen- or fourteen-year-old boy in the whole world, for all he knew, could have gotten a hit off Trammel D. Jones on that day.

Trammel did not, could not, unravel all these threads to his torment as he looked out the window of his father's car and into the beautiful trees shrouding the familiar passage down Shady

Brook Lane. His soul ached as he grieved over his decision and wondered whether he would ever get close to pitching such a game again. He concluded that there was a world of difference between a one-hitter and a perfect game. Having achieved the former, for a third or fourth time that season, he might get a mere by-line in the sports page the next day. Had he accomplished the former, his full picture—an action shot of his whole fearsome frame bearing down the mound while launching yet another rocket of a pitch—would be on the front page of the local paper. On top of that, the Dallas papers would have likely picked up his story: in the same way the perfect game his father threw had been covered when he was that same age, pitching in that same league.

As they pulled into the garage and Trammel began to open the car door, the father said simply to the son, "Tram . . . You poured your heart out inta that game today, boy. 'At's all I cou'd ever ask of ya. 'At's all you can ask a' yourself."

"Yes, sir. I reckon so," returned the son, leaving the car to hide the tears in his eyes. The young man went upstairs to clean up for dinner, another season finished and waiting for the history books.

Chapter 11: "'At Ain't Right"

Three months later, the almost perfect game had been all but been forgotten in the Joneses' house. Trammel's mother had mentioned a couple of times at the dinner table that Joey was still talking to his mother about "my hit off Trammel." Trammel resisted the urge to say what he naturally would have in such cases—"Eb'm a blind hog finds an acorn ever now an' 'en"—replacing it with the respectful, "Well, I reckon 'e deserved it."

It was football season. His mind was now engaged with his favorite—his father's second favorite—sport. "Football is not a contact sport," a great man once said, as the father reminded the boy at the beginning of every season. "Dancing is a contact sport. Football is a collision sport." So Trammel played the game. He was the quarterback. He had the arm, the quickness, the discipline, the command of the other players, the mind. His temperament, however, was that of a defender. He pleaded with the coach before and during every game to put him in on defense and special teams so he could hit somebody. "It ain't right fer *them* always ta be takin' shots at me if *I* can't put some hurt on 'em ever now an' 'en." And hurt them he did—given the chance. Though the coach did not like risking his star player, he often relented during what promised to be close games and put Trammel on the field for the opening kick-off. Three out of four times he was first to the kick returner and on several occasions simply laid the poor boy out with a hit heard round the stadium. Lanny—his friend and teammate—always offered the same response: "Way ta put a *hush* on 'em, Tram. 'Ey ain't got no Mo now."

It was on offense, though, that Trammel led the team. Several games into the season they were undefeated, as they had been for the last two years, and no opposition seemed capable of stopping them in their quest for city and district championships. Yesterday's game against a rival North Texas town had brought out the team's and Trammel's best: the far-from-expected 28-7 rout in which Trammel had pitched out to Charlie on the option for one touchdown, thrown to Lanny on the fly for a second, run back a 60-yard punt return for a third, and, late in the game, scored a fourth on a broken play in which he was almost sacked by two defenders. He also held for extra points and field goals.

During football season Trammel had little time for the leisurely pastimes of the easy summer. He spent seven hours in school and practiced for two hours afterwards. He had also begun his own physical training regime, regularly lifting weights for the first time in a gym he and his father had set up in the garage and running three miles at least twice a week, once on the weekend and once on a morning before school.

Despite his pious loyalty to the Texan vernacular, whose offenses against (though not colorings of) the English language he would not abandon until he encountered a grammar book in high school, Trammel was an exceptional student. He had been named "student of the quarter" twice, once for each grade in middle school, and was the odds-on favorite for the same award in the present quarter. He had also been awarded top student trophies in two different subjects at last year's middle-school awards assembly, in science and English. The rumor circulated that Trammel would have also won the award for history, especially given that it was his favorite subject, had he not persisted in asking questions the teacher could not answer and found so many basic factual mistakes on her tests. Just as he wasted no time in practice for sports, so Trammel took every moment of his classes seriously and became impatient whenever a teacher had nothing to offer (which was all too often). The teachers were so happy with his interest in class (and so little bothered by their own want of preparation) that they invariably responded to his queries with, "That's a great question, Tram. I'll have to look that one up." They never did. He also made it his policy to transfer directly out of a coach's class whenever he was put into one. "No offense, Coach, but I gotta learn sump'm." No offense was taken. To supplement the less-than-challenging assignments required by his classes, Trammel read books he found in the school library, to which he often escaped after eating lunch; or in the town library which had a surprising number of good books in the areas which interested him; and at a used book store in Dallas his mother frequented. The rigors of Texas football combined with his self-imposed demands in school left Trammel little time in the fall for "hanging out" with his friends or even with family. He had been over to see his grandparents only a couple of times this semester, though they came to his games and most every Sunday took him out for a "man-sized" brunch after church, specifically, two different orders at the best pancake house in town.

So little spare time did Trammel have that he had turned down Lanny's invitation to go duck hunting that weekend. His immediate concern was finishing an assignment he had been working on several weeks already. The assignment was to read a book about a famous or important person and then write a report on it. Trammel had chosen George Washington, who seemed to him to have been the most famous and important person to any American, and had read *two* biographies. Lanny had taken a different route. He had not finished or even begun his report but had shown Trammel his title page to convince him that the assignment was "easy" and there was no good reason not to go duck hunting.

Country Boys Can Survive
The Life And Times Of Hank Williams, Jr.
By Lance "Lanny" Freeman

When Trammel asked him what book he had read, Lanny responded that no book was necessary. "All ya gotta know's in 'a songs. I can make all 'a res' a' stuff up in my head." Trammel's remonstrance that a book report without a book "ain't no real book report" fell on deaf ears. For his part, Trammel found that he needed, in addition to his reading, to spend a fair amount of time *writing* his paper. He enjoyed this enterprise, especially since the story of the founding father turned out to be somewhat more complex than the lives of Hank, Jr., Willie Nelson, Clint Eastwood, or even Tom Landry.

One acquaintance from the summer Trammel had not seen much of at all was Joey. The two boys did not have any classes together that semester and had different lunches, so they encountered each other only on rare occasions in the halls. A couple of weeks back Joey had approached Trammel in the hall as the latter was talking to a few of his teammates about something that had happened in the previous day's practice. Joey stood off at a distance and clearly wished to talk. Once Trammel made his point he looked at the shy, slight boy who appeared to be pulling an object of some importance out of his backpack.

"Hey, man. What's goin' on?"

"Not much, Trammel. I just wanted to give you this."

Joey handed Trammel a blue envelope with his name written on it.

"Hey, thanks, man. I'll take a look at it when I git home." Trammel never knew the protocol of whether you were supposed to open up a present or a card in front of the giver or wait until some private moment. It always seemed to him somewhat mercenary just to open it up right there in front of him, as though you could not wait to get to the good stuff without sufficiently acknowledging the thought behind it.

Joey hesitated, not knowing exactly what to say or do.

Trammel reassured him. "I 'preciate it, man. Where you been hidin', anyhow? I ain't seen ya 'round much."

Joey blushed at Trammel's concern. He replied that he had been fine, seemed for an instant to want to say something, looked inward with his bright blue eyes and thought better of it, waved, and disappeared into the crowded hallway.

The two teammates waited upon their captain to see whether the King of All Chaps might offer one of his wry witticisms at the expense of the unexpected visitor. Hearing none, they, too, left for class. Having no classes together, Trammel had not noticed that Joey had already missed quite a lot of school that year.

The envelope turned out to contain an invitation to Joey's fourteenth birthday party. The prospect of a party on the same weekend Lanny wanted him to go duck hunting led to a slight conflict of conscience, but Trammel reasoned that the hunting trip was "an overnight deal," whereas he could easily slip over to Joey's for a couple of hours and then get back to work on his

Washington report. This past Saturday morning Trammel had informed his mother that he would be off on his bike since he had some "shufflin' ta do." His mother asked whether he would be shopping for Joey's present. She *always* knew. Trammel ended up spending the whole morning on this errand. He looked over all of Big Luke's inventory before deciding upon the right gift. In addition, he had to listen to Big Luke himself opining on how the season was going and what sort of future Trammel could expect— in football and baseball—when he got to the high school and beyond. Big Luke clearly intended Trammel for bigger things than TCU, "no disrespec' ta your daddy, fer sure the best young ball player I ever seen 'til you come along." Big Luke seemed to think that UT might have Trammel's "name on it."

Trammel took even more time in finding Joey "a decent card." The ones at the first grocery store he visited were, he pronounced under his breath, "stupid." So he stopped in a drugstore and at last a better grocery store until he landed upon one that seemed to send the right message.

As he headed down a deserted hallway late that Friday afternoon, having just come from a light practice the day after a big game and facing an easier opponent the next week, Trammel ran through his mental list of the things he would attend to that weekend: the report, the party, a good run, church, pancakes. Some other event or duty he knew was looming but could not remember what. He had forgotten for the moment the social minefield he had been dodging through all week. He was less sure-footed in this type of minefield because the mines were far more explosive and unpredictable than the normal duties and claims upon his time. They were girls.

It would be an understatement to say that the girls of Dogwood West had Trammel's "number." He just wasn't answering— literally. Girls called the house rather frequently. Since she was always first to pick up the phone and the person most often on it, Christie functioned as the family secretary. She had standing orders to tell anyone calling for her brother that he was not at home, except for certain male friends he had named or any of his customers. He farmed out his lawn business to a couple of younger boys once school started, and since they did not always do a perfect job, he urged his clients to call him directly. No lover of telephones in the first place, the last thing Trammel wanted to do was to get caught on the line with some girl, or worse, two girls at the same time who would just giggle and whisper to each other about what they should say to him. Christie proved to be a great sister in that respect. Often she ended up talking to the girl or girls, sometimes for quite a while, and as long as she did not divulge any information about him, Trammel encouraged her to run such interference. It was not that he had anything against girls. He was unfailingly polite to them. A few, like Jill, he considered "decent" enough. It was mostly a case of his having nothing to say to girls and no interest in the things they were saying. In principle he "liked" girls. In practice he did not. As he told his mother once when she was exploring in her discreet, maternal manner whether to help him along in this way, Trammel thought girls were "perty dad-gum silly." His mother just smiled in agreement and promised that one day they would not be quite so silly, and the least silly among them would be looking for a man of his mind and character.

The specific danger Trammel had thus far dexterously avoided was the annual Sadie Hawkins sock hop to be held the following Friday night that functioned as an eighth-grade Homecoming. All week long the girls in his grade had been acting sillier—in Trammel's mind—and more covertly than they normally did. Every time he turned a corner or passed a group of girls at their lockers, the whispers and giggles would stop and then start up again. Each girl passed every other girl in the hall with smiles and knowing glances. The notes were flying back and forth, both in and out of class. He did not know exactly how, but in some definite way he must have fit into their grand scheme of who would be going with whom to this annual travesty. Trammel did not know who Sadie Hawkins was or had been. But whoever she was, he sensed that she had fundamentally upset the order of things. It was bad enough to have to ask a girl out on your own, in the middle of the season, when the football team should have been thinking about the game rather than some dumb dance. At least then a fellow could have some control over who his date would be and how much energy he would put into the whole business. But to be witness to and a target of the gossipry and machinations of the adolescent female for a week or more was almost more than this uncommonly reserved and fiercely independent young man could endure.

As he loaded the books he needed into the cleaner part of his backpack and stuffed a sweatshirt in as well, he felt a tall, thin, blond specter approaching noiselessly from his right side. He pretended to rearrange some papers in a folder in hopes that the specter would pass, but instead it stopped a few feet from him. He shut his locker and turned to face the inevitable. It was Cindy Bristol. Now it all made perfect sense.

Since the beginning of the school year Cindy had been exceedingly nice to him and not in an obviously conniving or overtly provocative way as in the past. Each time he passed her in the hall she smiled big and gave him one of those quick waves girls do as though they are washing the window of a car. Once she called the house and made it past Christie's screening, to his consternation, by pleading the need for help on an assignment. Though she had resorted to him before for such help, it appeared this time that the school work was more a pretext to talk to him than a way to get an easy "A" without her really understanding the homework. If anything, she had tried to appear smarter in class lately by being sometimes the first to raise her hand when the teacher asked a question. More surprising, after nearly every game she had complimented him on his performance: not in just a general way but by mentioning exact plays he had scored on. In one of the earlier games of the season she had composed a cheer in his honor that soon became a favorite with the fans:

> Tram, Tram, he's our man,
> You can't stop him; no one can!

Another indication of her game plan was her becoming better buds with Jana, who was now officially "going with" Lanny. To be sure, none of these individual acts, nor her design as a whole, surprised him. He had figured out during the summer that she meant to date him in some way during the coming school year and had used her intentions to gain one of the best sandwiches he had ever eaten. What surprised him was how patient, how unassuming, and how genuinely nice she had been every step of the way. She did not, for example, cease being friends with Jill when the summer was over, as she would certainly have done a year ago, though she had no immediate use for Jill once school was back in session. His own observations seemed confirmed by his overhearing at least two girls say, "Cindy's really nice this year."

Now that she was standing in front of him in the hall with no one else around it was clear that by some common agreement girls come to, through dozens of phone calls and scores of hallway conversations, Trammel had become the exclusive prerogative of one Cindy Bristol for the annual sock hop. And, since it had been decided, no one, least of all Trammel, could question the inviolability of this perfect match.

"He-ey, Tra-am," Cindy opened cheerfully.

"Hidee," he replied in a low voice, still holding his cards close.

Cindy had just come from cheerleading practice, or rather the gaggle of girls that had worked on cheers for half an hour and then stood around for forty-five minutes planning the social events of the coming week. She was wearing shorts and a tee shirt of blue and gold, the school colors. Trammel did not know, though it would not have surprised him, that Cindy had touched up her make-up and taken the ponytail holder out of her hair just before tracking him down in the hall. That she found him in such an opportune setting owed to her studying his movements well enough to know that he was the only player to come get his books after practice from his locker, keeping them there lest they get lost or stepped on in the mayhem of the boys' locker room.

"So-o, are you gonna be workin' on your report this weekend?" she began, choosing a safe, neutral topic.

"Yeah, I reckon. It's due on Mondee."

"Yea-ah, I need ta finish, too. I've been workin' on it for a whi-ile, though." When no response came, she continued, "I'm writin' about Laura Ingalls Wilder."

"You mean 'at lady 'at did *Little House on 'a Prairie?*"

"Yea-ah. That one."

"I didn't know you 'as inta all 'at kinda stuff."

"Yea-ah, I been watchin' it a lo-ot lately. I read one a' the books for the book report an' some stuff about how she grew u-up. . . . Did you ever watch it?"

"When I's a kid, my mom perty much roped me into it. Me an' my dad. I 'member 'er cryin' a lot whene'er sump'm sad happened, er eb'm sump'm happy. I don't watch it no more, though. I'm usually studyin'. My mom an' Chris still watch it. I reckon it's kinda a girls' thang." Trammel surprised himself by offering so much detail about his own family to someone he had never spoken more than twenty words to at one time.

"Oh, it's *really* good. I watched it when I was a kid, too, but I didn't really get it all, ya know, like what you're s'posed ta thank. I been watchin' it lately, though, an', ya know, thankin' about thangs . . . like how you're s'posed ta be nicer ta people an' stuff."

Trammel reflected on this revelation but said nothing. He looked at her with his dark, intense eyes, as yet unaware of the effect they had on the other sex.

"So-o, Tra-am, I was kinda wonderin'," Cindy ventured, visibly nervous as Trammel had never seen her, yet maintaining her full composure and sweetness of voice. As she spoke, she rose to her tiptoes, bent the fingers of one hand back with the other, bit her lip, and partially shut one eye, the combined effect betraying an apprehension that he might say "no," an altogether cute and arresting apprehension. "I heard you didn't have a date for the Sadie Hawkins da-ance, an', ya know, you're like the smartest an' coolest guy in the whole school. So-o, I was hopin' you might not mind goin' with me. I mean, I'd really like ta take ya. My mom said if you say 'yes' we oughta have ya over ta dinner beforehand. Me an' her been cookin' a lo-ot lately."

Trammel was not buying the part about his not having a date, knowing full well that these girls had orchestrated the whole deal—how was she so *sure* that he was not already going with someone else?—but the rest of what she said did not sound that bad. He knew she had him trapped—he had to hand it to her—but in this instance he did not mind being trapped, not as much as he would have a year or so ago. He ran through all the possible objections in his head of why he might not want to go with her but found them each to be of history and not of the present.

"Yeah, I reckon 'at'd be a'right. I mean, we'd pro'lly have a a'right time."

"Yaaaay!" Cindy cheered softly as she sprung up in the air, clapping her hands, a look of joy, of real joy, spreading across her cover-girl face and into her crystalline blue eyes. Trammel maintained his naturally aloof and critical expression.

"We'll talk more next week. Oh, this'll be so much fun!" Triumphantly, ecstatically, Cindy sealed the deal by leaning over and kissing the startled, rigid young man on the cheek, then gracefully turned and ran, or rather bounded off, her arms held straight at acute angles from her sides, her smiling gaze cast downward just beyond the reach of her long legs, her train of blond curls bouncing behind her, as cheerleaders always run.

"Geez," muttered Trammel softly, shaking his head and making no attempt to unravel the utterly incomprehensible.

As Trammel rode down the long driveway that swept around to the back of his house, he found the garage door open and his father's car already parked in it. His father often came home early on a Friday but with his long commute rarely made it home before five. Trammel parked his bike and entered the house, immediately seeing and smelling a pizza on the kitchen table as he dropped his bag and took off his shoes. He looked around to see where everyone was. Christie lay on the floor of the family room, flipping through a magazine, a third sign that something was amiss, since normally she would have been on the phone, playing the piano, or watching television.

She looked up. "Dad's home."

"I figur'd 'at out. 'Is car's in 'a garage. How come?"

"I don't know. Nobody's tellin' me anythang."

"'Bout what?" Trammel asked, as he sat down at the table and helped himself to a slice of the large pizza, which he knew must have been intended for him.

"All I know is that mom's been pretty upset since I got home. She's been talkin' ta people on the phone all day and tol' me ta stay off it. She's been cryin' a lot, too."

"'Bout what?"

"Like I said, she won't tell me. I already asked her if everythang's okay or if I could do somethin', but she just said she'd talk to me later. Right now she just wants me ta stay off the phone and try ta be quiet."

"Well, 'd'ya hear what she 'as sayin' on 'a phone?"

"No. She's been talkin' up in their room. An' she's been answerin' the phone herself, so don't ask me who she's been talkin' to."

"When 'id Dad git home?"

"Oh, around twenty minutes ago, maybe. He ordered a pizza right away and told me ta tell ya ta go ahead an' eat. He said I could have some, too, so try not ta eat the whole thang like you always do."

Trammel could see that this interrogation of his sister was not yielding any worthwhile information. She was as in the dark as he was, but clearly something was amiss. He tried to recall whether anything out of the ordinary had happened that morning but could think of nothing. His mother had actually said that they might go out to dinner that night. His father often took the family out to dinner on a Friday night. Whenever Trammel had won a big game as decisively as he had the day before, he could count on it being his favorite chicken fried steak place in town, or maybe a great Mexican restaurant they had found on the outskirts of Plano. That his father had unceremoniously ordered him pizza meant that those plans had been scuttled, that his mother was unable to cook, and, strangely, that his father would be occupied as well for a while. Otherwise, he would have taken Trammel and Christie to get burgers, leaving a quiet house to their mother.

Trammel kept eating, but he had no heart in it. The thing that he could not keep from passing through his mind on such occasions, as much as his reason and his soul told him the thing to be impossible, was the eventuality that his parents were talking about getting a divorce. He knew—he was ninety-five percent sure—this horrible possibility could not be the case. His parents loved each other; he knew that. They argued occasionally—not often in front of him and his sister—rather in "discussions" in their bedroom, and never did these discussions seem too vehement or too prolonged. The parents always made up quickly and became more loving, more patient towards each other than before. Still, Trammel could not help thinking about the remote chance, the terrible prospect, that his parents, too—even they—might get a divorce. So many of his classmates' parents had gotten a divorce, seemingly out of the blue, with no more of an excuse than some vague mumblings beginning with "Your mother and I . . ." or "Sometimes adults just can't . . ." What Trammel had seen of the unhappiness that came from divorce caused him to know and unconsciously to resolve that he would never, never get a divorce, never put his own children through that emotional turmoil and pain. It always came as a great relief, then, when these secret discussions turned out only to be strategy meetings prior to the parents confronting either him or his sister with some stupid thing one of them had done. These strategy meetings had become longer and longer, to be sure, presumably so the parents could prepare for their son's disarming logic or, which was more often, figure out a way to make their daughter care about her crime and punishment for more than half an hour.

So Trammel sat, eating his pizza, brooding.

"Hey, son," his father called to him from the landing on the stairs in a weak, ominous, and almost apologetic voice that he had never heard before from the strong, commanding man. "Cou'd we see ya a minute?"

"Yes, sir," the son returned immediately, choking down a bite and leaving the table.

As he entered the master bedroom, the boy saw his mother sitting on a small, faded, comfortable sofa that had been the first family couch, from which as a toddler he had leapt countless times into his father's arms, only to be thrown back on it, laughing and saying, "Again." His mother's head was buried in her hands, her hair in disarray, as it would be seen only early in the morning, if even then. She looked up at him reluctantly as he entered and folded her arms into a tight embrace of her lower abdomen as though she were cold or felt sick. Around her eyes were the redness and swollenness of crying, but their hue was the brilliant, piercing aquamarine that could not fail in their magnetic powers out of a crowd of a thousand. She looked at him tenderly, hopefully, proudly, as she would if he had been a kind of remedy for her obvious pain, though also with no small amount of regret and compassion. It was a look not unlike the one she had given him after the last baseball game that summer, though this time with grief. She glanced from him to her husband, taking his place at his wife's side and putting one arm around her, the hand of the other grasping her upper arm. Trammel sat down just in front of them on the tall, king-size bed. The son sat a full two feet above his parents. He had no idea what was going on. There was not a trace of anger in his mother; her body language and expression indicated that she was reaching out both to him and his father for support while searching for some internal strength of her own.

"Son," she began, "you probably haven't noticed anything different happening with Joey lately because, you know, you've been really busy. But he's been really sick. For the last couple of months his chemo has been stepped up, but it hasn't worked like it has in the past. . . Oh, what am I tryin' ta say?" left off the mother, frustrated that she could not find the words and had lapsed into medical jargon.

"Are ya sayin' 'e's startin' ta git sicker instead a' better?" offered the son.

"No, honey, no. You see, there was never any way he could've gotten better. He's been getting sicker this last little bit because, well, because, I guess . . . it was his time . . ." She could not go on but rather lifted one of her hands to cover her trembling lip and flow of tears as her whole frame began heaving with sobs.

"Are ya sayin'," Trammel asked, though he had perceived the answer as soon as his mother had slipped into the simple past tense, "'at Joey's . . . I mean, 'at Joey died?"

His mother could only nod.

"It happened all'v'a sudden," the father confirmed. "Joey went inta the hospital yesterdee mornin', an' thangs got worse over the night. 'E passed early 'is mornin'. 'E 'as conscious an' talkin' almos' up ta the very last, but 'ey say 'ere wudn't much pain, no pain at all, really. Pastor 'as with eem most a' the time an' so was 'is mother. Ya know, as 'ese thangs go, it wasn't as bad as it cou'da been. Joey's mother called your mom 'is mornin'."

For a moment Trammel was simply stunned. As he began to confront the full import, though, the horrible finality of the message, he began to reject its validity, its possibility even, because there was too much evidence to the contrary.

"'Ere ain't no way. 'Ere ain't no way 'at cou'd be right. I mean, 'e's got a birthday 'is weekend. Yeah, 'e'll be fourteen. All kindsa kids is pro'lly goin' to 'is party. I got eem a card an' a little sump'm. . . . Why, we 'as jus' playin' ball th'other day, like it 'as yesterdee. I's showin' eem all about knuckle balls. An' 'e 'as swangin' at 'em. Missin' a bunch, but hittin' a few, but 'e 'as swangin'. 'At's 'a point. An' I'd say, 'Look at 'at, man, now 'at's what I'm talkin' 'bout. 'At's really takin' 'a cover off 'a ball.'

An' 'e'd say, 'Yeah, Tram, I thank I'm gettin' 'a hang of it.' An' we'd go back at it. Don't ya see? 'E can't be gone! 'E can't be." And so the same boy who at all other times was so unfailingly, mercilessly, coldly logical now grasped at straws.

The son's recounting of the summer's activities only caused the mother's silent sobs to become audible throes of grief whose dolorous truth silenced the boy's argument. She again looked up at her son, proudly, once she could almost speak.

"Yes," she whispered. "Yes. It was a wonderful, wonderful summer and you . . ." She broke off again for a moment into sobbing but recovered. "You were a big, such a big part of that."

"The doctors said," the father continued, "'at Joey had kind of a last burst 'a strangth 'is summer, whatcha might call a Indian Summer. 'E felt real good, an' stronger 'n usual, which is why 'e cou'd play ball with ya an' ride 'is bike an' thangs. An', like 'is mother tol' your mom jus' 'is morning, 'e'd never been in better spirits. An' son," his father paused, clearing his throat and wiping a tear from his own cheek, "'at boy jus' thought 'a world a' you. An' fer you ta take 'a time ta play ball with eem all summer meant a lot to eem. It 'as real, real special. I don't thank me er your mother ever been prouder of ya, boy. You became a big part a' that boy's life: a big, big part."

Trammel was having none of it. The young man spent not an instant reflecting upon the rectitude of his own conduct, which now seemed a moot point since it had not done any good in keeping Joey alive. Resigned to the reality of Joey's death, he now began to attack its justice. Yes, yes he had died all right. Trammel remembered the pencil thin arms, the lack of any weightiness, resistance, or strength in the boy's frame. Joey could not have withstood one hit on the football field, not one punch in some backyard boxing, not one tackle in a game of "smear the queer." Trammel's sister could have fared much better. There had always been something vulnerable, unearthly about Joey. So it was unreasonable to be surprised. Die he must. But why did he have to die in the first place? Why now? The poor kid was just getting started. One thing Trammel had figured out that summer was that, however feeble or un-athletic or otherwise unlike one of the guys, the kid had some spark in him, some real guts.

"'At ain't right. 'At ain't right at all. Can't a kid eb'm have a birthday? At least a crummy birthday? 'At wou'dn't 'a' made it right, but at least it'd be better'n nut'n'. But now 'ere ain't nut'n': ain't no kinda, ya know, closin' ceremonies er last shoot-out er . . . nut'n'. Jus' a poor kid dyin' alone in a hospital. . . . Naw, ain't nut'n' right about it." He looked from the floor up into the eyes of his mother. He looked at her intently, in defiance, even angrily, as though she had been responsible, as though her resigning herself to the boy's death had made her an accomplice in it. He enunciated the three words distinctly:

"'At—ain't—*right*."

Then he left the room.

Trammel went into his own room and shut the door behind him. He did not slam it, at least did not mean to. But the doors in this house were not the paper-thin pressed wood doors of the other house, rather stout oak on newly lubed brass hinges. Sometimes just shutting the door made it sound like a person was slamming it. Trammel instinctively picked up his glove that had a ball lodged into the webbing. He had thrown the glove aside—into the bottom level of his bookshelf—the day he had come back from the Little League state tournament and taken his football from the same shelf. Trammel now began throwing the baseball into his glove—not something he did often—not as often as did his dad, anyway, who regularly watched televised baseball games glove-in-hand.

Trammel kept repeating to himself the phrases, "'E's jus' a kid" and "'At ain't right" and variations on this theme. In his mind, the "kid" did not get "half a chance." He was just getting started. Trammel was not unaware of death. He knew people, even young people, died in accidents every day. He knew people were shot and killed unjustly. He knew young men died in wars. One of the heroes he had come to know in his reading about George Washington was this fellow named John Laurens. The fiery young patriot, a South Carolinian who had proposed freeing and arming the slaves in the middle of the Revolutionary War, had been one of Washington's most loyal officers and the best friend of Alexander Hamilton. Laurens had even fought a duel to defend Washington's honor. That same young man, at the very end of the war in a worthless skirmish, had been killed, making him one of the last men to die for independence. Trammel considered such a death a terrible shame and thought about it a while. John Laurens could have gone on to become one of the great heroes of the Revolution, become President or even figured out the slavery problem. But Trammel knew that every soldier risked death every day in a war. He thought he might one day have to go to war and face death. Doing so would be heroic. That was the way to die. What made no sense to him was how inevitable, how unpreventable, how *settled from the beginning* Joey's death had been. The "kid" had not been given a fighting chance at life.

Trammel reclined on his bed, throwing the baseball into the glove for an hour or so, recalling everything that had happened with Joey that past summer, imagining what kind of practices they might have had together the following summer. They still had a lot to work on, after all. Trammel could have turned him into a real hitter, a pitcher's worst nightmare, given half a chance. But there would be no next summer—not for Joey.

Still angry, but more in possession of himself, Trammel sought out his mother in her bedroom. She had been crying, all day long as far as her son could tell, but she had at the moment no more tears in her. She was alone, her husband having gone down to take care of Christie after they had told her about Joey. Christie had cried; Trammel had heard her from his room. Yet her grief was the momentary, emotional peal of an adolescent girl. It came as a storm but did not last long. It could never have become the abiding resentment steadily growing in her brother's heart. Without too much emotion, though with a softer voice than the one he had left her with, Trammel spoke to his mother.

"Mom, I been thankin'. Ya know we gotta go ta the funeral."

"Yes, son. It's on Sunday—in the afternoon."

"Mom, ya know, I'm real sad, too. I'm pretty broke up about it. 'Is ain't like Uncle Buck's funeral," the boy said, in reference to the death of his great uncle, the only death of someone close he had experienced. "'Is'n don't make no sense." With that the boy returned to his room and was not seen again that night.

Chapter 12: "Why, God?"

That Sunday morning Trammel did not go to church with the rest of the family. He would have enough of church later on that day. Instead he sat at home in the empty house—trying to finish his report—but mostly desponding. The return of his parents and sister just before noon did not change his unhappy thoughts nor his countenance. He did not say much at lunch and hardly ate a thing. Indeed, he could barely look at his family or even himself in the mirror. No one else had much to say beyond the simply necessary. Trammel's melancholy spoke for the whole house.

A full hour before it was time to go, Trammel had already gotten dressed in his best attempt at a suit of mourning and could be found slumped into an antique chair in the front room. The present and card he had bought for Joey rested on his lap, his mother having told him that those invited to the party were still to bring their gifts to the funeral. The young man, for once, was not impatient. He did not wonder whether his mother's customary last-minute care of her person would make them late. He did not have his eye on the clock to see how much time he had left to complete the important tasks he had to do. He did not have his mind set to a certain day, which was a certain number of other days away from a game or an assignment. He cared neither for the day nor for the hour. What did all that matter? What did that matter now?

The hour did come, so Trammel and his mother got in the car. His father was staying at home with his sister, who was not thought ready for a funeral of someone so young and whom she did not know that well to begin with. As his mother turned down the familiar road leading to the church, Trammel's dread became a sharp pang of disaffection and not a little resentment such as he had never felt before in going to church. This sensation did not owe to his going to a funeral per se. Where else would one go to a funeral other than a church? He remembered Pastor McGuffey saying in a sermon once that in the old days churches were surrounded by graveyards. To go to church meant every Sunday passing by the graves of your family member and friends who had died, as well as those of others you might know only by name or reputation, and many, many you would not know. For a reason Trammel could not now remember, Pastor had considered that walking through a cemetery to get to church was somehow more appropriate than just getting out of your car and walking across a parking lot. No, Trammel was not opposed to churches or to funerals. He was opposed to *this* funeral.

Over the last couple of days Trammel had thought about little else. His mind dwelled wholly on uneasy thoughts. He deeply regretted and resented the sad fact that Joey never got his birthday party. Even before the boy's death, particularly on that morning he rode around on his bike in search of a card, Trammel had come around to thinking he might actually enjoy the party. It would not be his typical scene, of course. Joey's friends were pretty different from Trammel's. They did different things than he did: they played corny board games, for example. But they never bothered anybody. Now that Joey was gone, the event seemed of vital importance. Trammel wished that he and Joey could have pulled away from the party for a while to go into the boy's room and maybe catch up on some things since the summer. He would have tried not to be as uncomfortable in the house, for all its unkemptness, as he had always been in the past. He would try to enjoy the games they would assuredly play at the party by pretending that they were not stupid or that he was a kid again. In the same spirit of friendship and gaming, he would show them how to play some poker. He guessed that, since Joey did not have a father, the boy was probably completely lost when it came to poker and gambling. That was no way for a kid to be, especially a teenager. Almost as much as the party, Trammel thought about that day in the hall, only a couple of weeks ago, when Joey had given him the invitation. The look on his face suggested he had wanted to say something. What was it? Trammel imagined the things Joey might have said. Was it something about his horrible sickness? Trammel had never heard Joey talk about it before. Did he want to thank Trammel for teaching him to play ball? Trammel hoped not. He did not want Joey going to his grave thinking he owed somebody something. If Joey had mentioned it, Trammel would have just shaken it off by saying, "'At ain't no big deal, man."

But it was not only Joey that Trammel had been thinking about. He had run straight up against the undeniable problem of his own mortality as well. Not that Trammel was selfish or heartless or only worried about himself. He had often imagined himself in someone else's situation in order to figure out that individual's greatness or plight. Once when he had read in school about Louis Braille, Trammel had walked home with his eyes closed, taking the back alleys and using a stick that he had found on the ground to feel out the fences and find his way. He came to the conclusion that not only was it hard to be blind—who would have disputed that?—but also that Braille had shown some real guts. Most people he knew would have just sat there in the dark, feeling sorry for themselves. But Braille had taken the bull by the horns; he had done the one thing that no one thought he could ever do. Trammel had thought the same about Helen Keller—at first. But by the time he had gotten to the fifth grade, he had had a belly full of Helen Keller. There was not a teacher in the building who had not read or told the kids the story of Helen Keller. The principal, whenever he talked to the whole school about doing good and needed to reach into his bag of stories—a bag hardly as deep as Trammel's by that point and not remotely close to the size of his grandfather's—likely as not would pull out old Helen Keller. Trammel caustically asked himself whether anyone in the history of the world had ever done anything worth doing besides Helen Keller, such as flown in a rocket ship or fought in a war.

Yet whenever Trammel tried to imagine the mysteries of death, he came up short. He could never get past the funeral and those who would be left behind. He did not think too much about his own funeral. He figured everybody in the school and a lot of other folks from the town would be there, all crying and saying what a "cool dude" or a "fine young man" he had been. He ruminated much more on how his death might affect others. He knew Lanny would have a tough time of it. Lanny was a survivor, though. He would no doubt honor Trammel in his own way: by taking Trammel's chair and tackle box and rod and reel down to the pond, casting out his buddy's line and watching it. Lanny would even talk to him, as though he were sitting right there, relating the long plots of movies and tales from school and football games, always ending by saying how much the team needed him. Little did Trammel realize when imagining these things that the two friends, pursuing other passions and interests, would go to the pond only twice the next summer and never again after that.

Trammel dwelled much more on how his death might affect his family, the people he loved and who really counted. He could not long bear to think of his mother's state. She would be beside herself with grief. In her own room she would alternate between long bouts of crying and desperate pleadings in prayer. In the rest of the house she would try to keep up a bold front, especially for Christie's sake. Yet it could only be a silent, distant, halfhearted effort to hide the wilting of her very being. Trammel wondered whether, if he died, she could ever sing again. He knew that she would continue to play the piano. That was how she thought things through and put aside the cares of the day. Playing was her study and her repose. But how could she continue to *sing*—how could she lift up her heart and her voice in joy and in faith— without her son to hear her?

His sister would have her own way of dealing with his death, more constructive than his mother's, he thought. She, too, would cry a lot at first. Yet Christie never stayed in an unhappy mood for long. From time to time she would slip into her brother's room, which he could only picture just as it was. She would rearrange all his trophies, as she sometimes did, in the way she liked them: that is, in a kind of pyramid with the tallest trophy in the middle, rather than the chronological order Trammel preferred that gave the appearance of an ascending stock market chart. After looking at them, though, she would put them back the way her brother liked them; they were *his* trophies, after all, as he had pointed out any number of times. She would also bring in one of her stuffed animals and place it on the pillow. She did that quite often in the early morning so that the first thing her brother would see when he woke up would be one of her dumb dolls. Trammel could also see his sister writing things to him on the notepad he kept on the nightstand beside his bed. Instead of her typical "you snore" or "wake up, dummy," she would reveal the sweeter side of her nature, along the lines of, "You're the best brother EVER," or simply, "I MISS YOU."

Yet it was his father's grief Trammel could barely contemplate. The quick, strong, authoritative, vigorous man the son had always known, so ready to laugh, so full of life, would simply be lost: lost in the memories of what once was and the dreams of what would never come to be. He would no doubt drive by the fields where Trammel had played—never when anyone was around—and park his car there for a while. He would recall the individual games, the plays, the hits, the searing throws, the victories, one after the other. He would say to himself, forgetting that he had himself competed on the same fields, "Here played a champion!" His father would also look out onto their back yard and drive by the old house from time to time, remembering the countless hours of playing catch, the windows broken with baseballs and footballs and golf balls— Trammel always being the one sent in first to placate his mother—, and all the jokes even amid the deadly serious business of making a young man. Trammel figured his father would sell the bass boat. He would never have the heart to go fishing again: not without his boy, not without his *compadre*. Altogether, Trammel's father would be worse off than his mother because he would find consolation in nothing. His son was everything to him.

As gloomy as these thoughts were, they gave Trammel a kind of peace, a peace which the wrestling with the actual death at hand did not give him. Every time he recalled Joey, he dilated upon the same themes, phrases that ran through his head and burned him up inside: "wudn't given half a chance," "jus' got started," "ain't done nut'n' ta nobody," "not a mean bone in 'is whole body." Trammel's indignation was not the moodiness or self-pity or hormonal anarchy of the typical adolescent. He despised the lack of self-control in a fair number of his peers. Indeed, he always sided with justice whenever they got caught doing something stupid and protested their innocence, and more than once he had told them to stop whining whenever they acted like the world was falling apart over a little thing they would forget in a day or two. He watched with incredulity as teenagers argued with—no, screamed at—their parents *in public*. Trammel was not of that cast of mind, and his father would have "worn him out" if he had been. There was no mopiness or post-modern angst in Trammel's present state of mind. Rather, his whole spirit was mounting into an implacable anger at the injustice, the senselessness, and the outrage of Joey's death. Worse still, Trammel had no vent for this particular anger, no object for his steady concentration to settle upon, none at least that he could admit to himself. And that feeling —of anger without an enemy—put the whole world at odds with him, indeed cast the supposed order of the world in a pretty sorry light.

The young man's soul found no rest upon entering the familiar church and making his way, alongside his mother, into the sanctuary. Once he quickly surveyed the scene, he grew a little uneasy, wondering what he was supposed to do. Apart from the choir, there were only forty or so people there, mostly adults, far fewer than Trammel had expected. No one was sitting down yet. Normally he would have headed straight for the pews to his own spot, but at a funeral sitting down immediately did not seem appropriate. As he waited for his mother's cue, he noticed some of the other friends of Joey huddled in a small circle. He did not know them by name. That is, he was not sure enough of their names to risk calling one out and being wrong, though he had seen them around school. They were the kids who all sat at the same table in the rear corner of the cafeteria during lunch and never went out after they finished eating to take part in the ongoing pickup game of football that the other boys played. For their part, seeing Trammel show up at the funeral of one of their closest chums was unfathomable.

"Hey, 'at's Trammel D. Jones," said one.

"Yeah, I thank he goes ta church here, same as Joey," said another.

"You thank 'ey knew each other perty good?" asked the first.

"Y'all didn't know? Joey an' Tram got ta be perty good friends over the summer," confirmed a boy called Robbie, who had been in Trammel's math class for the last two years and knew him better than the other boys present. "Tram eb'm took eem out ta show eem how ta play baseball, an' Joey ended up gettin' a hit off Tram in 'a last game a' the season. It was a big deal. I can't b'lieve y'all didn't hear about it."

"Yeah, I remember eem talkin' about 'a hit a lot, but I didn't hear nut'n' 'bout 'em practicin' together."

"Yeah, 'at's how it happened. Joey wasn't a very good baseball player b'fore that."

"Man, 'at's unb'lievable."

Trammel, who had noticed the attention of the group of boys furtively directed his way, raised his head slightly in acknowledgement. Yet he was at the moment occupied with Joey's mother, who had left off talking quietly with and at times hugging some older people—who must have been Joey's grandparents—in order to greet Trammel and his mother. Like Mrs. Jones, Mrs. Lorne wore black. Trammel, though still a novitiate in understanding the eternal feminine, could not help but see the difference between his mother's tasteful and tailored elegance, whose purpose was not to upstage but rather to recede into the background, as much as a woman of her glow and presence ever could, and Mrs. Lorne's overdone attempt of dressing up to the occasion. He was careful not to criticize Joey's mother in his mind, but instead felt very sorry for her. He was learning not to judge women—at least not harshly and hypercritically—by the standard of his mother's perfection. He was more bothered by what seemed to him the fuss Joey's mother was making over his arrival. She gave him the same look she did whenever he had visited the house and expressed how she was "so glad" that he could make it to the funeral, as though he would have had something better to do on such a day. And how could anybody be "glad"—for whatever reason—at a funeral, Trammel asked himself, particularly at the funeral for one's own son? Trammel reasoned that the grieving mother could not have really understood what she was saying, and he felt even more sorry for her. Still, he was terribly uncomfortable in becoming the center of attention when all thoughts ought to be directed at the deceased.

His mother apparently recognized his discomfort and asked him to show Mrs. Lorne the card and present. Trammel had seen that a small, round table had been set up below and just to the side of the pulpit in order to receive the gifts of those who had been invited to the party.

"Yes, ma'am. Thanks fer lettin' us brang our gifts. It ain't nut'n' really, ya know, jus' a battin' glove I figur'd 'e cou'd use. Ya know, Joey 'as jus' gittin' started when it come ta bein' a real stick. What I mean is a hitter."

Trammel told her his gift in part to make conversation, in part to satisfy whatever curiosity she might have, and in part to relieve her of the need of opening up the gift right there on the spot. Mrs. Lorne, however, as women so often do, put more store in what the card had to say than the gift itself. She pulled out the flap of the envelope, which had only been tucked in, then thought better of it and asked, "Can I?"

"Yes, ma'am, a' course."

The card was drawn in comic strip style. It was an aerial view of a baseball stadium. At home plate, a batter with strawlike blond hair sticking out from under his cap and big arm muscles had just taken a swing with an outsized bat. The players on the field and the hardly discernible fans packing the stadium were miniscule compared to the hitter at the plate, but the impression was conveyed that all heads were turned upwards towards the sky. The top third of the card was occupied by a baseball, placed in the foreground of the viewer, whose immense size made it appear that it had been hit clear out of the stadium. The whole scene suggested triumph and joy. Mrs. Lorne studied the card with great intensity, more than the artist of this cartoon probably ever hoped for. She then opened the card to find the printed words, "You're a big hit!" and underneath them those written in Trammel's own hand:

> To Joey, a real slugger. Keep beltin' 'em out there.
> Your friend, Tram.

On first reading these lines, Mrs. Lorne seemed not to grasp them fully or to be in a state of disbelief because she read them over several times and even mouthed the words to herself. After a few moments in this daze she broke down crying, pressing the card to her chest with one hand and trying to hide the tears streaming down her face with the other. She recovered and looked at Trammel in a kind of melancholic rapture.

"Oh, thank you so much. This would have meant so much to him." The mother was overtaken by sobbing again but only for a moment. She recovered enough to gasp a few words.

"This would have meant the world to him."

"Ma'am, I'm jus' real sorry. Joey 'as about 'a best kid I ever met. Pro'lly *the* best."

Rather than evoking tears, these words seemed bracing to Mrs. Lorne. She looked at Trammel, but more than looking at him she looked inward, to her memories or her own reflections, in the same way that Joey used to do when something important occurred to him or he struck a happy thought.

"Yes. Yes, you're right," she said, now with a proud, though faint, smile. "He *was* about the best kid around. Thank you for saying so, Trammel."

Trammel felt his mother's hand on his shoulder. But he thought he should leave Mrs. Lorne alone for a while and had said all he could, so he told her he was going to put his gift on the table and made his way from the presence of the two mothers.

To reach the table with the gifts one had to walk near the casket, which was open. Trammel did not know how properly to reverence the body of the deceased boy and wondered whether he should make some kind of sign of the cross as he had seen done by the few Catholics he knew whenever they prayed. Yet now was not a time, he thought, to start making up stuff, so instead he just approached the casket slowly. He looked steadily at the thin, ashen face of the boy and was overcome by a feeling of disbelief. The whole thing still did not make any sense to him. They had *just been* playing ball, Trammel kept saying to himself. And there he was, *right there*. Joey did not even look much different, except that the overwhelming impression Trammel used to have of the boy's frailty, an impression that had largely disappeared during the summer, returned in force now that the breath of life had departed from the feeble form. Still holding his gift, Trammel just thought out to Joey what he would have liked to say.

"Man, I wish you didn't have ta go so soon. We 'as jus' gettin' started, ya know. I thought ya might like a battin' glove, ya know, 'cause ya had a lotta hits left in ya. A lotta hits. Anybody could see that. Anyway, I never gotta chance ta tell ya. An' I thank all 'ese people in here would say the same thang: You were the best,

Joey. You never did nut'n' er said nut'n' ta nobody 'at ya had ta be sorry for. I reckon I ain't never met a kid like 'at. An' I sure ain't 'at way. So I know you're in a place where ya can hear me now. So jus' remember, jus' remember: we're thankin' 'bout ya. An' missin' ya."

The young man did not know what else to say, or rather to think, to Joey. Far from being satisfied with what he had intimated, sensing that it was a hopeless attempt to cast events in the best light he could, Trammel took his leave from the open casket and placed his gift on the table at the base of the altar.

There were still several minutes left before the service began. Trammel's mother had just left the sanctuary, and he knew it always took about ten minutes for her to put on her robe and return with the rest of the choir, at least in the case of a regular church service. Still, no one was sitting down, so he made his way over to the small circle of boys who had been looking at him earlier.

"Hey, Tram," they greeted him as he ambled up, causing them to open their circle.

"How're y'all?"

"Perty good," they answered.

"Can't be too good, I reckon, on a day like t'day, though," meditated Trammel, as much to himself as to the other boys.

"No, 'at's right, Tram."

"Yeah, Tram."

Like Trammel, the other boys wore blue blazers of a polyester blend adorned with shiny gold buttons, each bearing the raised image of an anchor. A couple of the boys had both buttoned, a couple only the bottom one, and a couple, like Trammel, had buttoned neither. The collars of their shirts were, in the main, two sizes too large for their necks. Their neckties were mostly borrowed from and tied by their fathers, the others wrestled into a giant double Windsor. They looked no different from boys their age anywhere who had been required to dress up for a formal occasion.

After a silent moment, Trammel continued. "It's a pretty sorry deal, ya know, a kid not eb'm gittin' a birthday. What's a kid gotta do ta git a birthday, anyhow?"

The boys nodded and offered up "yeahs" in agreement, though surprised both by the revelation that Trammel would have gone to

Joey's party and by the verdict of the judge, having not tried the case in their own minds. As no one else spoke, the normally taciturn Trammel continued the thread.

"Was y'all all goin' ta the party?"

They said yes.

"Yeah, i'd 'a' been a good 'un. Yep, 'e'd 'a' got a real kick out of it, I reckon."

No one else could think of anything appropriate to say, so Trammel finally broke up the group by saying it was probably about time they got to their seats, at which point he took up his normal station on the right side of the church, close to the center aisle, though he sat much nearer to the front than he normally did. Just then the music of the organ began, and others fanned out over a rather sparsely populated sanctuary. As Trammel was looking at the order of service, someone unexpectedly slid into his pew and sat next to him. He looked up to see Jill.

"Hi, Tram," she whispered sadly. "It's good you could make it."

"Yeah, a' course."

The choir entered from a side door off the chancel, wearing robes of white trimmed in gold, and filled up the risers to the right of the communion table. Joey lay in front of that table. As the organ played softly "Rock of Ages," Pastor McGuffey, wearing his robe, made his way slowly down the center aisle. On reaching the casket, the pastor stopped in front of the body of Joey, holding his Bible in front of him with his hands crossed, and prayed silently for a moment. Then he nodded to two men sitting on the front row who closed the casket and draped it with a white funeral pall as the pastor wearily ascended the steps, made his way into the pulpit, and looked up to face the small congregation. The pastor Trammel had known his whole life appeared to have changed considerably. He somehow looked older, or just terribly worn, though nothing in particular about him was different. Only over the course of the service would the young man, so little aware of small things like age in adults, come to see that the older man's eyes, normally radiating energy and humor and hope, had taken on a morose and mortal character, thus casting the rest of his features in their actual rather than their borrowed light. The veteran pastor began to say something, but, being barely heard, he caught himself and spoke up in the voice that had for so many years filled the sanctuary.

"Bles . . . Blessed are they that mourn, for they shall be comforted."

Then the pastor invited the congregation to stand and sing "How Great Thou Art." In the order of service Trammel noticed an asterisk, leading to a note at the bottom of the page: "Music and arrangement and Scripture passages chosen by Joey Fuller."

The words of the hymn, which Trammel had sung dozens of times, and heard his mother sing countless times more, now raised up for Joey and in a way coming from Joey, took on new worth.

> O Lord my God, when I in awesome wonder,
> Consider all the worlds Thy Hands have made;
> I see the stars; I hear the rolling thunder,
> Thy power throughout the universe displayed.

Trammel was, in fact, not a little jolted by the hymn's hearty and unequivocal praise of God's boundless creativity and might at so sad a moment, at the very moment of death. He mouthed the words, though his voice was barely audible.

> Then sings my soul, My Savior God, to Thee,
> How great Thou art, how great Thou art.

As he sang, Trammel could not help noticing that others—his mother in the choir, Joey's mother, sitting in front of him and to the left, Jill standing just next to him—offered their voices more fervently than he, with a kind of fragile, desperate hope, as though they were holding on to something for dear life.

> And when I think that God, His Son not sparing;
> Sent Him to die, I scarce can take it in;
> That on the Cross, my burden gladly bearing,
> He bled and died to take away my sin.

Once the singing stopped Pastor McGuffey asked the congregation to bow their heads, and he offered a short prayer:

Eternal God, we bless you for those who
have kept the faith, who have finished the
race, and who now rest from strife and labor.
We praise you for the life of Joseph
Christopher Fuller, whom we commend,
unworthy as we are, to your divine presence.
Help us to believe where we have not seen.
Help us to know the truth we allow
    ourselves to doubt.
And bring us one day to our true home,
Through Jesus Christ, our Lord and Savior.

The pastor then recited from memory two passages of Scripture that were printed in the order of service, these too chosen by Joey.

Death is swallowed up in victory.
O death, where is thy sting?
O grave, where is thy victory?
The sting of death is sin;
and the strength of sin is the law.
But thanks be to God, which giveth us
the victory through our Lord Jesus Christ.
Therefore, my beloved brethren, be ye
steadfast, unmoveable, always abounding
in the work of the Lord, forasmuch as
ye know that your labor is not in vain
    in the Lord.

I have fought the good fight, I have finished
    the race, I have kept the faith.

The pastor paused for an instant and closed his eyes in prayer. He spoke intimately familiar words adapted to the present occasion.

"Dear Heavenly Father, as we gather to mourn the passing of Joseph Christopher Fuller from our troubled world and at the same time to celebrate his arrival into your blessed kingdom, we pray that the words of my mouth and the meditations of all our hearts will be acceptable unto You, O Lord, our Rock and our Redeemer. Amen."

The pastor opened his eyes but did not look up. He stared for a moment at the top of his podium, the place where he normally kept his sermon notes but which was today bare of any paper. Only his Bible sat there, off to the side. After a few breaths, he recovered and looked into the faces of the congregation: to the grandparents and Joey's mother, to Jill and Trammel, sitting together, the only ones among the young people he knew. The pastor, who had delivered untold sermons and conducted scores of funerals, now seemed troubled, perplexed, and unsure of what exactly he should say. Yet he forced himself to speak, as though making good on a promise.

"I know what my duty is here today," he began solemnly. "As a Christian and as a minister of God's Word, I am given the task of telling you that today is *not really* a day of mourning, *not really* a day of somber regret and sorrow, *not really* a day of despair. Far, far from those things, it is my responsibility to tell you, today is a day of great hope, a day in which we can rejoice in the victory of our Lord and Savior Jesus Christ over the horrors of sin and death and therefore also rejoice in the triumph of our own Joey Fuller over the sicknesses, the struggles, and the sadness of our fallen world; that we can take great joy and comfort in his passing, his journey, to a better place, to a perfect place." Whatever his words, it was clear to all that the pastor's heart was not in this message.

"You know, I have been to and been a part of many, many funerals. And no matter who has died or the circumstances of his death, always the same kinds of things are said, depending on the situation. If the deceased went quickly and unexpectedly, the mourners say, 'At least he didn't suffer. It was better this way.' If the deceased lived for months or years in unspeakable agony, people say, 'At least his suffering is over now. It's better this way.' If his wife has died before him, we will say, 'He's going to join her now.' If he dies before her, we just say, 'He lived a long life.' And there is always that note of hope, to hide our doubt about what may happen to the deceased, and to us, after death. 'He lived a good life.' 'He was a good man.' 'He meant well.' 'He loved life.' 'He, well . . . he made us laugh.' And when the circumstances of the death are just too impossible, too tragic, we comfort ourselves with the innocuous, resigned truism, 'The Lord works in mysterious ways.' And then what invariably happens after these words have been passed back and forth several times and the preacher has thought it good and helpful enough to offer his preacherly perspective and the body has been lowered into the cold ground, then, well . . . then we all go home. Those who knew him well but weren't family offer prayers at the dinner table for a few nights, prayers for the family and for the deceased. Those who *are* family are left in their own homes, sometimes alone, to mourn, to cry. But they—even they—after many tears, begin to, dare I say . . . go on with their lives. You see, a kind of routine sets in, in the lives of men, even in death. But I ask you, do we honor death—do we honor life—when we treat them both as things so . . . so . . . *routine*?

"Please do not misunderstand me. I realize the need and the use of comforting words, however commonplace, at the moment of death. I understand the pattern of grieving, or what we call 'the healing process.' And, as a Presbyterian minister, I can hardly doubt the wisdom or advantages of order and routine. In fact, I am inclined to think that we fall into these routines because if we human beings, we frail human beings, were required to face the full force of what this life never ceases to throw at us, or of the speed at which our looming death is catching up to us, that we would be simply unable to bear it.

"Furthermore," the pastor continued, after a pause, "when we join together in order to celebrate the life of a man or woman who has lived a 'full life,' as we say, who has lived seventy or eighty years on this earth; when we have seen his former vitality and energy give way to frailty, whether physical or mental or both; then we can more easily and in good conscience say that that man is going to his much deserved resting place. There even seems to be something natural in the occasion. We can certainly see God's hand at work in that.

"But when a child, when a fourteen-year-old boy dies before our very eyes, not due to an accident or any tragedy that we can blame, but because it was in the *very of nature of things* for him to die, then I wonder . . . then I wonder: where are the words of our Savior, where is the crying out of our Savior, even as He was on the cross,

'My God, my God, why hast thou forsaken me?'?

Or if not that—if not the Divine Cry—where are the passions, the very human passions of the poet: 'Rage, rage against the dying of the light!'?

"Joey Fuller was just about to turn fourteen. His birthday would have been yesterday. He had planned a party and invited many of his friends, many of you. But Joey was not able to have that party. Nor will there ever be another party for him. He will not go on to do the things that most people do. He will never go to high school. He will never have a girlfriend or go to Prom. He will, of course, not go to college. Nor will he embark upon a career, some occupation or calling that puts bread on the table but also gives meaning to life. It goes without saying that he will not meet a woman he loves and marry her and with her have children, who will be the source of many worries in his life—and most of his joy. He will not vote in an election; he will not serve his country or his community in any capacity. He will achieve none of the milestones that we widely regard as being the sure signs of living life to the fullest. He will never be able to answer for himself the oft-repeated question that children ask of each other, the question that dreams are made of, that even men carry well into adulthood, 'What do you want to be when you grow up?'

"These are our complaints. These are our regrets: over the life that Joey Fuller *didn't have*. And yet we as Christians know that human life, any human life, however short it may be cut, has dignity, has worth, has something to offer. Every human life plays a part in the grand theatre that is our world, and it may be that every life offers a lesson to us. In some cases that life may offer a complete and beautiful and awe-inspiring lesson, one that we the living can only hope to emulate and can never afford to forget."

The pastor paused to reach to the shelf on the inside of the podium where he always kept a glass of water to refresh himself when he had been talking a long time or gotten "carried away" with the vehemence of his sermon. He took no drink now but rather took out a tissue to wipe his moist eyes. Glancing up toward the back rafters, he continued.

"In many ways Joey Fuller was your average boy. He went to school. He loved to play games, mostly board games involving strategy or chance. Joey had his favorite movies, especially adventures. . . . I recall one time Joey telling me after he had seen the Indiana Jones movie that if he could do anything, anything at all, that he would like to discover something, something that the whole world had thought was lost. But he would find it, just like Indiana Jones, he said, because he had thought the whole thing through and not given up on its being there like everybody else had."

Mrs. Lorne, who had sat quietly until then, broke out crying, presumably because this was just the sort of thing that Joey would say. The pastor looked down from the pulpit but had to raise his eyes quickly to keep from crying himself. Again he brought the tissue to his eyes and looked toward that high place at the back of the sanctuary from whence he seemed to pull his words.

"Yes, in so many ways," the pastor went on, "Joey was like any other boy his age. He loved baseball. He had all the typical likes and dislikes when it came to what he ate and what he wore and what he had to do around the house. In these ways he was no different from any other boy. But in one important way, in one heartrending way, Joey was not like any other boy his age. Nor was he like any of us. From a very early age little Joey knew an important truth that escapes the wisest of us most of the time. Joey Fuller was born to die.

"Of course, all of us are born to die . . . at some point. But we, we frail human beings, are good, so very good at hiding that fact from ourselves. We are masters in the art of self-deception. We obscure the fact of our inevitable death with the disguises of all sorts: with health and fitness and wealth and success and fun in any number of forms, and, a few of us, with fame. If we did not have these disguises, if we had to face the fact of our impending deaths every day of our lives, it is almost certain that many of us would hardly be able to live or to act, to carry on any kind of meaningful existence. It is almost certain that few of us could go through life without a stinging resentment against our fate and the Maker of that fate.

"We all learn about death at some point when we are children, in a vague way when an older relative of ours dies. As a child,

Joey realized he was different from other boys. He was not as strong as they were. He had to go to the doctor more often than they did and have special treatments that simply exhausted him. He began to ask questions since he was smart, observant, curious, and intuitive. His mother told him he was 'special.' What else could she have said? What else could a mother have told her dying son? His being 'special' led to 'treatments' called *chemotherapy*. 'Special' was another word for physical pain and weakness. 'Special' meant having a body that could never keep up with the stirring life within him. In this way Joey learned about death—first-hand. At the moment he was learning to read, he also learned that his own life would not be long, that it might already be half over. And yet that information, that cruel knowledge, never seemed to touch Joey, to burden him, to defeat him, in the way it would have defeated one of us. That knowledge—I wish I knew how to explain it—that knowledge gave him a strength, a life, that his frail body did not. This makes no sense, I know. But Joey's sense of his own death is what gave strength, immeasurable strength, to his short life."

Again the flow of words stopped. The pastor looked toward the choir in order to gather strength or to give strength. Trammel's mother had buried her head in her hand. She knew—more than anyone other than Joey's mother and the pastor—the quiet, mature strength of which Pastor McGuffey spoke. She had talked to Joey privately and had read passages of Scripture with him during vacation Bible school. After class, when the other kids went out to play and to wait to be picked up by their mothers, he would tell her what the things they had talked about that day meant to him, never with sadness, always with hope. He had spoken to her not about things in general but from within.

Pastor McGuffey now looked down into the congregation, particularly to Trammel and Jill, the latter who had been crying softly the whole time. Trammel remembered now how much Jill and Joey used to talk together, after church usually, and how Joey wore his brightest smiles around her. Trammel did not know what they talked about. But he got the impression that Joey could tell Jill things since she had that same caring nature that Trammel's mother had. The pastor returned his gaze to his lectern, pulled the Bible nearer to him, and spoke again.

"What would we do with such knowledge, with the harsh reality of our own death almost taunting us each moment of our lives? I honestly do not know what I would do, especially at that age. But Joey Fuller never doubted, never questioned, and was never resentful. Joey once told me in my office—and we had many conversations in my office, more for my sake than for his, I think—he told me that he was sure God put him on this earth for a reason. He admitted that he did not know what that reason was. But, as he put it, 'God does.' That was enough for Joey. '*God does*': so simple, so heartbreaking, so mysterious, and so true. Those two words express the beauty of Joey's life.

"As some of you know, I had the pleasure of having Joey in our confirmation class this last spring. A couple of you were in that class. To be honest, to this day I do not know who was the better teacher. Joey asked many questions of me, probing questions that I had not been forced to answer in my twenty years as a pastor. My answer to one of those questions took us to one of Paul's epistles. Whatever Joey asked me, I suggested that we look at a passage from the Second Letter to the Corinthians. It reads," the pastor quoted without looking at his Bible,

> "'And He said to me, "My grace is sufficient for you, for My strength is made perfect in weakness." Therefore most gladly I will rather boast in my infirmities, that the power of Christ may rest upon me.'

What is remarkable to me as I think back on that moment in confirmation class, when young men and women are supposed to be learning from their preacher about the truths, the often impenetrable truths, of our Christian faith, is not the life-giving words of Christ nor the appropriate lesson drawn by the Apostle, both of which we have come to expect. What amazed me was Joey's reaction. He simply shut his eyes for a moment, looked, I would say, inward, and then said to me, 'Yes, Pastor. Yes, that's right.' As long as I live I shall never forget that moment, that wise and miraculous and knowing *Yes, Pastor*.

"Unlike the rest of us who knew him, Joey never complained, never wondered, as I did, as I still do, 'Why, God?' He was satisfied with a Reason that was beyond his own comprehension. He treasured the life that he did have. We talked about his life that last day in the hospital. He told me about the things he had done that he was proud of. He told me about how so many people had been kind to him, about how he had become good friends with people he never thought he would know but from afar. He spoke of the joy and goodness of life as his own life was leaving him. His biggest worry was his mother. He said he hoped she would not be too sad. Then he told me how he wanted his funeral to be. One of the things he was particularly insistent upon was this picture board you see below me here. Joey laughed as he recalled how his mother was always making him let her take pictures of anything he did, no matter how small or ordinary. He knew why. He knew that some day that would be all she would have of him: pictures and her memories. So he posed for these pictures gladly and tried to say something to her through them. He told me he wanted all of you to look at these pictures and remember the great times y'all had together. He said these times meant more to him than any of you could ever know."

Again the pastor broke off, this time because he was weeping and losing control of his voice. But he managed to whisper out these words: "He told me to tell all of y'all not to be too sad for him and that, most of all . . . he loves you . . . And then he said . . . then he said, 'You, too, Pastor.'"

The pastor, the choir, and the congregation sat motionless for a while, every one of them crying. Jill, who had been crying since the service began, leaned against Trammel for support. The young man pulled out some more tissues from his inside coat pocket (his mother had given them to him on the drive over without a word) and squeezed them into her hand as if to say, "I know. I'm here."

"My friends, I do not have any faith in myself at this moment. I have no faith in my words as being able to comfort or to heal. I am still stuck with this question of 'Why God?' and can only hope that since our Lord asked it, it cannot be wrong for us to ask it. Yet I have to cling to the belief of what I have been saying my whole adult life, that in Jesus Christ we have an answer. And I suspect that in Joey Fuller, the purest heart I have ever known, we also have an answer. That is, there are some who come to us—call them chosen, call them blessed—who are put on this earth, for however short a time, in order to teach *us*, we weaker souls, how to live. These purer souls, these great ones, teach us that there is more to live for than for ourselves, as we normally understand ourselves. They teach us that most of our present concerns—so many, many do we have, as did the busy Martha—are not our ultimate concerns, not the concerns that elevate us as we walk on this earth or that sustain us in death. They teach us that our lives are happier and more promising than we make them out to be, if we but seek out the hidden treasures that the rest of the world has forgotten. And they teach us one of the hardest lessons of all, that of finding joy in what little we may have—or seem to have—rather than envying others for the great abundance they have—or seem to have. A pure soul like Joey reminds us, we who have forgotten, how to live with faith, with hope, and with love in this world we have been given, in this world we must make our home. But more than that, they teach us there is the world that awaits us if we should but claim it as our own. As we return Joey Fuller's frail body back to this earth from whence it came, we do so in great faith, and, yes, great joy—that his giant heart has gone to a better place, a place made for him."

Silent for a time, the pastor asked the congregation to join him in The Lord's Prayer. The mourners prayed with one voice.

After the prayer, the pastor remained in the pulpit for a moment, looked down at the gray casket that contained Joey's remains, and slumped: as though he had not done what he had set out to do, had not done Joey justice, or had not said enough. Or maybe it had just struck him that he would never again talk to Joey. He stepped down from the pulpit, leaving his Bible on the lectern, and took his place on the preacher's bench.

The choir rose in one motion as Trammel's mother stepped forward. Trammel looked into the order of service again to see that Joey had chosen the music and its arrangement. He was not unaccustomed to hearing his mother sing solos in church, but the knowledge that Joey had chosen it that way surprised him a little. Even more of a surprise was the hymn itself. Trammel had expected something soothing or promising in the way church hymns usually are, something about the afterlife or getting closer to God. For the last couple of days his mother had been playing "Just a Closer Walk With Thee," the very hymn she had sung this last spring when he, Joey, Jill, and the others from the confirmation class had taken communion for the first time. This music was a very far cry from that sort of thing. He was not sure that it belonged in church, much less at a funeral.

> Mine eyes have seen the glory
> Of the coming of the Lord;
> He is trampling out the vintage
> Where the grapes of wrath are stored;
> He hath loosed the fateful lightning
> Of his terrible swift sword;
> His truth is marching on.

As she sang, with the rest of the choir backing her up on the chorus, as she spirited the words into every space of the resonant sanctuary, Trammel's mother wept a continuous stream of tears, yet whose effect seemed only to bring out the brilliance of her sky blue eyes and the power of her celestial voice. Trammel had never really considered how his mother's voice might have affected others, but he now realized, seeing things from Joey's point of view, how his mother's great gift could bring peace—or courage—to others.

> I have seen Him in the watchfires
> Of a hundred circling camps
> They have builded Him an altar
> In the evening dews and damps;
> I can read His righteous sentence
> By the dim and flaring lamps;
> His day is marching on.
> *Glory! Glory! Hallelujah!*
> *Glory! Glory! Hallelujah!*
> *Glory! Glory! Hallelujah!*
> *His truth is marching on.*

As incongruous as the theme seemed to be with the occasion, Trammel could not but admire the power and beauty of the message, its spirit of triumph. It felt like winning.

> I have read a fiery gospel writ
> In burnished rows of steel:
> "As you deal with my contemners,
> So with you My grace shall deal":
> Let the Hero born of woman
> Crush the serpent with His heel,
> Since God is marching on.

Yet it was the fourth verse that most spoke to Trammel through his mother's perfect pitch.

> He has sounded forth the trumpet
> That shall never call retreat;
> He is sifting out the hearts of men
> Before his judgment seat;
> Oh, be swift, my soul, to answer Him;
> Be jubilant, my feet;
> Our God is marching on.

That verse and the last three lines of the hymn, before the chorus, seized Trammel in a way that no music, no words, no commands ever had. He felt called to action.

> As He died to make men holy,
> Let us die to make men free;
> While God is marching on.

After the hymn, the choir sat down. Six men emerged from the congregation: a couple of Joey's coaches, including Coach Cobbs, and four of his teachers. Mr. Joseph, Joey and Trammel's current Sunday School teacher, who ran several businesses in town, took off the funeral pall. As the pallbearers bore out the body of Joey Fuller, Mrs. Lorne cried out, as it was the last time she would be in the presence of her son.

While these men were performing their duty, the congregation sat stunned. They, too, were almost in shock over the "Battle Hymn of the Republic," the strangest of ways to end the funeral of a child. Joey had thrown everyone a curve. The crying went on softly, but a few incongruous smiles came across the faces of those who understood, or thought they understood, his message. The mourners sat in silence for a time until the organ music began. On this cue they went to pay their respects to Mrs. Lorne and to look at Joey's display the pastor had spoken of.

Trammel's mind was racing with the things the pastor had said, the meaning behind the hymns, and scattered memories of Joey, some flatly contradicting what his own ideas of Joey had always been. One matter Trammel put to rest in an instant. As he first heard it, he could not fully endorse his pastor's statement about Joey loving baseball and felt bad about not being able to do so. True, Trammel had spent a great deal of time showing Joey how to play the game that summer, and Joey had obviously enjoyed this experience. Likewise, Trammel quite naturally got Joey a birthday present and a card dealing with baseball. Still, Trammel had always thought that to love something a person would have to be good at it. At the same time, anyone who was good at something would certainly love doing it. Now Trammel was sure about neither of these propositions. He now saw a real value to a kid liking to play baseball even if he was not a very good athlete. He also thought it might be a shame and a waste to work so hard getting good at the game while not really being able to love it. He thought about what his father had said about playing golf. Once he had told Trammel that he never really enjoyed golf until he played it while in the Army; he found it too frustrating a game. Trammel asked his father why being in the Army made a difference. "Ever round on 'a golf course 'as a day I wudn't shipped out ta Nam." His father called that way of looking at things "perspective." "See, boy, 'ere ain't nut'n' like a war 'at'll give a man 'a right perspective on thangs." Trammel figured that what often made the difference between dread and joy must be just that: of getting the right perspective, of getting "your mind right," to quote a line from one of his and Lanny's favorite movies. If a man did not have his mind right then he would never love or take pride in much of anything. So Pastor was right about Joey loving baseball. Every day on the baseball field, whether hitting or striking out, was a day Joey was alive.

Trammel's mind worked over the other things Pastor McGuffey had said. He now remembered their talks in the confirmation class. It seemed ages ago, though it had only been in the spring.

Trammel recalled how moved he was in those sessions, sometimes feeling as though he was being lifted up out of his chair as the pastor explained passages of Scripture. Jill had been affected, too, even to the point of crying once or twice. Yet, just as Pastor said, Joey had been the one whose comments and questions were the most apt and true. In the silence of the sanctuary Trammel could still almost hear Joey asking Pastor questions and sometimes giving answers that went right to the heart of the matter, some about things that had passed through Trammel's mind from time to time, others that seemed wholly unlike the thoughts of a child. Joey wanted to know about the commands of Jesus: what it meant to walk "an extra mile" with someone, what it really meant to turn the other cheek, what it took to be a good Samaritan, obligations that Trammel had heard about since he was a child but had never entirely figured out. Yet Joey's other questions concerned matters that Trammel, normally so astute in everything he read or heard, had not noticed: why Jesus had said the disciples had little faith and why He *rebuked* the sea, by what means Christ had driven the moneychangers out of the Temple, what it meant to bring not peace but the sword, how Jesus could baptize with the Holy Spirit and with *fire*. Trammel recalled thinking at the time that Jesus, who had always seemed so, well, not so tough, was much more like a hero than most people said. He now remembered—he was ashamed to have forgotten so easily—how impressed he had been with Joey's insights and comments. He had wanted to ask him some questions later on, but Trammel did not know how to talk about these matters without Pastor being in the room. In all the time they had spent together that summer, Joey and Trammel, the subject had never come up.

Trammel remembered the comment that Joey had made which the pastor had referred to. Yet it did not happen quite as he had described it. It was much more like a debate, a friendly debate— they were not arguing—but a debate nonetheless. Pastor had been talking about Jesus healing the sick and raising Lazarus from the dead. Joey had asked a question, which prompted the pastor to quote the passage from Corinthians. But a few minutes later Joey said they should look at Second Timothy: "I have fought the good fight, I have finished the race, I have kept the faith." Try as he might, Trammel could not now recall what Joey had found in that verse. But he was so impressed by the passage that he put his ribbon bookmark in that place in his Bible and had kept it there ever since. He would sometimes turn to it when he sat down in church. What Trammel found most interesting now was that the passage from Timothy rather than the one from Corinthians had been proclaimed in this service, presumably because Joey had requested that reading.

There were other parts of Pastor's eulogy Trammel subjected to scrutiny. Not that he disagreed with what had been said. Far from it. Everything the pastor said was perfectly right and true. At the same time, Trammel had gotten to know Joey over the summer in a way that the older man had not. It was true, for instance, that Joey really enjoyed Indiana Jones. Joey, Trammel, and Lanny talked about it the second time Joey came to the pond. But that was not Joey's favorite movie. His favorite was *Rocky*, which had been playing on cable that summer. The three of them had seen it at least half a dozen times and could quote virtually all the lines, which they traded back and forth that day. They talked about the fight scenes and the training scenes, and they loved Rocky hitting the meat. Trammel and Lanny had to explain the basics of boxing to Joey, since he did not know a jab from a hook from an uppercut. But once he learned he took great delight in the information. At one point Lanny complained that *Rocky* would have been the best movie ever except for there being too much "lovey-dovey crap" in it. Joey, in his innocent way, reflected a minute and then said, "That's funny. I thought the point was that Rocky couldn't be a great fighter until he had something to fight for." In response to this oracle, Lanny could say nothing other than, "Well, I'll be damned."

For whatever reason, something else came into Trammel's mind now that had to be resolved: the last baseball game of the season when Joey had gotten the hit. Whenever Trammel had considered it, he had done so from his own perspective: about how he had taken the break out of the ball or placed it perfectly. He had not thought too much about what Joey had brought to the plate that day. True, Trammel had understood that Joey had gained immensely from their Monday outings. But now what came back to him forcibly were their last couple of practices. Joey had proudly told Trammel about the hits he was starting to get. More than that, he had very specific questions about whether his stance was just right, whether he was getting the bat around fast enough, when he should take a pitch and when he should swing. Trammel could now recall a statement Joey made that did not seem like much at the time. He had said, "I don't want to get hits just 'cause of luck. I want to get real hits, just like you get." And so Trammel started throwing the ball even faster, having already sped things up gradually over the summer. He threw fastballs at about the speed of the better-than-average pitchers in the league. Joey managed to foul them off and occasionally get around on one. Trammel had not put these final practices together in his mind with Joey's hit. Yet when he did so, Trammel saw more clearly Joey at the plate that day. Trammel had to admit that Joey's swing was textbook. Given the limitations of Joey's strength, it was a perfect swing.

Yet the most amazing and surprising revelation to Trammel was the fact that Joey had known he would die: *soon* as it turned out to be. And yet he never breathed a word about it. He never moped about it. On the contrary, Joey seemed to be about the happiest kid Trammel had ever known. That took guts. Trammel knew Joey had guts. He had seen so himself over the summer. But Trammel had no idea what kind of guts. He was now amazed at Joey's real guts, his *life-and-death guts*, and wondered whether he himself had that kind of strength and fearlessness in him. He hoped so.

By now Trammel was standing last in the line of those waiting to see Joey's pictures. He wanted to be the last to see Joey, the last to commune with him. They had already passed by to pay their respects to Mrs. Lorne, who was grieving as any mother would after losing a teenage son. As he added up all the things that had occurred to him, as he tried to penetrate the mystery of the hymn, as he kept looking down to the verse printed on the memorial, he could come to only one conclusion, to only one thing that made any sense. Joey was a fighter. That might not be how the world saw him. That might not even be how Pastor saw him. But that was what his words and his actions really said. Though his body held him back, Joey was a fighter through and through. He fought *the good fight* every day of his life. This spirit, this tenacity, this kind of guts that Joey had reminded Trammel of what his father always said about it being not "the size of the dog in the fight, but the size of the fight in the dog" that mattered. Joey had all kinds of fight in him—a more than human fight. Trammel thought that if he had the kind of fight in him that Joey had, that if he could combine Joey's fight with his own, not just now but as a man, he could take on the world. He could do something great.

At last Trammel got his turn at Joey's picture board. It seemed vital that he took in all that the pictures had to tell him, particularly since he had blown it the day that Joey meant to tell him something in the hall. It was clear that Joey put the pictures into a chronology, much in the way Trammel had arranged his own trophies. The earlier pictures of Joey began in the top left corner but then moved around the board in a circle, swirling inward to the center. Pastor was right; Joey had been a weakly child. But there he was doing the same things that babies always do, sitting in bathtubs and whatnot. For reasons Trammel could not understand, parents always took stupid pictures of their babies lying on their stomachs with their bare bottoms in the air, smiling at the camera with no idea that they are just setting themselves up for a lifetime of humiliation at the visit of the most distant relative. A kid got interesting, in Trammel's view, only when he began to do real things, such as ride his bike or throw a football. Joey had done a fair bit of that. In every one of these pictures Joey was smiling: a somewhat shy, genuine, good-natured smile. Yet the smile took a back seat to Joey's eyes: bright blue eyes that had a life in them that would have singled out their host in a crowd of ten thousand. Trammel had known no one but his mother who had eyes like that. A few of the pictures brought back events Trammel had been a part of but forgotten. Two of these were choral performances. The first was in church. Both Trammel and Joey had been in the children's choir at church when the former's mother was music director. Trammel had hated that choir and begged to be let out of it, and, after some lobbying of his father, he finally was. The picture of the choir and Trammel's mother confirmed the memory. With a furrowed brow, at the end of the row opposite his mother, Trammel glared at the camera while everyone else smiled with childish glee. The other choir picture solved, at least partly, one mystery. It featured a whole class of third-graders: half of whom were dressed in red, white, and blue, the other half in blue and gray. What he remembered now was some concert featuring historical or patriotic songs. All the boys in the Civil War part of the show, Trammel included, had wanted to sing "Dixie." Mrs. Ball had corrected one kid about not wanting to sing "no damn Yankee song." That's right! thought Trammel. Joey had been the only boy who wanted to sing "Glory, Glory," as the kids called it then. So he ended up singing a solo. The crowd gave Joey a standing ovation despite the fact that twenty years before they would have stood, by custom, to the playing of "Dixie." Trammel was amazed at how much guts Joey had even back then and was somewhat ashamed that he, for once, had gone along with the crowd.

The three photographs Joey had placed in the center of the picture board, though, were the ones that stood out, that finished the story, and that would linger in Trammel's mind throughout his youth and in some ways throughout the rest of his life. The picture on the right had been taken the first day Joey had come fishing at the pond. Joey stood with his back to the pond. In the distance Trammel and Lanny were discernible though having no idea they were in the picture. Nor would they have understood the import of the moment. Only today had Pastor made it clear why Joey's mother would care so much about a few measly fish. Joey stood there, smiling and holding the stringer of three fish in one hand, including the bream whose mystery they had never figured out, and his fishing rod in the other, as if to say, "See what I've caught." He was obviously happy and proud. Trammel was glad Joey got to go fishing a few times and have a few laughs. Trammel thought of a couple of pictures that his own father kept on his desk at work taken after the family had been fishing. In one of those snapshots Trammel held up a full stringer of fish, on the other side of which stood his sister, pointing her thumb at herself as if to say, "I caught them all." She had not caught them all, of course, only the biggest one (with a little help from her father), much to Trammel's consternation at the time. Trammel would not have traded those times with his sister and dad out on the lake for anything. Maybe Joey had felt the same way about fishing with him and Lanny. It stood to reason that, since Joey never had any other family in the house besides his mom, maybe he and Lanny had been sort of like brothers.

The photograph Joey had put on the left-hand side of the middle three had been taken at the end of their confirmation class. Trammel could almost hear them lining up for it as the church secretary had tried to arrange them according to height, however unavailing her attempt. Pastor stood in the very middle. He rested his right hand on the shoulder of Joey, standing to his right, and had his other hand on Trammel's near shoulder, not so much resting it as pushing the larger boy forward a little. Everyone wore a broad smile—Pastor had just cracked one of his jokes—except Trammel, who seemed, as always, awfully serious for a teenage boy. The rest of the boys fanned out from the middle. Off to the side stood Jill, facing inward, with a big smile but keeping her distance from the class made up only of boys, save her. Trammel now remembered Pastor saying, "C'mon, Jill, get with the program," to which she responded, "No way, Pastor, especially if I have to stand next to *Tram*," and then winked. And thus she remained a bit apart, as though presiding over the rest of them. Trammel now realized how much he had enjoyed that confirmation class and how much they had learned. It helped to go really slowly over their readings, to ask questions, and to talk about them with Pastor, and, in a way, with Joey, who knew so many things. He thought that was just a start. He wanted to know more—about a lot of things. He realized he was just beginning to learn.

The central photograph of the three, the center of the entire picture board, surprised Trammel a little. In it Joey wore his baseball uniform and stood at the home plate up at their Little League field. In his right hand he held his bat, resting over his shoulder in the way that ballplayers took pictures back in the fifties. In his other hand he held up a ball. It must have been the ball he hit in the last game of the season playing against Trammel. No other hit would have meant that much. Joey and his mother must have waited until everyone else was gone and then taken the picture. There was no other explanation. The look on Joey's face was, although in many respects similar to his expressions at other moments, noticeably different from the rest. His smile was no bigger; his eyes were no brighter. But his face shone with an unmistakable confidence, a look of victory. It was the sort of picture Trammel had taken many times before, at the behest of his father, his mother, his various coaches. Joey stood there as a real ballplayer. Trammel blinked the tears away as he remembered how much work—but good work—it took to get Joey to that point, how hopeless his initial efforts seemed to be, how utterly pointless seemed to be the enterprise. But Joey was not a kid to mess around. They had talked sometimes after practice or while getting a drink, but mainly it was all business: about how to get the bat around faster or what to look for in the ball right as it came out of the pitcher's hand. Trammel missed that time. He even found the whole thing quite natural now. After his mother made him play ball with Joey—which he was not too crazy about at first, he was ashamed to admit to himself—after that it had just been the two of them. There were no coaches, no parents, no umpires, no fans— just two kids playing some ball and figuring out how to get better at it. Trammel thought he might have gotten better himself showing Joey how to hit and how to field and how to throw. When they started out, Trammel did not know anything about coaching another kid. He had never done it before. But put on the spot like that, he figured it out pretty soon. He thought maybe that was the way it was supposed to be.

Trammel felt a sense of ease or relief come over him. He understood, or hoped he was at least beginning to understand, what Joey might have meant by these pictures. After a few moments, Trammel took a step back to take it all in. It had all come so fast, so very fast. He closed his eyes for a moment, then opened them again, overcome with tears. He took in somehow the whole of Joey's life, the joy conveyed by Joey's disarming smile. Trammel was not angry any more. He did not resent the death of his unlikely friend. Instead, he was grateful. He found himself inestimably grateful that he had been there, grateful to have known Joey, really to know him, even in so short a stretch of time. And he was glad to have been a big part of it all. He had contributed in his own way to the happiest day in that young man's brief but beautiful life, the day that Joey Fuller got a hit off Trammel D. Jones.